BIRTH OF A LOST NATION . . .

The young man was dressed only in walking shorts and soft bush shoes. "Friends," he said, "we are gathered here tonight to found a new nation."

He paused to let the idea sink in. "You know our situation. We fervently hope to be rescued. I will even go so far as to say that I think we will be rescued . . . eventually.

"It might be tomorrow . . . it might be our descendants a thousand years from now. But when the main body of our great race reestablishes contact with us, it is up to us whether they find a civilized society, or flea-bitten animals without language, without art—with the light of reason grown dim. Or no survivors at all, nothing but bones picked clean!"

"Heinlein has produced another ingenious piece of scientific imagination."
—*Saturday Review*

Tunnel
IN THE
Sky

Robert A. Heinlein

A Del Rey Book

BALLANTINE BOOKS • NEW YORK

A Del Rey Book
Published by Ballantine Books

Library of Congress Catalog Card Number: 55-10142

ISBN 0-345-33212-1

This edition published by arrangement with
Charles Scribner's Sons

Printed in Canada

First Ballantine Books Edition: March 1977
Eighth Printing: September 1985

Cover art by Darrell Sweet

For **Jeannie** and **Bibs**

Contents

1. The Marching Hordes   1
2. The Fifth Way   19
3. Through the Tunnel   36
4. Savage   60
5. The Nova   68
6. "I Think He Is Dead"   75
7. "I Should Have Baked a Cake"   86
8. "Fish, or Cut Bait"   95
9. "A Joyful Omen"   116
10. "I So Move"   123
11. The Beach of Bones   140
12. "It Won't Work, Rod"   151
13. Unkillable   156
14. Civilization   173
15. In Achilles' Tent   191
16. The Endless Road   208

1

The Marching Hordes

THE BULLETIN BOARD OUTSIDE LECTURE HALL 1712-A of Patrick Henry High School showed a flashing red light. Rod Walker pushed his way into a knot of students and tried to see what the special notice had to say. He received an elbow in the stomach, accompanied by: "Hey! Quit shoving!"

"Sorry. Take it easy, Jimmy." Rod locked the elbow in a bone breaker but put no pressure on, craned his neck to look over Jimmy Throxton's head. "What's on the board?"

"No class today."

"Why not?"

A voice near the board answered him. "Because tomorrow it's 'Hail, Caesar, we who are about to die—' "

"So?" Rod felt his stomach tighten as it always did before an examination. Someone moved aside and he managed to read the notice:

PATRICK HENRY HIGH SCHOOL
Department of Social Studies

SPECIAL NOTICE to all students Course 410
      (elective senior seminar) *Advanced Survival,*
      instr. Dr. Matson, 1712-A MWF
1.   There will be no class Friday the 14th.
2.   *Twenty-Four Hour Notice* is hereby given of final examination in Solo Survival. Students will present themselves for physical check at 0900 Saturday in the dispensary of Templeton Gate and will start passing through the gate at 1000, using three-minute intervals by lot.

1

3. *TEST CONDITIONS:*
    (a) ANY planet, ANY climate, ANY terrain;
    (b) NO rules, ALL weapons, ANY equipment;
    (c) TEAMING IS PERMITTED but teams will not be allowed to pass through the gate in company;
    (d) TEST DURATION is not less than forty-eight hours, not more than ten days.
4. Dr. Matson will be available for advice and consultation until 1700 Friday.
5. Test may be postponed only on recommendation of examining physician, but any student may withdraw from the course without administrative penalty up until 1000 Saturday.
6. Good luck and long life to you all!

                              (s) **B. P. Matson, Sc.D.**

Approved:
J. R. ROERICH, *for the Board*

Rod Walker reread the notice slowly, while trying to quiet the quiver in his nerves. He checked off the test conditions—why, those were not "conditions" but a total lack of conditions, no limits of any sort! They could dump you through the gate and the next instant you might be facing a polar bear at forty below—or wrestling an octopus deep in warm salt water.

Or, he added, faced up to some three-headed horror on a planet you had never heard of.

He heard a soprano voice complaining, " 'Twenty-four hour notice!' Why, it's less than twenty hours now. That's not fair."

Another girl answered, "What's the difference? I wish we were starting this minute. I won't get a wink of sleep tonight."

"If we are supposed to have twenty-four hours to get ready, then we ought to have them. Fair is fair."

Another student, a tall, husky Zulu girl, chuckled softly. "Go on in. Tell the Deacon that."

Rod backed out of the press, taking Jimmy Throxton with him. He felt that he knew what "Deacon" Matson would say . . . something about the irrelevancy of fairness to survival. He chewed over the bait in paragraph five; nobody would say boo if he dropped the course.

2

After all, "Advanced Survival" was properly a college course; he would graduate without it.

But he knew down deep that if he lost his nerve now, he would never take the course later.

Jimmy said nervously, "What d'you think of it, Rod?"

"All right, I guess. But I'd like to know whether or not to wear my long-handled underwear. Do you suppose the Deacon would give us a hint?"

"Him? Not him! He thinks a broken leg is the height of humor. That man would eat his own grandmother—without salt."

"Oh, come now! He'd use salt. Say, Jim? You saw what it said about teaming."

"Yeah . . . what about it?" Jimmy's eyes shifted away.

Rod felt a moment's irritation. He was making a suggestion as delicate as a proposal of marriage, an offer to put his own life in the same basket with Jimmy's. The greatest risk in a solo test was that a fellow just had to sleep sometime . . . but a team could split it up and stand watch over each other.

Jimmy must know that Rod was better than he was, with any weapon or bare hands; the proposition was to his advantage. Yet here he was hesitating as if he thought Rod might handicap him. "What's the matter, Jim?" Rod said bleakly. "Figure you're safer going it alone?"

"Uh, no, not exactly."

"You mean you'd rather not team with *me*?"

"No, no, I didn't mean that!"

"Then what did you mean?"

"I meant—Look, Rod, I surely do thank you. I won't forget it. But that notice said something else, too."

"What?"

"I said we could dump this durned course and still graduate. And I just happened to remember that I don't need it for the retail clothing business."

"Huh? I thought you had ambitions to become a wide-angled lawyer?"

"So exotic jurisprudence loses its brightest jewel . . . so what do I care? It will make my old man very happy

3

to learn that I've decided to stick with the family business."

"You mean you're scared."

"Well, that's one way of putting it. Aren't you?"

Rod took a deep breath. "Yes. I'm scared."

"Good! Now let's both give a classic demonstration of how to survive and stay alive by marching down to the Registrar's office and bravely signing our names to withdrawal slips."

"Uh, no. You go ahead."

"You mean you're sticking?"

"I guess so."

"Look, Rod, have you looked over the statistics on last year's classes?"

"No. And I don't want to. So long." Rod turned sharply and headed for the classroom door, leaving Jimmy to stare after him with a troubled look.

The lecture room was occupied by a dozen or so of the seminar's students. Doctor Matson, the "Deacon," was squatting tailor-fashion on one corner of his desk and holding forth informally. He was a small man and spare, with a leathery face, a patch over one eye, and most of three fingers missing from his left hand. On his chest were miniature ribbons, marking service in three famous first expeditions; one carried a tiny diamond cluster that showed him to be the last living member of that group.

Rod slipped into the second row. The Deacon's eye flicked at him as he went on talking. "I don't understand the complaints," he said jovially. "The test conditions say 'all weapons' so you can protect yourself any way you like . . . from a slingshot to a cobalt bomb. I think final examination should be bare hands, not so much as a nail file. But the Board of Education doesn't agree, so we do it this sissy way instead." He shrugged and grinned.

"Uh, Doctor, I take it then that the Board knows that we are going to run into dangerous animals?"

"Eh? You surely will! The most dangerous animal known."

"Doctor, if you mean that literally—"

"Oh, I do, I do!"

"Then I take it that we are either being sent to

4

Mithra and will have to watch out for snow apes, or we are going to stay on Terra and be dumped where we can expect leopards. Am I right?"

The Deacon shook his head despairingly. "My boy, you had better cancel and take this course over. Those dumb brutes aren't dangerous."

"But Jasper says, in *Predators and Prey,* that the two trickiest, most dangerous—"

"Jasper's maiden aunt! I'm talking about the *real* King of the Beasts, the only animal that is always dangerous, even when not hungry. The two-legged brute. Take a look around you!"

The instructor leaned forward. "I've said this nineteen dozen times but you still don't believe it. Man is the one animal that can't be tamed. He goes along for years as peaceful as a cow, when it suits him. Then when it suits him not to be, he makes a leopard look like a tabby cat. Which goes double for the female of the species. Take another look around you. All friends. We've been on group-survival field tests together; we can depend on each other. So? Read about the Donner Party, or the First Venus Expedition. Anyhow, the test area will have several other classes in it, all strangers to you." Doctor Matson fixed his eye on Rod. "I hate to see some of you take this test, I really do. Some of you are city dwellers by nature; I'm afraid I have not managed to get it through your heads that there are no policemen where you are going. Nor will I be around to give you a hand if you make some silly mistake."

His eye moved on; Rod wondered if the Deacon meant him. Sometimes he felt that the Deacon took delight in rawhiding him. But Rod knew that it was serious; the course was required for all the Outlands professions for the good reason that the Outlands were places where you were smart—or you were dead. Rod had chosen to take this course before entering college because he hoped that it would help him to get a scholarship—but that did not mean that he thought it was just a formality.

He looked around, wondering who would be willing to team with him now that Jimmy had dropped out. There was a couple in front of him, Bob Baxter and Carmen Garcia. He checked them off, as they undoubtedly would team together; they planned to become medical missionaries and intended to marry as soon as they could.

How about Johann Braun? He would make a real partner, all right—strong, fast on his feet, and smart. But Rod did not trust him, nor did he think that Braun would want him. He began to see that he might have made a mistake in not cultivating other friends in the class besides Jimmy.

That big Zulu girl, Caroline something-unpronounceable. Strong as an ox and absolutely fearless. But it would not do to team with a girl; girls were likely to mistake a cold business deal for a romantic gambit. His eyes moved on until at last he was forced to conclude that there was no one there to whom he wished to suggest partnership.

"Prof, how about a hint? Should we take suntan oil? Or chilblain lotion?"

Matson grinned and drawled, "Son, I'll tell you every bit that I know. This test area was picked by a teacher in Europe . . . and I picked one for his class. But I don't know what it is any more than you do. Send me a post card."

"But—" The boy who had spoken stopped. Then he suddenly stood up. "Prof, this isn't a fair test. I'm checking out."

"What's unfair about it? Not that we meant to make it fair."

"Well, you could dump us any place—"

"That's right."

"—the back side of the Moon, in vacuum up to our chins. Or onto a chlorine planet. Or the middle of an ocean. I don't know whether to take a space suit, or a canoe. So the deuce with it. Real life isn't like that."

"It isn't, eh?" Matson said softly. "That's what Jonah said when the whale swallowed him." He added, "But I will give you some hints. We mean this test to be passed by anyone bright enough to deserve it. So we won't let you walk into a poisonous atmosphere, or a vacuum, without a mask. If you are dumped into water, land won't be too far to swim. And so on. While I don't know where you are going, I did see the list of test areas for this year's classes. A smart man can survive in any

6

of them. You ought to realize, son, that the Board of Education would have nothing to gain by killing off all its candidates for the key professions."

The student sat down again as suddenly as he had stood up. The instructor said, "Change your mind again?"

"Uh, yes, sir. If it's a fair test, I'll take it."

Matson shook his head. "You've already flunked it. You're excused. Don't bother the Registrar; I'll notify him."

The boy started to protest; Matson inclined his head toward the door. "Out!" There was an embarrassed silence while he left the room, then Matson said briskly, "This is a class in applied philosophy and I am sole judge of who is ready and who is not. Anybody who thinks of the world in terms of what it 'ought' to be, rather than what it is, isn't ready for final examination. You've got to relax and roll with the punch . . . not get yourself all worn out with adrenalin exhaustion at the slings and arrows of outrageous fortune. Any more questions?"

There were a few more but it became evident that Matson either truthfully did not know the nature of the test area, or was guarding the knowledge; his answers gained them nothing. He refused to advise as to weapons, saying simply that the school armorer would be at the gate ready to issue all usual weapons, while any unusual ones were up to the individual. "Remember, though, your best weapon is between your ears and under your scalp—provided it's loaded."

The group started to drift away; Rod got up to leave. Matson caught his eye and said, "Walker, are you planning to take the test?"

"Why, yes, of course, sir."

"Come here a moment." He led him into his office, closed the door and sat down. He looked up at Rod, fiddled with a paperweight on his desk and said slowly, "Rod, you're a good boy . . . but sometimes that isn't enough."

Rod said nothing.

"Tell me," Matson continued, "why you want to take this test?"

"Sir?"

7

" 'Sir' yourself," Matson answered grumpily. "Answer my question."

Rod stared, knowing that he had gone over this with Matson before he was accepted for the course. But he explained again his ambition to study for an Outlands profession. "So I have to qualify in survival. I couldn't even get a degree in colonial administration without it, much less any of the planetography or planetology specialties."

"Want to be an explorer, huh?"

"Yes, sir."

"Like me."

"Yes, sir. Like you."

"Hmm . . . would you believe me if I told you that it was the worst mistake I ever made?"

"Huh? No, sir!"

"I didn't think you would. Son, the cutest trick of all is how to know *then* what you know *now*. No way to, of course. But I'm telling you straight: I think you've been born into the wrong age."

"Sir?"

"I think you are a romantic. Now this is a very romantic age, so there is no room in it for romantics; it calls for practical men. A hundred years ago you would have made a banker or lawyer or professor and you could have worked out your romanticism by reading fanciful tales and dreaming about what you might have been if you hadn't had the misfortune to be born into a humdrum period. But this happens to be a period when adventure and romance are a part of daily existence. Naturally it takes very practical people to cope with it."

Rod was beginning to get annoyed. "What's the matter with *me?*"

"Nothing. I like you. I don't want to see you get hurt. But you are 'way too emotional, too sentimental to be a real survivor type."

Matson pushed a hand toward him. "Now keep your shirt on. I know you can make fire by rubbing a couple of dry words together. I'm well aware that you won merit badges in practically everything. I'm sure you can devise a water filter with your bare hands and know which side of the tree the moss grows on. But I'm not sure that you can beware of the Truce of the Bear."

8

" 'The Truce of the Bear?' "

"Never mind. Son, I think you ought to cancel this course. If you must, you can repeat it in college."

Rod looked stubborn. Matson sighed. "I could drop you. Perhaps I should."

"But *why,* sir?"

"That's the point. I couldn't give a reason. On the record, you're as promising a student as I have ever had." He stood up and put out his hand. "Good luck. And remember—when it gets down to fundamentals, do what you have to do and shed no tears."

Rod should have gone straight home. His family lived in an out-county of Greater New York City, located on the Grand Canyon plateau through Hoboken Gate. But his commuting route required him to change at Emigrants' Gap and he found himself unable to resist stopping to rubberneck.

When he stepped out of the tube from school he should have turned right, taken the rotary lift to the level above, and stepped through to Arizona Strip. But he was thinking about supplies, equipment, and weapons for tomorrow's examination; his steps automatically bore left, he got on the slideway leading to the great hall of the planetary gates.

He told himself that he would watch for only ten minutes; he would not be late for dinner. He picked his way through the crowd and entered the great hall—not onto the emigration floor itself, but onto the spectator's balcony facing the gates. This was the new gate house he was in, the one opened for traffic in '68; the original Emigrants' Gap, now used for Terran traffic and trade with Luna, stood on the Jersey Flats a few kilometers east alongside the pile that powered it.

The balcony faced the six gates. It could seat eighty-six hundred people but was half filled and crowded only in the center. It was here, of course, that Rod wished to sit so that he might see through all six gates. He wormed his way down the middle aisle, squatted by the railing, then spotted someone leaving a front row seat. Rod grabbed it, earning a dirty look from a man who had started for it from the other aisle.

Rod fed coins into the arm of the seat; it opened out,

he sat down and looked around. He was opposite the replica Statue of Liberty, twin to the one that had stood for a century where now was Bedloe Crater. Her torch reached to the distant ceiling; on both her right and her left three great gates let emigrants into the outer worlds.

Rod did not glance at the statue; he looked at the gates. It was late afternoon and heavily overcast at east coast North America, but gate one was open to some planetary spot having glaring noonday sun; Rod could catch glimpses through it of men dressed in shorts and sun hats and nothing else. Gate number two had a pressure lock rigged over it; it carried a big skull & crossbones sign and the symbol for chlorine. A red light burned over it. While he watched, the red light flickered out and a blue light replaced it; the door slowly opened and a traveling capsule for a chlorine-breather crawled out. Waiting to meet it were eight humans in diplomatic full dress. One carried a gold baton.

Rod considered spending another half pluton to find out who the important visitor was, but his attention was diverted to gate five. An auxiliary gate had been set up on the floor, facing gate five and almost under the balcony. Two high steel fences joined the two gates, forming with them an alley as wide as the gates and as long as the space between, about fifteen meters by seventy-five. This pen was packed with humanity moving from the temporary gate toward and through gate five—and onto some planet light-years away. They poured out of nowhere, for the floor back of the auxiliary gate was bare, hurried like cattle between the two fences, spilled through gate five and were gone. A squad of brawny Mongol policemen, each armed with a staff as tall as himself, was spread out along each fence. They were using their staves to hurry the emigrants and they were not being gentle. Almost underneath Rod one of them prodded an old coolie so hard that he stumbled and fell. The man had been carrying his belongings, his equipment for a new world, in two bundles supported from a pole balanced on his right shoulder.

The old coolie fell to his skinny knees, tried to get up, fell flat. Rod thought sure he would be trampled, but somehow he was on his feet again—minus his baggage.

10

He tried to hold his place in the torrent and recover his possessions, but the guard prodded him again and he was forced to move on barehanded. Rod lost sight of him before he had moved five meters.

There were local police outside the fence but they did not interfere. This narrow stretch between the two gates was, for the time, extraterritorial; the local police had no jurisdiction. But one of them did seem annoyed at the brutality shown the old man; he put his face to the steel mesh and called out something in lingua terra. The Mongol cop answered savagely in the same simple language, telling the North American what he could do about it, then went back to shoving and shouting and prodding still more briskly.

The crowd streaming through the pen were Asiatics—Japanese, Indonesians, Siamese, some East Indians, a few Eurasians, but predominantly South Chinese. To Rod they all looked much alike—tiny women with babies on hip or back, or often one on back and one in arms, endless runny-nosed and shaven-headed children, fathers with household goods in enormous back packs or pushed ahead on barrows. There were a few dispirited ponies dragging two-wheeled carts much too big for them but most of the torrent had only that which they could carry.

Rod had heard an old story which asserted that if all the Chinese on Terra were marched four abreast past a given point the column would never pass that point, as more Chinese would be born fast enough to replace those who had marched past. Rod had taken his slide rule and applied arithmetic to check it—to find, of course, that the story was nonsense; even if one ignored deaths, while counting all births, the last Chinese would pass the reviewing stand in less than four years. Nevertheless, while watching this mob being herded like brutes into a slaughterhouse, Rod felt that the old canard was true even though its mathematics was faulty. There seemed to be no end to them.

He decided to risk that half pluton to find out what was going on. He slid the coin into a slot in the chair's speaker; the voice of the commentator reached his ears: "—the visiting minister. The prince royal was met by officials of the Terran Corporation including the Direc-

11

tor General himself and now is being escorted to the locks of the Ratoonian enclave. After the television reception tonight staff level conversations will start. A spokesman close to the Director General has pointed out that, in view of the impossibility of conflict of interest between oxygen types such as ourselves and the Ratoonians, any outcome of the conference must be to our advantage, the question being to what extent.

"If you will turn your attention again to gate five, we will repeat what we said earlier: gate five is on forty-eight hour loan to the Australasian Republic. The temporary gate you see erected below is hyperfolded to a point in central Australia in the Arunta Desert, where this emigration has been mounting in a great encampment for the past several weeks. His Serene Majesty Chairman Fung Chee Mu of the Australasian Republic has informed the Corporation that his government intends to move in excess of two million people in forty-eight hours, a truly impressive figure, more than forty thousand each hour. The target figure for this year for all planetary emigration gates taken together—Emigrants' Gap, Peter the Great, and Witwatersrand Gates —is only seventy million emigrants or an average of eight thousand per hour. This movement proposes a rate five times as great using only *one* gate!"

The commentator continued: "Yet when we watch the speed, efficiency and the, uh—*forthrightness* with which they are carrying out this evolution it seems likely that they will achieve their goal. Our own figures show them to be slightly ahead of quota for the first nine hours. During those same nine hours there have been one hundred seven births and eighty-two deaths among the emigrants, the high death rate, of course, being incident to the temporary hazards of the emigration.

"The planet of destination, GO-8703-IV, to be called henceforth 'Heavenly Mountains' according to Chairman Fung, is classed as a bounty planet and no attempt had been made to colonize it. The Corporation has been assured that the colonists are volunteers." It seemed to Rod that the announcer's tone was ironical. "This is understandable when one considers the phenomenal population pressure of the Australasian Republic. A brief historical rundown may be in order. After the re-

12

moval of the remnants of the former Australian population to New Zealand, pursuant to the Peiping Peace Treaty, the first amazing effort of the new government was the creation of the great inland sea of—"

Rod muted the speaker and looked back at the floor below. He did not care to hear school-book figures on how the Australian Desert had been made to blossom like the rose . . . and nevertheless had been converted into a slum with more people in it than all of North America. Something new was happening at gate four—

Gate four had been occupied by a moving cargo belt when he had come in; now the belt had crawled away and lost itself in the bowels of the terminal and an emigration party was lining up to go through.

This was no poverty-stricken band of refugees chivvied along by police; here each family had its own wagon . . . long, sweeping, boat-tight Conestogas drawn by three-pair teams and housed in sturdy glass canvas . . . square and businesslike Studebakers with steel bodies, high mudcutter wheels, and pulled by one or two-pair teams. The draft animals were Morgans and lordly Clydesdales and jug-headed Missouri mules with strong shoulders and shrewd, suspicious eyes. Dogs trotted between wheels, wagons were piled high with household goods and implements and children, poultry protested the indignities of fate in cages tied on behind, and a little Shetland pony, riderless but carrying his saddle and just a bit too tall to run underneath with the dogs, stayed close to the tailgate of one family's rig.

Rod wondered at the absence of cattle and stepped up the speaker again. But the announcer was still droning about the fertility of Australasians; he muted it again and watched. Wagons had moved onto the floor and taken up tight echelon position close to the gate, ready to move, with the tail of the train somewhere out of sight below. The gate was not yet ready and drivers were getting down and gathering at the Salvation Army booth under the skirts of the Goddess of Liberty, for a cup of coffee and some banter. It occurred to Rod that there probably was no coffee where they were going and might not be for years, since Terra never exported food —on the contrary, food and fissionable metals were almost the only permissible imports; until an Outland

13

colony produced a surplus of one or the other it could expect precious little help from Terra.

It was extremely expensive in terms of uranium to keep an interstellar gate open and the people in this wagon train could expect to be out of commercial touch with Earth until such a time as they had developed surpluses valuable enough in trade to warrant reopening the gate at regular intervals. Until that time they were on their own and must make do with what they could take with them . . . which made horses more practical than helicopters, picks and shovels more useful than bulldozers. Machinery gets out of order and requires a complex technology to keep it going—but good old "hayburners" keep right on breeding, cropping grass, and pulling loads.

Deacon Matson had told the survival class that the real hardhips of primitive Outlands were not the lack of plumbing, heating, power, light, nor weather conditioning, but the shortage of simple things like coffee and tobacco.

Rod did not smoke and coffee he could take or let alone; he could not imagine getting fretful over its absence. He scrunched down in his seat, trying to see through the gate to guess the cause of the holdup. He could not see well, as the arching canvas of a prairie schooner blocked his view, but it did seem that the gate operator had a phase error; it looked as if the sky was where the ground ought to be. The extradimensional distortions necessary to match places on two planets many light-years apart were not simply a matter of expenditure of enormous quantities of energy; they were precision problems fussy beyond belief, involving high mathematics and high art—the math was done by machine but the gate operator always had to adjust the last couple of decimal places by prayer and intuition.

In addition to the dozen-odd proper motions of each of the planets involved, motions which could usually be added and canceled out, there was also the rotation of each planet. The problem was to make the last hyperfold so that the two planets were internally tangent at the points selected as gates, with their axes parallel and their rotations in the *same* direction. Theoretically it was possible to match two points in contra-rotation,

14

twisting the insubstantial fabric of space-time in exact step with "real" motions; practically such a solution was not only terribly wasteful of energy but almost unworkable—the ground surface beyond the gate tended to skid away like a slidewalk and tilt at odd angles.

Rod did not have the mathematics to appreciate the difficulties. Being only about to finish high school his training had gone no farther than tensor calculus, statistical mechanics, simple transfinities, generalized geometries of six dimensions, and, on the practical side, analysis for electronics, primary cybernetics and robotics, and basic design of analog computers; he had had no advanced mathematics as yet. He was not aware of his ignorance and simply concluded that the gate operator must be thumb-fingered. He looked back at the emigrant party.

The drivers were still gathered at the booth, drinking coffee and munching doughnuts. Most of the men were growing beards; Rod concluded from the beavers that the party had been training for several months. The captain of the party sported a little goatee, mustaches, and rather long hair, but it seemed to Rod that he could not be many years older than Rod himself. He was a professional, of course, required to hold a degree in Outlands arts—hunting, scouting, jackleg mechanics, gunsmithing, farming, first aid, group psychology, survival group tactics, law, and a dozen other things the race has found indispensable when stripped for action.

This captain's mount was a Palomino mare, lovely as a sunrise, and the captain was dressed as a California don of an earlier century—possibly as a compliment to his horse. A warning light flashed at the gate's annunciator panel and he swung into saddle, still eating a doughnut, and cantered down the wagons for a final inspection, riding toward Rod. His back was straight, his seat deep and easy, his bearing confident. Carried low on a fancy belt he wore two razor guns, each in a silver-chased holster that matched the ornate silver of his bridle and saddle.

Rod held his breath until the captain passed out of sight under the balcony, then sighed and considered studying to be like him, rather than for one of the more intellectual Outlands professions. He did not know just what he did want to be . . . except that he meant to get off Earth as soon as he possibly could and get out there where things were going on!

Which reminded him that the first hurdle was tomorrow; in a few days he would either be eligible to matriculate for whatever it was he decided on, or he would be—but no use worrying about *that*. He remembered uneasily that it was getting late and he had not even decided on equipment, nor picked his weapons. This party captain carried razor guns; should he carry one? No, this party would fight as a unit, if it had to fight. Its leader carried that type of weapon to enforce his authority—not for solo survival. Well, what should he take?

A siren sounded and the drivers returned to their wagons. The captain came back at a brisk trot. "Reins up!" he called out. "Reeeeeeiiiins UP!" He took station by the gate, facing the head of the train; the mare stood quivering and tending to dance.

The Salvation Army lassie came out from behind her counter carrying a baby girl. She called to the party captain but her voice did not carry to the balcony.

The captain's voice did carry. "Number four! Doyle! Come get your child!" A red-headed man with a spade beard climbed down from the fourth wagon and sheepishly reclaimed the youngster to a chorus of cheers and cat calls. He passed the baby up to his wife, who upped its skirt and commenced paddling its bottom. Doyle climbed to his seat and took his reins.

"Call off!" the captain sang out.

"One."

"Tuh!"

"Three!"

"Fo*ah!*"

"*Five!*"

The count passed under the balcony, passed down the chute out of hearing. In a few moment it came back, running down this time, ending with a shouted *"ONE!"* The captain held up his right arm and watched the lights of the order panel.

A light turned green. He brought his arm down smartly with a shout of "Roll 'em! *Ho!*" The Palomino took off like a race horse, cut under the nose of the nigh lead horse of the first team, and shot through the gate.

Whips cracked. Rod could hear shouts of "Git, Molly! Git, Ned!" and "No, no, you jugheads!" The train begin to roll. By the time the last one on the floor was through the gate and the much larger number which had been in the chute below had begun to show it was rolling at a gallop, with the drivers bracing their feet wide and their wives riding the brakes. Rod tried to count them, made it possibly sixty-three wagons as the last one rumbled through the gate . . . and was gone, already half a galaxy away.

He sighed and sat back with a warm feeling sharpened with undefined sorrow. Then he stepped up the speaker volume: "—onto New Canaan, the premium planet described by the great Langford as 'The rose without thorns.' These colonists have paid a premium of sixteen thousand four hundred per person—not counting exempt or co-opted members—for the privilege of seeking their fortunes and protecting their posterity by moving to New Canaan. The machines predict that the premium will increase for another twenty-eight years; therefore, if you are considering giving your children the priceless boon of citizenship on New Canaan, the time to act is now. For a beautiful projection reel showing this planet send one pluton to 'Information, Box One, Emigrants' Gap, New Jersey County, Greater New York.' For a complete descriptive listing of all planets now open plus a special list of those to be opened in the near future add another half pluton. Those seeing this broadcast in person may obtain these at the information booth in the foyer outside the great hall."

Rod did not listen. He had long since sent for every free item and most of the non-free ones issued by the Commission for Emigration and Trade. Just now he was wondering why the gate to New Canaan had not relaxed.

He found out at once. Stock barricades rose up out of the floor, forming a fenced passage from gate four to the chute under him. Then a herd of cattle filled the gate and came flooding toward him, bawling and snorting. They were prime Hereford steers, destined to become tender steaks and delicious roasts for a rich but

17

slightly hungry Earth. After them and among them rode New Canaan cowpunchers armed with long goads with which they urged the beasts to greater speed—the undesirability of running weight off the animals was offset by the extreme cost of keeping the gate open, a cost which had to be charged against the cattle.

Rod discovered that the speaker had shut itself off; the half hour he had paid for was finished. He sat up with sudden guilt, realizing that he would have to hurry or he would be late for supper. He rushed out, stepping on feet and mumbling apologies, and caught the slideway to Hoboken Gate.

This gate, being merely for Terra-surface commuting, was permanently dilated and required no operator, since the two points brought into coincidence were joined by a rigid frame, the solid Earth. Rod showed his commuter's ticket to the electronic monitor and stepped through to Arizona, in company with a crowd of neighbors.

"The (almost) solid Earth—" The gate robot took into account tidal distortions but could not anticipate minor seismic variables. As Rod stepped through he felt his feet quiver as if to a small earthquake, then the *terra* was again *firma*. But he was still in an airlock at sea-level pressure. The radiation from massed bodies triggered the mechanism, the lock closed and air pressure dropped. Rod yawned heavily to adjust to the pressure of Grand Canyon plateau, North Rim, less than three quarters that of New Jersey. But despite the fact that he made the change twice a day he found himself rubbing his right ear to get rid of an earache.

The lock opened, he stepped out. Having come two thousand miles in a split second he now had ten minutes by slide tube and a fifteen minute walk to get home. He decided to dogtrot and be on time after all. He might have made it if there had not been several thousand other people trying to use the same facilities.

18

2

The Fifth Way

ROCKET SHIPS DID NOT CONQUER SPACE; THEY MERELY challenged it. A rocket leaving Earth at seven miles per second is terribly slow for the vast reaches beyond. Only the Moon is reasonably near—four days, more or less. Mars is thirty-seven weeks away, Saturn a dreary six years, Pluto an impossible half century, by the elliptical orbits possible to rockets.

Ortega's torch ships brought the Solar System within reach. Based on mass conversion, Einstein's deathless $e = Mc^2$, they could boost for the entire trip at any acceleration the pilot could stand. At an easy one gravity the inner planets were only hours from Earth, far Pluto only eighteen days. It was a change like that from horseback to jet plane.

The shortcoming of this brave new toy was that there was not much anywhere to go. The Solar System, from a human standpoint, is made up of remarkably unattractive real estate—save for lovely Terra herself, lush and green and beautiful. The steel-limbed Jovians enjoy gravity 2.5 times ours and their poisonous air at inhuman pressure keeps them in health. Martians prosper in near vacuum, the rock lizards of Luna do not breathe at all. But these planets are not for men.

Men prosper on an oxygen planet close enough to a G-type star for the weather to cycle around the freezing point of water . . . that is to say, on Earth.

When you are already there why go anywhere? The reason was babies, too many babies. Malthus pointed it out long ago; food increases by aritmetical progression, people increase by geometrical progression. By World War I half the world lived on the edge of starvation;

by World War II Earth's population was increasing by 55,000 people *every day;* before World War III, as early as 1954, the increase had jumped to 100,000 mouths and stomachs per day, 35,000,000 additional people each year . . . and the population of Terra had climbed well beyond that which its farm lands could support.

The hydrogen, germ, and nerve gas horrors that followed were not truly political. The true meaning was more that of beggars fighting over a crust of bread.

The author of *Gulliver's Travels* sardonically proposed that Irish babies be fattened for English tables; other students urged less drastic ways of curbing population—none of which made the slightest difference. Life, *all* life, has the twin drives to survive and to reproduce. Intelligence is an aimless byproduct except as it serves these basic drives.

But intelligence *can* be made to serve the mindless demands of life. Our Galaxy contains in excess of one hundred thousand Earth-type planets, each as warm and motherly to men as sweet Terra. Ortega's torch ships could reach the stars. Mankind could colonize, even as the hungry millions of Europe had crossed the Atlantic and raised more babies in the New World.

Some did . . . hundreds of thousands. But the entire race, working as a team, cannot build and launch a hundred ships a day, each fit for a thousand colonists, and keep it up day after day, year after year, time without end. Even with the hands and the will (which the race never had) there is not that much steel, aluminum, and uranium in Earth's crust. There is not one hundredth of the necessary amount.

But intelligence can find solutions where there are none. Psychologists once locked an ape in a room, for which they had arranged only four ways of escaping. Then they spied on him to see which of the four he would find.

The ape escaped a fifth way.

Dr. Jesse Evelyn Ramsbotham had not been trying to solve the baby problem; he had been trying to build a time machine. He had two reasons: first, because time machines are an impossibility; second, because his hands would sweat and he would stammer whenever in the

20

presence of a nubile female. He was not aware that the first reason was compensation for the second, in fact he was not aware of the second reason—it was a subject his conscious mind avoided.

It is useless to speculate as to the course of history had Jesse Evelyn Ramsbotham's parents had the good sense to name their son Bill instead of loading him with two girlish names. He might have become an All-American halfback and ended up selling bonds and adding his quota of babies to a sum already disastrous. Instead he became a mathematical physicist.

Progress in physics is achieved by denying the obvious and accepting the impossible. Any nineteenth century physicist could have given unassailable reasons why atom bombs were impossible if his reason were not affronted at the question; any twentieth century physicist could explain why time travel was incompatible with the real world of space-time. But Ramsbotham began fiddling with the three greatest Einsteinian equations, the two relativity equations for distance and duration and the mass-conversion equation; each contained the velocity of light. "Velocity" is first derivative, the differential of distance with respect to time; he converted those equations into differential equations, then played games with them. He would feed the results to the Rakitiac computer, remote successor to Univac, Eniac and Maniac. While he was doing these things his hands never sweated nor did he stammer, except when he was forced to deal with the young lady who was chief programmer for the giant computer.

His first model produced a time-stasis or low-entropy field no bigger than a football—but a lighted cigarette placed inside with full power setting was still burning a week later. Ramsbotham picked up the cigarette, resumed smoking and thought about it.

Next he tried a day-old chick, with colleagues to witness. Three months later the chick was unaged and no hungrier than chicks usually are. He reversed the phase relation and cut in power for the shortest time he could manage with his bread-boarded hook-up.

In less than a second the newly-hatched chick was long dead, starved and decayed.

He was aware that he had simply changed the slope

21

of a curve, but he was convinced that he was on the track of true time travel. He never did find it, although once he thought that he had—he repeated by request his demonstration with a chick for some of his colleagues; that night two of them picked the lock on his lab, let the little thing out and replaced it with an egg. Ramsbotham might have been permanently convinced that he had found time travel and then spent the rest of his life in a blind alley had they not cracked the egg and showed him that it was hard-boiled.

But he did not give up. He made a larger model and tried to arrange a dilation, or anomaly (he did not call it a "Gate") which would let him get in and out of the field himself.

When he threw on power, the space between the curving magnetodes of his rig no longer showed the wall beyond, but a steaming jungle. He jumped to the conclusion that this must be a forest of the Carboniferous Period. It had often occurred to him that the difference between space and time might simply be human prejudice, but this was not one of the times; he believed what he wanted to believe.

He hurriedly got a pistol and with much bravery and no sense crawled between the magnetodes.

Ten minutes later he was arrested for waving firearms around in Rio de Janeiro's civic botanical gardens. A lack of the Portuguese language increased both his difficulties and the length of time he spent in a tropical pokey, but three days later through the help of the North American consul he was on his way home. He thought and filled notebooks with equations and question marks on the whole trip.

The short cut to the stars had been found.

Ramsbotham's discoveries eliminated the basic cause of war and solved the problem of what to do with all those dimpled babies. A hundred thousand planets were no farther away than the other side of the street. Virgin continents, raw wilderness, fecund jungles, killing deserts, frozen tundras, and implacable mountains lay just beyond the city gates, and the human race was again going out where the street lights do not shine, out where there was no friendly cop on the corner nor indeed a corner, out where there were no well-hung, tender steaks, no boneless hams, no packaged, processed foods suitable for delicate minds and pampered bodies. The biped omnivore again had need of his biting, tearing, animal teeth, for the race was spilling out (as it had so often before) to kill or be killed, eat or be eaten.

But the human race's one great talent is survival. The race, as always, adjusted to conditions, and the most urbanized, mechanized, and civilized, most upholstered and luxurious culture in all history trained its best children, its potential leaders, in primitive pioneer survival —man naked against nature.

Rod Walker knew about Dr. J. E. Ramsbotham, just as he knew about Einstein, Newton, and Columbus, but he thought about Ramsbotham no oftener than he thought about Columbus. These were figures in books, each larger than life and stuffed with straw, not real. He used the Ramsbotham Gate between Jersey and the Arizona Strip without thinking of its inventor the same way his ancestors used elevators without thinking of the name "Otis." If he thought about the miracle at all, it was a half-formed irritation that the Arizona side of Hoboken Gate was so far from his parents' home. It was known as Kaibab Gate on this side and was seven miles north of the Walker residence.

At the time the house had been built the location was at the extreme limit of tube delivery and other city utilities. Being an old house, its living room was above ground, with only bedrooms, pantry, and bombproof buried. The living room had formerly stuck nakedly above ground, an ellipsoid monocoque shell, but, as Greater New York spread, the neighborhood had been zoned for underground apartments and construction above ground which would interfere with semblance of virgin forest had been forbidden.

The Walkers had gone along to the extent of covering the living room with soil and planting it with casual native foliage, but they had refused to cover up their view window. It was the chief charm of the house, as it looked out at the great canyon. The community corporation had tried to coerce them into covering it up and had offered to replace it with a simulacrum window

23

such as the underground apartments used, with a relayed view of the canyon. But Rod's father was a stubborn man and maintained that with weather, women, and wine there was nothing "just as good." His window was still intact.

Rod found the family sitting in front of the window, watching a storm work its way up the canyon—his mother, his father, and, to his great surprise, his sister. Helen was ten years older than he and an assault captain in the Amazons; she was seldom home.

The warmth of his greeting was not influenced by his realization that her arrival would probably cause his own lateness to pass with little comment. "Sis! Hey, this is *swell*—I thought you were on Thule."

"I was . . . until a few hours ago." Rod tried to shake hands; his sister gathered him in a bear hug and bussed him on the mouth, squeezing him against the raised ornaments of her chrome corselet. She was still in uniform, a fact that caused him to think that she had just arrived—on her rare visits home she usually went slopping around in an old bathrobe and go-ahead slippers, her hair caught up in a knot. Now she was still in dress armor and kilt and had dumped her side arms, gauntlets, and plumed helmet on the floor.

She looked him over proudly. "My, but you've grown! You're almost as tall as I am."

"I'm taller."

"Want to bet? No, don't try to wiggle away from me; I'll twist your arm. Slip off your shoes and stand back to back."

"Sit down, children," their father said mildly. "Rod, why were you late?"

"Uh . . ." He had worked out a diversion involving telling about the examination coming up, but he did not use it as his sister intervened.

"Don't heckle him, Pater. Ask for excuses and you'll get them. I learned that when I was a sublieutenant."

"Quiet, daughter. I can raise him without your help."

Rod was surprised by his father's edgy answer, was more surprised by Helen's answer: "So? Really?" Her tone was odd.

Rod saw his mother raise a hand, seem about to speak, then close her mouth. She looked upset. His sister and father looked at each other; neither spoke. Rod looked from one to the other, said slowly, "Say, what's all this?"

His father glanced at him. "Nothing. We'll say no more about it. Dinner is waiting. Coming, dear?" He turned to his wife, handed her up from her chair, offered her his arm.

"Just a minute," Rod said insistently. "I was late because I was hanging around the Gap."

"Very well. You know better, but I said we would say no more about it." He turned toward the lift.

"But I wanted to tell you something else, Dad. I won't be home for the next week or so."

"Very well—*eh?* What did you say?"

"I'll be away for a while, sir. Maybe ten days or a bit longer."

His father looked perplexed, then shook his head. "Whatever your plans are, you will have to change them. I can't let you go away at this time."

"But, Dad—"

"I'm sorry, but that is definite."

"But, Dad, I *have* to!"

"No."

Rod looked frustrated. His sister said suddenly, "Pater, wouldn't it be well to find out why he wants to be away?"

"Now, daughter—"

"Dad, I'm taking my solo survival, starting tomorrow morning!"

Mrs. Walker gasped, then began to weep. Her husband said, "There, there, my dear!" then turned to his son and said harshly, "You've upset your mother."

"But, Dad, I . . ." Rod shut up, thinking bitterly that no one seemed to give a hoot about *his* end of it. After all, *he* was the one who was going to have to sink or swim. A lot they knew or—

"You see, Pater," his sister was saying. "He does have to be away. He has no choice, because—"

"I see nothing of the sort! Rod, I meant to speak about this earlier, but I had not realized that your test would take place so soon. When I signed permission for you to take that course, I had, I must admit, a mental reservation. I felt that the experience would be valuable

25

later . . . when and if you took the course in college. But I never intended to let you come up against the final test while still in high school. You are too young."

Rod was shocked speechless. But his sister again spoke for him. "Fiddlesticks!"

"Eh? Now, daughter, please remember that—"

"Repeat fiddlesticks! Any girl in my company has been up against things as rough and many of them are not much older than Buddy. What are you trying to do, Pater? Break his nerve?"

"You have no reason to . . . I think we had best discuss this later."

"I think that is a good idea." Captain Walker took her brother's arm and they followed their parents down to the refectory. Dinner was on the table, still warm in its delivery containers; they took their places, standing, and Mr. Walker solemnly lighted the Peace Lamp. The family was evangelical Monist by inheritance, each of Rod's grandfathers having been converted in the second great wave of proselyting that swept out of Persia in the last decade of the previous century, and Rod's father took seriously his duties as family priest.

As the ritual proceeded Rod made his responses automatically, his mind on this new problem. His sister chimed in heartily but his mother's answers could hardly be heard.

Nevertheless the warm symbolism had its effect; Rod felt himself calming down. By the time his father intoned the last "—one Principle, one family, one flesh!" he felt like eating. He sat down and took the cover off his plate.

A yeast cutlet, molded to look like a chop and stripped with real bacon, a big baked potato, and a grilled green lobia garnished with baby's buttons . . . Rod's mouth watered as he reached for the catsup.

He noticed that Mother was not eating much, which surprised him. Dad was not eating much either but Dad often just picked at his food . . . he became aware with sudden warm pity that Dad was thinner and greyer than ever. How old was Dad?

His attention was diverted by a story his sister was telling: "—and so the Commandant told me I would have to clamp down. And I said to her, 'Ma'am, girls will be girls. If I have to bust a petty officer everytime one of them does something like that, pretty soon I won't have anything but privates. And Sergeant Dvorak is the best gunner I have.' "

"Just a second," her father interrupted. "I thought you said 'Kelly,' not 'Dvorak.' "

"I did and she did. Pretending to misunderstand which sergeant she meant was my secret weapon—for I had Dvorak cold for the same offense, and Tiny Dvorak (she's bigger than I am) is the Squadron's white hope for the annual corps-wide competition for best trooper. Of course, losing her stripes would put her, and us, out of the running.

"So I straightened out the 'mix up' in my best wide-eyed, thick-headed manner, let the old gal sit for a moment trying not to bite her nails, then told her that I had both women confined to barracks until that gang of college boys was through installing the new 'scope, and sang her a song about how the quality of mercy is not strained, it droppeth as the gentle rain from heaven, and made myself responsible for seeing to it that she was not again embarrassed by scandalous—her word, not mine —scandalous incidents . . . especially when she was showing quadrant commanders around.

"So she grumpily allowed as how the company commander was responsible for her company and she would hold me to it and now would I get out and let her work on the quarterly training report in peace? So I threw her my best parade ground salute and got out so fast I left a hole in the air."

"I wonder," Mr. Walker said judicially, "if you should oppose your commanding officer in such matters? After all, she is older and presumably wiser than you are."

Helen made a little pile of the last of her baby's buttons, scooped them up and swallowed them. "Fiddle-sticks squared and cubed. Pardon me, Pater, but if you had any military service you would know better. I am as tough as blazes to my girls myself . . . and it just makes them boast about how they've got the worst fire-eater in twenty planets. But if they're in trouble higher up, I've got to take care of my kids. There always comes a day when there is something sticky up ahead and I have to stand up and walk toward it. And it will be all right because I'll have Kelly on my right flank and Dvorak on my left and each of them trying to take care of Maw Walker all by her ownself. I know what I'm doing. 'Walker's Werewolves' are a team."

Mrs. Walker shivered. "Gracious, darling, I wish you had never taken up a calling so . . . well, so *dangerous*."

Helen shrugged. "The death rate is the same for us as for anybody . . . one person, one death, sooner or later. What would you want, Mum? With eighteen million more women than men on this continent did you want me to sit and knit until my knight comes riding? Out where I operate, there are more men than women; I'll wing one yet, old and ugly as I am."

Rod asked curiously, "Sis, would you really give up your commission to get married?"

"Would I! I won't even count his arms and legs. If he is still warm and can nod his head, he's had it. My target is six babies and a farm."

Rod looked her over. "I'd say your chances are good. You're quite pretty even if your ankles are thick."

"Thanks, pardner. Thank you too much. What's for dessert, Mum?"

"I didn't look. Will you open it, dear?"

Dessert turned out to be iced mangorines, which pleased Rod. His sister went on talking. "The Service isn't a bad shake, on active duty. It's garrison duty that wears. My kids get fat and sloppy and restless and start fighting with each other from sheer boredom. For my choice, barracks casualties are more to be dreaded than combat. I'm hoping that our squadron will be tagged to take part in the pacification of Byer's Planet."

Mr. Walker looked at his wife, then at his daughter. "You have upset your mother again, my dear. Quite a bit of this talk has hardly been appropriate under the Light of Peace."

"I was asked questions, I answered."

"Well, perhaps so."

Helen glanced up. "Isn't it time to turn it out, anyway? We all seem to have finished eating."

"Why, if you like. Though it is hardly reverent to hurry."

"The Principle knows we haven't all eternity." She

turned to Rod. "How about making yourself scarce, mate? I want to make palaver with the folks."

"Gee, Sis, you act as if I was—"

"Get lost, Buddy. I'll see you later."

Rod left, feeling affronted. He saw Helen blow out the pax lamp as he did so.

He was still making lists when his sister came to his room. "Hi, kid."

"Oh. Hello, Sis."

"What are you doing? Figuring what to take on your solo?"

"Sort of."

"Mind if I get comfortable?" She brushed articles from his bed and sprawled on it. "We'll go into that later."

Rod thought it over. "Does that mean Dad won't object?"

"Yes, I pounded his head until he saw the light. But, as I said, we'll go into that later. I've got something to tell you, youngster."

"Such as?"

"The first thing is this. Our parents are not as stupid as you probably think they are. Fact is, they are pretty bright."

"I never said they were stupid!" Rod answered, uncomfortably aware of what his thoughts had been.

"No. But I heard what went on before dinner and so did you. Dad was throwing his weight around and not listening. But, Buddy, it has probably never occurred to you that it is hard work to be a parent, maybe the hardest job of all—particularly when you have no talent for it, which Dad hasn't. He knows it and works hard at it and is conscientious. Mostly he does mighty well. Sometimes he slips, like tonight. But, what you did not know is this: Dad is going to die."

"What?" Rod looked stricken. "I didn't know he was ill!"

"You weren't meant to know. Now climb down off the ceiling; there is a way out. Dad is terribly ill, and he would die in a few weeks at the most—unless something drastic is done. But something is going to be. So relax."

29

She explained the situation bluntly: Mr. Walker was suffering from a degenerative disease under which he was slowly starving to death. His condition was incurable by current medical art; he might linger on, growing weaker each day, for weeks or months—but he would certainly die soon.

Rod leaned his head on his hands and chastised himself. Dad dying . . . and he hadn't *even noticed.* They had kept it from him, like a baby, and he had been too stupid to see it.

His sister touched his shoulder. "Cut it out. If there is anything stupider than flogging yourself over something you can't help, I've yet to meet it. Anyhow, we are doing something about it."

"What? I thought you said nothing could be done?"

"Shut up and let your mind coast. The folks are going to make a Ramsbotham jump, five hundred to one, twenty years for two weeks. They've already signed a contract with Entropy, Incorporated. Dad has resigned from General Synthetics and is closing up his affairs; they'll kiss the world good-by this coming Wednesday—which is why he was being stern about your plans to be away at that time. You're the apple of his eye—Heaven knows why."

Rod tried to sort out too many new ideas at once. A time jump . . . of course! It would let Dad stay alive another twenty years. But— "Say, Sis, this doesn't get them anything! Sure, it's twenty years but it will be just two weeks to them . . . and Dad will be as sick as ever. I know what I'm talking about; they did the same thing for Hank Robbin's great grandfather and he died anyhow, right after they took him out of the stasis. Hank told me."

Captain Walker shrugged. "Probably a hopeless case to start with. But Dad's specialist, Dr. Hensley, says that he is morally certain that Dad's case is not hopeless . . . twenty years from now. I don't know anything about metabolic medicine, but Hensley says that they are on the verge and that twenty years from now they ought to be able to patch Dad up as easily they can graft on a new leg today."

"You really think so?"

"How should I know? In things like this you hire the

best expert you can, then follow his advice. The point is, if we don't do it, Dad is finished. So we do it."

"Yeah. Sure, sure, we've got to."

She eyed him closely and added, "All right. Now do you want to talk with them about it?"

"Huh?" He was startled by the shift. "Why? Are they waiting for me?"

"No. I persuaded them that it was best to keep it from you until it happened. Then I came straight in and told you. Now you can do as you please—pretend you don't know, or go have Mum cry over you, and listen to a lot of last-minute, man-to-man advice from Dad that you will never take. About midnight, with your nerves frazzled, you can get back to your preparations for your survival test. Play it your own way—but I've rigged it so you can avoid that, if you want to. Easier on everybody. Myself, I like a cat's way of saying good-by.'"

Rod's mind was in a turmoil. Not to say good-by seemed unnatural, ungrateful, untrue to family sentiment—but the prospect of saying good-by seemed almost unbearably embarrassing. "What's that about a cat?"

"When a cat greets you, he makes a big operation of it, bumping, stropping your legs, buzzing like mischief. But when he leaves, he just walks off and never looks back. Cats are smart."

"Well . . ."

"I suggest," she added, "that you remember that they are doing this for their convenience, not yours."

"But Dad has to—"

"Surely, Dad must, if he is to get well." She considered pointing out that the enormous expense of the time jump would leave Rod practically penniless; she decided that this was better left undiscussed. "But Mum does not have to."

"But she has to go with Dad!"

"So? Use arithmetic. She prefers leaving you alone for twenty years in order to be with Dad for two weeks. Or turn it around: she prefers having you orphaned to having herself widowed for the same length of time."

"I don't think that's quite fair to Mum," Rod answered slowly.

31

"I wasn't criticizing. She's making the right decision. Nevertheless, they both have a strong feeling of guilt about you and—"

"About *me?*"

"About you. I don't figure into it. If you insist on saying good-by, their guilt will come out as self-justification and self-righteousness and they will find ways to take it out on you and everybody will have a bad time. I don't want that. You are all my family."

"Uh, maybe you know best."

"I didn't get straight A's in emotional logic and military leadership for nothing. Man is not a rational animal; he is a rationalizing animal. Now let's see what you plan to take with you."

She looked over his lists and equipment, then whistled softly. "Whew! Rod, I never saw so much plunder. You won't be able to move. Who are you? Tweedledum preparing for battle, or the White Knight?"

"Well, I was going to thin it down," he answered uncomfortably.

"I should think so!"

"Uh, Sis, what sort of gun should I carry?"

"Huh? Why the deuce do you want a gun?"

"Why, for what I might run into, of course. Wild animals and things. Deacon Matson practically said that we could expect dangerous animals."

"I doubt if he advised you to carry a gun. From his reputation, Dr. Matson is a practical man. See here, infant, on this tour you are the rabbit, trying to escape the fox. You aren't the fox."

"What do you mean?"

"Your only purpose is to stay alive. Not to be brave, not to fight, not to dominate the wilds—but just stay breathing. One time in a hundred a gun might save your life; the other ninety-nine it will just tempt you into folly. Oh, no doubt Matson would take one, and I would, too. But we are salted; we know when not to use one. But consider this. That test area is going to be crawling with trigger-happy young squirts. If one shoots you, it won't matter that you have a gun, too—because you will be dead. But if you carry a gun, it makes you feel cocky; you won't take proper cover. If you don't

32

have one, then you'll *know* that you are the rabbit. You'll be careful."

"Did you take a gun on your solo test?"

"I did. And I lost it the first day. Which saved my life."

"How?"

"Because when I was caught without one I ran away from a Bessmer's griffin instead of trying to shoot it. You savvy Bessmer's griffin?"

"Uh, Spica V?"

"Spica IV. I don't know how much outer zoology they are teaching you kids these days—from the ignoramuses we get for recruits I've reached the conclusion that this new-fangled 'functional education' has abolished studying in favor of developing their cute little personalities. Why, I had one girl who wanted to— never mind; the thing about the griffin is that it does not really have vital organs. Its nervous system is decentralized, even its assimilation system. To kill it quickly you would have to grind it into hamburger. Shooting merely tickles it. But I did not know that; if I had had my gun I would have found out the hard way. As it was, it treed me for three days, which did my figure good and gave me time to think over the philosophy, ethics, and pragmatics of self-preservation."

Rod did not argue, but he still had a conviction that a gun was a handy thing to have around. It made him feel good, taller, stronger and more confident, to have one slapping against his thigh. He didn't have to use it—not unless he just had to. And he knew enough to take cover; nobody in the class could do a silent sneak the way he could. While Sis was a good soldier, still she didn't know everything and—

But Sis was still talking. "I know how good a gun feels. It makes you bright-eyed and bushy-tailed, three meters tall and covered with hair. You're ready for anything and kind of hoping you'll find it. Which is exactly what is dangerous about it—because you aren't anything of the sort. You are a feeble, hairless embryo, remarkably easy to kill. You could carry an assault gun with two thousand meters precision range and isotope charges that will blow up a hill, but you still would not have eyes in the back of your head like a janus bird,

33

nor be able to see in the dark like the Thetis pygmies. Death can cuddle up behind you while you are drawing a bead on something in front."

"But, Sis, your own company carries guns."

"Guns, radar, bombs, black scopes, gas, warpers, and some things which we light-heartedly hope are secret. What of it? You aren't going to storm a city. Buddy, sometimes I send a girl out on an infiltration patrol, object: information—go out, find out, come back alive. How do you suppose I equip her?"

"Uh—"

"Never mind. In the first place I don't pick an eager young recruit; I send some unkillable old-timer. She peels down to her underwear, darkens her skin if it is not dark, and goes out bare-handed and bare-footed, without so much as a fly swatter. I have yet to lose a scout that way. Helpless and unprotected you do grow eyes in the back of your head, and your nerve ends reach out and feel everything around you. I learned that when I was a brash young j.o., from a salty trooper old enough to be my mother."

Impressed, Rod said slowly, "Deacon Matson told us he would make us take this test bare-handed, if he could."

"Dr. Matson is a man of sense."

"Well, what would *you* take?"

"Test conditions again?"

Rod stated them. Captain Walker frowned. "Mmm . . . not much to go on. Two to ten days probably means about five. The climate won't be hopelessly extreme. I suppose you own a Baby Bunting?"

"No, but I've got a combat parka suit. I thought I would carry it, then if the test area turned out not to be cold, I'd leave it at the gate. I'd hate to lose it; it weighs only half a kilo and cost quite a bit."

"Don't worry about that. There is no point in being the best dressed ghost in Limbo. Okay, besides your parka I would make it four kilos of rations, five of water, two kilos of sundries like pills and matches, all in a vest pack . . . and a knife."

"That isn't much for five days, much less ten."

"It is all you can carry and still be light on your feet. Let's see your knife, dear."

Rod had several knives, but one was "his" knife, a lovely all-purpose one with a 21-cm. molysteel blade and a fine balance. He handed it to his sister, who cradled it lightly. "Nice!" she said, and glanced around the room.

"Over there by the outflow."

"I see." She whipped it past her ear, let fly, and the blade sank into the target, sung and quivered. She reached down and drew another from her boot top. "This is a good one, too." She threw and it bit into the target a blade's width from the first.

She retrieved both knives, stood balancing them, one on each hand. She flipped her own so that the grip was toward Rod. "This is my pet, 'Lady Macbeth.' I carried her on my own solo, Buddy. I want you to carry her on yours."

"You want to trade knives? All right." Rod felt a sharp twinge at parting with "Colonel Bowie" and a feeling of dismay that some other knife might let him down. But it was not an offer that he could refuse, not from Sis.

"My very dear! I wouldn't deprive you of your own knife, not on your solo. I want you to carry both, Buddy. You won't starve nor die of thirst, but a spare knife may be worth its weight in thorium."

"Gee, Sis! But I shouldn't take your knife, either—you said you were expecting active duty. I can carry a spare of my own."

"I won't need it. My girls haven't let me use a knife in years. I want you to have Lady Macbeth on your test." She removed the scabbard from her boot top, sheathed the blade, and handed it to him. "Wear it in good health, brother."

3

Through the Tunnel

ROD ARRIVED AT TEMPLETON GATE THE NEXT MORNING feeling not his best. He had intended to get a good night's sleep in preparation for his ordeal, but his sister's arrival in conjunction with overwhelming changes in his family had defeated his intention. As with most children Rod had taken his family and home for granted; he had not thought about them much, nor placed a conscious value on them, any more than a fish treasures water. They simply were.

Now suddenly they were not.

Helen and he had talked late. She had begun to have strong misgivings about her decision to let him know of the change on the eve of his test. She had weighed it, decided that it was the "right" thing to do, then had learned the ages-old sour truth that right and wrong can sometimes be determined only through hindsight. It had not been fair, she later concluded, to load anything else on his mind just before his test. But it had not seemed fair, either, to let him leave without knowing ... to return to an empty house.

The decision was necessarily hers; she had been his guardian since earlier that same day. The papers had been signed and sealed; the court had given approval. Now she found with a sigh that being a "parent" was not unalloyed pleasure; it was more like the soul-searching that had gone into her first duty as member of a court martial.

When she saw that her "baby" was not quieting, she had insisted that he go to bed anyhow, then had given him a long back rub, combining it with hypnotic instructions to sleep, then had gone quietly away when he seemed asleep.

But Rod had not been asleep; he had simply wanted to be alone. His mind raced like an engine with no load for the best part of an hour, niggling uselessly at the matter of his father's illness, wondering what it was going to be like to greet them again after twenty years —why, he would be almost as old as Mum!—switching over to useless mental preparations for unknown test conditions.

At last he realized that he had to sleep—forced himself to run through mental relaxing exercises, emptying his mind and hypnotizing himself. It took longer than ever before but finally he entered a great, golden, warm cloud and was asleep.

His bed mechanism had to call him twice. He woke bleary-eyed and was still so after a needle shower. He looked in a mirror, decided that shaving did not matter where he was going and anyhow he was late—then decided to shave after all . . . being painfully shy about his sparse young growth.

Mum was not up, but she hardly ever got up as early as that. Dad rarely ate breakfast these days . . . Rod recalled why with a twinge. But he had expected Sis to show up. Glumly he opened his tray and discovered that Mum had forgotten to dial an order, something that had not happened twice in his memory. He placed his order and waited for service—another ten minutes lost.

Helen showed up as he was leaving, dressing surprisingly in a dress. "Good morning."

"Hi, Sis. Say, you'll have to order your own tucker. Mother didn't and I didn't know what you wanted."

"Oh, I had breakfast hours ago. I was waiting to see you off."

"Oh. Well, so long. I've got to run, I'm late."

"I won't hold you up." She came over and embraced him. "Take it easy, mate. That's the important thing. More people have died from worry than ever bled to death. And if you do have to strike, strike low."

"Uh, I'll remember."

"See that you do. I'm going to get my leave extended

today so that I'll be here when you come back." She kissed him. "Now run."

Dr. Matson was sitting at a desk outside the dispensary at Templeton Gate, checking names on his roll. He looked up as Rod arrived. "Why, hello, Walker. I thought maybe you had decided to be smart."

"I'm sorry I'm late, sir. Things happened."

"Don't fret about it. Knew a man once who didn't get shot at sunrise because he overslept the appointment."

"Really? Who was he?"

"Young fellow I used to know. Myself."

"Hunh? You really did, sir? You mean you were—"

"Not a word of truth in it. Good stories are rarely true. Get on in there and take your physical, before you get the docs irritated."

They thumped him and x-rayed him and made a wavy pattern from his brain and did all the indignities that examining physicians do. The senior examiner listened to his heart and felt his moist hand. "Scared, son?"

"Of course I am!" Rod blurted.

"Of course you are. If you weren't, I wouldn't pass you. What's that bandage on your leg?"

"Uh—" The bandage concealed Helen's knife "Lady Macbeth." Rod sleepishly admitted the fact.

"Take it off."

"Sir?"

"I've known candidates to pull dodges like that to cover up a disqualification. So let's have a look."

Rod started removing it; the physician let him continue until he was sure that it was a cache for a weapon and not a wound dressing. "Get your clothes on. Report to your instructor."

Rod put on his vest pack of rations and sundries, fastened his canteen under it. It was a belt canteen of flexible synthetic divided into half-litre pockets. The weight was taken by shoulder straps and a tube ran up the left suspender, ending in a nipple near his mouth so that he might drink without taking it off. He planned, if possible, to stretch his meager supply through the whole test, avoiding the hazards of contaminated water and the greater hazards of the water hole—assuming that fresh water could be found at all.

He wrapped twenty meters of line, light, strong, and thin, around his waist. Shorts, overshirt, trousers, and boot moccasins completed his costume; he belted "Colonel Bowie" on outside. Dressed, he looked fleshier than he was; only his knife showed. He carried his parka suit over his left arm. It was an efficient garment, hooded, with built-in boots and gloves, and with pressure seams to let him use bare hands when necessary, but it was much too warm to wear until he needed it. Rod had learned early in the game that Eskimos don't dare to sweat.

Dr. Matson was outside the dispensary door. "The late Mr. Walker," he commented, then glanced at the bulkiness of Rod's torso. "Body armor, son?"

"No, sir. Just a vest pack."

"How much penalty you carrying?"

"Eleven kilograms. Mostly water and rations."

"Mmm . . . well, it will get heavier before it gets lighter. No Handy-Dandy Young Pioneer's Kit? No collapsible patent wigwam?"

Rod blushed. "No, sir."

"You can leave that snow suit. I'll mail it to your home."

"Uh, thank you, sir." Rod passed it over, adding, "I wasn't sure I'd need it, but I brought it along, just in case."

"You did need it."

"Sir?"

"I've already flunked five for showing up without their snuggies . . . and four for showing up *with* vacuum suits. Both ways for being stupid. They ought to know that the Board would not dump them into vacuum or chlorine or such without specifying space suits in the test notice. We're looking for graduates, not casualties. On the other hand, cold weather is within the limits of useful test conditions."

Rod glanced at the suit he had passed over. "You're sure I won't need it, sir?"

"Quite. Except that you would have flunked if you hadn't fetched it. Now bear a hand and draw whatever pig shooter you favor; the armorer is anxious to close up shop. What gun have you picked?"

Rod gulped. "Uh, I was thinking about not taking one, Deacon—I mean 'Doctor.' "

"You can call me 'Deacon' to my face—ten days from now. But this notion of yours interests me. How did you reach that conclusion?"

"Uh, why, you see, sir . . . well, my sister suggested it."

"So? I must meet your sister. What's her name?"

"Assault Captain Helen Walker," Rod said proudly, "Corps of Amazons."

Matson wrote it down. "Get on in there. They are ready for the drawing."

Rod hesitated. "Sir," he said with sudden misgiving, "if I did carry a gun, what sort would you advise?"

Matson looked disgusted. "I spend a year trying to spoon-feed you kids with stuff I learned the hard way. Comes examination and you ask me to slip you the answers. I can no more answer that than I would have been justified yesterday in telling you to bring a snow suit."

"Sorry, sir."

"No reason why you shouldn't ask; it's just that I won't answer. Let's change the subject. This sister of yours . . . she must be quite a girl."

"Oh, she is, sir."

"Mmm . . . maybe if I had met a girl like that I wouldn't be a cranky old bachelor now. Get in there and draw your number. Number one goes through in six minutes."

"Yes, Doctor." His way led him past the school armorer, who had set up a booth outside the door. The old chap was wiping off a noiseless Summerfield. Rod caught his eye. "Howdy, Guns."

"Hi, Jack. Kind of late, aren't you? What'll it be?"

Rod's eye ran over the rows of beautiful weapons. Maybe just a little needle gun with poisoned pellets . . . He wouldn't have to *use* it . . .

Then he realized that Dr. Matson had answered his question, with a very broad hint. "Uh, I'm already heeled, Guns. Thanks."

"Okay. Well, good luck, and hurry back."

"Thanks a lot." He went into the gate room.

The seminar had numbered more than fifty students;

40

there were about twenty waiting to take the examination. He started to look around, was stopped by a gate attendant who called out, "Over here! Draw your number."

The lots were capsules in a bowl. Rod reached in, drew one out, and broke it open. "Number seven."

"Lucky seven! Congratulations. Your name, please."

Rod gave his name and turned away, looking for a seat, since it appeared that he had twenty minutes or so to wait. He walked back, staring with interest at what his schoolmates deemed appropriate for survival, any and all conditions.

Johann Braun was seated with empty seats on each side of him. The reason for the empty seats crouched at his feet—a big, lean, heavily-muscled boxer dog with unfriendly eyes. Slung over Braun's shoulder was a General Electric Thunderbolt, a shoulder model with telescopic sights and cone-of-fire control; its power pack Braun wore as a back pack. At his belt were binoculars, knife, first aid kit, and three pouches.

Rod stopped and admired the gun, wondering how much the lovely thing cost. The dog raised his head and growled.

Braun put a hand on the dog's head. "Keep your distance," he warned. "Thor is a one-man dog."

Rod gave back a pace. "Yo, you are certainly equipped."

The big blond youth gave a satisfied smile. "Thor and I are going to live off the country."

"You don't need him, with that cannon."

"Oh, yes, I do. Thor's my burglar alarm. With him at my side I can sleep sound. You'd be surprised at the things he can do. Thor's smarter than most people."

"Shouldn't wonder."

"The Deacon gave me some guff that the two of us made a team and should go through separately. I explained to him that Thor would tear the joint apart if they tried to separate us." Braun caressed the dog's ears. "I'd rather team with Thor than with a platoon of Combat Pioneers."

"Say, Yo, how about letting me try that stinger? After we come out, I mean."

"I don't mind. It really is a honey. You can pick off

41

a sparrow in the air easily as you can drop a moose at a thousand meters. Say, you're making Thor nervous. See you later."

Rod took the hint, moved on and sat down. He looked around, having in mind that he might still arrange a survival team. Near the shuttered arch of the gateway there was a priest with a boy kneeling in front of him, with four others waiting.

The boy who had been receiving the blessing stood up—and Rod stood up hastily. "Hey! *Jimmy!*"

Jimmy Throxton looked around, caught his eye and grinned, hurried over. "Rod!" he said, "I thought you had ducked out on me. Look, you haven't teamed?"

"No."

"Still want to?"

"Huh? Sure."

"Swell! I can declare the team as I go through as long as you don't have number two. You don't, do you?"

"No."

"Good! Because I'm—"

"NUMBER ONE!" the gate attendant called out. " 'Throxton, James.' "

Jimmy Throxton looked startled. "Oh, gee!" He hitched at his gun belt and turned quickly away, then called over his shoulder, "See you on the other side!" He trotted toward the gate, now unshuttered.

Rod called out, "Hey, Jimmy! How are we going to find—" But it was too late. Well, if Jimmy had sense enough to drive nails, he would keep an eye on the exit.

"Number two! Mshiyeni, Caroline." Across the room the big Zulu girl who had occurred to Rod as a possible team mate got up and headed for the gate. She was dressed simply in shirt and shorts, with her feet and legs and hands bare. She did not appear to be armed but she was carrying an overnight bag.

Someone called out, "Hey, Carol! What you got in the trunk?"

She threw him a grin. "Rocks."

"Ham sandwiches, I'll bet. Save me one."

"I'll save you a rock, sweetheart."

Too soon the attendant called out, "Number seven—Walker, Roderick L."

Rod went quickly to the gate. The attendant shoved a paper into his hand, then shook hands. "Good luck, kid. Keep your eyes open." He gave Rod a slap on the back that urged him through the opening, dilated to man size.

Rod found himself on the other side and, to his surprise, still indoors. But that shock was not as great as immediate unsteadiness and nausea; the gravity acceleration was much less than earth-normal.

He fought to keep from throwing up and tried to figure things out. Where was he? On Luna? On one of Jupiter's moons? Or somewhere 'way out there?

The Moon, most likely—Luna. Many of the longer jumps were relayed through Luna because of the danger of mixing with a primary, particularly with binaries. But surely they weren't going to leave him here; Matson had promised them no airless test areas.

On the floor lay an open valise; he recognized it absent-mindedly as the one Caroline had been carrying. At last he remembered to look at the paper he had been handed.

It read:

SOLO SURVIVAL TEST—Recall Instructions

1.   You must pass through the door ahead in the three minutes allowed you before another candidate is started through. An overlapping delay will disqualify you.
2.   Recall will be by standard visual and sound signals. You are warned that the area remains hazardous even after recall is sounded.
3.   The exit gate will not be the entrance gate. Exit may be as much as twenty kilometers in the direction of sunrise.
4.   There is no truce zone outside the gate. Test starts at once. Watch out for stobor. Good luck!

—B. P. M.

Rod was still gulping at low gravity and staring at the paper when a door opened at the far end of the long,

43

narrow room he was in. A man shouted, "Hurry up! You'll lose your place."

Rod tried to hurry, staggered and then recovered too much and almost fell. He had experienced low gravity on field trips and his family had once vacationed on Luna, but he was not used to it; with difficulty he managed to skate toward the far door.

Beyond the door was another gate room. The attendant glanced at the timer over the gate and said, "Twenty seconds. Give me that instruction sheet."

Rod hung onto it. "I'll use the twenty seconds."—*as much as twenty kilometers in the direction of sunrise.* A nominal eastward direction—call it "east." But what the deuce was, or were, "stobor"?

"Time! Through you go." The attendant snatched the paper, shutters rolled back, and Rod was shoved through a dilated gate.

He fell to his hands and knees; the gravity beyond was something close to earth-normal and the change had caught him unprepared. But he stayed down, held perfectly still and made no sound while he quickly looked around him. He was in a wide clearing covered with high grass and containing scattered trees and bushes; beyond was dense forest.

He twisted his neck in a hasty survey. Earth-type planet, near normal acceleration, probably a G-type sun in the sky . . . heavy vegetation, no fauna in sight—but that didn't mean anything; there might be hundreds within hearing. Even a stobor, whatever that was.

The gate was behind him, tall dark-green shutters which were in reality a long way off. They stood unsupported in the tall grass, an anomalism unrelated to the primitive scene. Rod considered wriggling around behind the gate, knowing that the tangency was one-sided and that he would be able to see through the locus from the other side, see anyone who came out without himself being seen.

Which reminded him that he himself could be seen from that exceptional point; he decided to move.

Where was Jimmy? Jimmy ought to be behind the gate, watching for him to come out . . . or watching from some other spy point. The only certain method of rendezvous was for Jimmy to have waited for Rod's appearance; Rod had no way to find him now.

Rod looked around more slowly and tried to spot anything that might give a hint as to Jimmy's whereabouts. Nothing . . . but when his scanning came back to the gate, the gate was no longer there.

Rod felt cold ripple of adrenalin shock trickle down his back and out his finger tips. He forced himself to quiet down and told himself that it was better this way. He had a theory to account for the disappearance of the gate; they were, he decided, refocusing it between each pair of students, scattering them possibly kilometers apart.

No, that could not be true—"twenty kilometers toward sunrise" had to relate to a small area.

Or did it? He reminded himself that the orientation given in the sheet handed him might not be that which appeared in some other student's instruction sheet. He relaxed to the fact that he did not really know anything . . . he did not know where he was, nor where Jimmy was, nor any other member of the class, he did not know what he might find here, save that it was a place where a man might stay alive if he were smart—and lucky.

Just now his business was to stay alive, for a period that he might as well figure as ten Earth days. He wiped Jimmy Throxton out of his mind, wiped out everything but the necessity of remaining unceasingly alert to all of his surroundings. He noted wind direction as shown by grass plumes and started crawling cautiously down wind.

The decision to go down wind had been difficult. To go up wind had been his first thought, that being the natural direction for a stalk. But his sister's advice had already paid off; he felt naked and helpless without a gun and it had reminded him that he was not the hunter. His scent would carry in any case; if he went down wind he stood a chance of seeing what might be stalking him, while his unguarded rear would be comparatively safe.

Something ahead in the grass!

He froze and watched. It had been the tiniest movement; he waited. There it was again, moving slowly from right to left across his front. It looked like a dark spike

45

with a tuft of hair on the tip, a tail possibly, carried aloft.

He never saw what manner of creature owned the tail, if it was a tail. It stopped suddenly at a point Rod judged to be directly down wind, then moved off rapidly and he lost sight of it. He waited a few minutes, then resumed crawling.

It was extremely hot work and sweat poured down him and soaked his overshirt and trousers. He began to want a drink very badly but reminded himself that five litres of water would not last long if he started drinking the first hour of the test. The sky was overcast with high cirrus haze, but the primary or "sun"—he decided to call it the Sun—seemed to burn through fiercely. It was low in the sky behind him; he wondered what it would be like overhead? Kill a man, maybe. Oh, well, it would be cooler in that forest ahead, or at least not be the same chance of sunstroke.

There was lower ground ahead of him and hawklike birds were circling above the spot, round and round. He held still and watched. Brothers, he said softly, if you are behaving like vultures back home, there is something dead ahead of me and you are waiting to make sure it stays dead before you drop in for lunch. If so, I had better swing wide, for it is bound to attract other things . . . some of which I might not want to meet.

He started easing to the right, quartering the light breeze. It took him onto higher ground and close to a rock outcropping. Rod decided to spy out what was in the lower place below, making use of cover to let him reach an overhanging rock.

It looked mightily like a man on the ground and a child near him. Rod reached, fumbled in his vest pack, got out a tiny 8-power monocular, took a better look. The man was Johann Braun, the "child" was his boxer dog. There was no doubt but that they were dead, for Braun was lying like a tossed rag doll, with his head twisted around and one leg bent under. His throat and the side of his head were a dark red stain.

While Rod watched, a doglike creature trotted out, sniffed at the boxer, and began tearing at it . . . then the first of the buzzard creatures landed to join the feast. Rod took the glass from his eye, feeling queasy. Old Yo had not lasted long—jumped by a "stobor" maybe—and his smart dog had not saved him. Too bad! But it did prove that there were carnivores around and it behooved him to be careful if he did not want to have jackals and vultures arguing over the leavings!

He remembered something and put the glass back to his eye. Yo's proud Thunderbolt gun was nowhere in sight and the corpse was not wearing the power pack that energized it. Rod gave a low whistle in his mind and thought. The only animal who would bother to steal a gun ran around on two legs. Rod reminded himself that a Thunderbolt could kill at almost any line-of-sight range—and now somebody had it who obviously took advantage of the absence of law and order in a survival test area.

Well, the only thing to do was not to be in line of sight. He backed off the rock and slid into the bushes.

The forest had appeared to be two kilometers away, or less, when he had started. He was close to it when he became uncomfortably aware that sunset was almost upon him. He became less cautious, more hurried, as he planned to spend the night in a tree. This called for light to climb by, since he relished a night on the ground inside the forest still less than he liked the idea of crouching helpless in the grass.

It had not taken all day to crawl this far. Although it had been morning when he had left Templeton Gate the time of day there had nothing to do with the time of day here. He had been shoved through into late afternoon; it was dusk when he reached the tall trees.

So dusky that he decided that he must accept a calculated risk for what he must do. He stopped at the edge of the forest, still in the high grass, and dug into his pack for his climbers. His sister had caused him to leave behind most of the gadgets, gimmicks, and special-purpose devices that he had considered bringing; she had not argued at these. They were climbing spikes of a style basically old, but refined, made small and light—the pair weighed less than a tenth of a kilogram—and made foldable and compact, from a titanium alloy, hard and strong.

He unfolded them, snapped them under his arches and around his shins, and locked them in place. Then he eyed the tree he had picked, a tall giant deep enough in the mass to allow the possibility of crossing to another tree if the odds made a back-door departure safer and having a trunk which, in spite of its height, he felt sure he could get his arms around.

Having picked his route, he straightened up and at a fast dogtrot headed for the nearest tree. He went past it, cut left for another tree, passed it and cut right toward the tree he wanted. He was about fifteen meters from it when something charged him.

He closed the gap with instantaneous apportation which would have done credit to a Ramsbotham hyperfold. He reached the first branch, ten meters above ground, in what amounted to levitation. From there on he climbed more conventionally, digging the spurs into the tree's smooth bark and setting his feet more comfortably on branches when they began to be close enough together to form a ladder.

About twenty meters above ground he stopped and looked down. The branches interfered and it was darker under the trees than it had been out in the open; nevertheless he could see, prowling around the tree, the denizen that had favored him with attention.

Rod tried to get a better view, but the light was failing rapidly. But it looked like . . . well, if he had not been certain that he was on some uncolonized planet 'way out behind and beyond, he would have said that it was a *lion*.

Except that it looked eight times as big as any lion ought to look.

He hoped that, whatever it was, it could not climb trees. Oh, quit fretting, Rod!—if it had been able to climb you would have been lunch meat five minutes ago. Get busy and rig a place to sleep before it gets pitch dark. He moved up the tree, keeping an eye out for the spot he needed.

He found it presently, just as he was beginning to think that he would have to go farther down. He needed two stout branches far enough apart and near enough the same level to let him stretch a hammock. Having found such, he worked quickly to beat the failing light. From a pocket of his vest pack he took out his hammock, a web strong as spider silk and almost as thin and light. Using the line around his waist he stretched it, made sure his lashings would hold and then started to get into it.

A double-jointed acrobat with prehensile toes might have found it easy; a slack-wire artist would simply have walked into it and sat down. But Rod found that he needed sky hooks. He almost fell out of the tree.

The hammock was a practical piece of equipment and Rod had slept in it before. His sister had approved it, remarking that it was a better model than the field hammock they gave her girls. "Just don't sit up in your sleep."

"I won't," Rod had assured her. "Anyway, I always fasten the chest belt."

But he had never slung it in this fashion. There was nothing to stand on under the hammock, no tree limb above it close enough to let him chin himself into it. After several awkward and breath-catching attempts he began to wonder whether he should perch like a bird the rest of the night, or drape himself in the notch of a limb. He did not consider spending the night on the ground—not with that *thing* prowling around.

There was another limb higher up almost directly over the hammock. Maybe if he tossed the end of his line over it and used it to steady himself . . .

He tried it. But it was almost pitch dark now; the only reason he did not lose his line was that one end was bent to the hammock. At last he gave up and made one more attempt to crawl into the hammock by main force and extreme care. Bracing both hands wide on each side of the head rope he scooted his feet out slowly and cautiously. Presently he had his legs inside the hammock, then his buttocks. From there on it was a matter of keeping his center of gravity low and making no sudden moves while he insinuated his body farther down into the cocoon.

At last he could feel himself fully and firmly supported. He took a deep breath, sighed, and let himself relax. It was the first time he had felt either safe or comfortable since passing through the gate.

After a few minute of delicious rest Rod located the nipple of his canteen and allowed himself two swallows of water, after which he prepared supper. This consisted in digging out a quarter-kilo brick of field ration, eleven hundred calories of yeast protein, fat, starch, and glucose, plus trace requirements. The label on it, invisible in the dark, certified that it was "tasty, tempting and pleasing in texture," whereas chewing an old shoe would have attracted a gourmet quite as much.

But real hunger gave Rod the best of sauces. He did not let any crumb escape and ended by licking the wrapper. He thought about opening another one, quelled the longing, allowed himself one more mouthful of water, then pulled the insect hood of the hammock down over his face and fastened it under the chest belt. He was immune to most insect-carried Terran diseases and was comfortably aware that humans were not subject to most Outlands diseases, but he did not want the night fliers to use his face as a drinking fountain, nor even as a parade ground.

He was too hot even in his light clothing. He considered shucking down to his shorts; this planet, or this part of this planet, seemed quite tropical. But it was awkward; tonight he must stay as he was, even if it meant wasting a day's ration of water in sweat. He wondered what planet this was, then tried to peer through the roof of the forest to see if he could recognize stars. But either the trees were impenetrable or the sky was overcast; he could see nothing. He attempted to draw everything out of his mind and sleep.

Ten minutes later he was wider awake than ever. Busy with his hammock, busy with his dinner, he had not paid attention to distant sounds; now he became aware of all the voices of the night. Insects buzzed and sang and strummed, foliage rustled and whispered, something coughed below him. The cough was answered by insane laughter that ran raggedly up, then down, and died in asthmatic choking.

Rod hoped that it was a bird.

He found himself straining to hear every sound, near and far, holding his breath. He told himself angrily to stop it; he was safe from at least nine-tenths of potential enemies. Even a snake, if this place ran to such, would be unlikely to crawl out to the hammock, still less likely to attack—if he held still. Snakes, button-brained as they were, showed little interest in anything too big to

50

swallow. The chances of anything big enough to hurt him—and interested in hurting him—being in this tree-top were slim. So forget those funny noises, pal, and go to sleep. After all, they're no more important than traffic noises in a city.

He reminded himself of the Deacon's lecture on alarm and could not see sky; he floated in a leafy cloud. The traced to the body's coming too urgently to battle sta-tions, remaining too long at full alert. Or, as his sister had put it, more people worry themselves to death than bleed to death. He set himself conscientiously to running through the mental routines intended to produce sleep.

He almost made it. The sound that pulled him out of warm drowsiness came from far away; involuntarily he roused himself to hear it. It sounded almost human . . . no, it *was* human—the terrible sound of a grown man crying with heartbreak, the deep, retching, bass sobs that tear the chest.

Rod wondered what he ought to do. It was none of his business and everyone there was on his own—but it went against the grain to hear such agony from a fellow human and ignore it. Should he climb down and feel his way through the dark to wherever the poor wretch was? Stumbling into tree roots, he reminded himself, and falling into holes and maybe walking straight into the jaws of something hungry and big.

Well, should he? Did he have any right *not* to?

It was solved for him by the sobs being answered by more sobs, this time closer and much louder. This new voice did not sound human, much as it was like the first, and it scared him almost out of his hammock. The chest strap saved him.

The second voice was joined by a third, farther away. In a few moments the peace of the night had changed to sobbing, howling ululation of mass fear and agony and defeat unbearable. Rod knew now that this was nothing human, nor anything he had ever heard, or heard of, before. He suddenly had a deep conviction that these were the stobor he had been warned to avoid.

But what were they? How was he to avoid them? The one closest seemed to be higher up than he was and no farther than the next tree . . . good grief, it might even be *this* tree!

51

When you meet a stobor in the dark what do you do? Spit in its face? Or ask it to waltz?

One thing was certain: anything that made that much noise in the jungle was not afraid of anything; therefore it behooved him to be afraid of it. But, there being nothing he could do, Rod lay quiet, his fear evidenced only by tense muscles, gooseflesh, and cold sweat. The hellish concert continued with the "stobor" closest to him sounding almost in his pocket. It seemed to have moved closer.

With just a bit more prodding Rod would have been ready to sprout wings and fly. Only at home on the North American continent of Terra had he ever spent a night alone in the wilderness. There the hazards were known and minor . . . a few predictable bears, an occasional lazy rattlesnake, dangers easily avoided.

But how could he guard against the utterly unknown? That stobor—he decided that he might as well call it that—that stobor might be moving toward him now, sizing him up with night eyes, deciding whether to drag him home, or eat him where it killed him.

Should he move? And maybe move right into the fangs of the stobor? Or should he wait, helpless, for the stobor to pounce? It was possible that the stobor could not attack him in the tree. But it was equally possible that stobor were completely arboreal and his one chance lay in climbing down quickly and spending the night on the ground.

What was a stobor? How did it fight? Where and when was it dangerous? The Deacon evidently expected the class to know what to do about them. Maybe they had studied the stobor those days he was out of school right after New Year's? Or maybe he had just plain forgotten . . . and would pay for it with his skin. Rod was good at Outlands zoology—but there was just too much to learn it all. Why, the zoology of Terra alone used to give oldstyle zoologists more than they could handle; how could they expect him to soak up all there was to learn about dozens of planets?

It wasn't *fair!*

When Rod heard himself think that ancient and useless protest he had a sudden vision of the Deacon's kindly, cynical smile. He heard his dry drawl: Fair? You expected this to be *fair,* son? This is not a game. I tried to tell you that you were a city boy, too soft and stupid for this. You would not listen.

He felt a gust of anger at his instructor; it drove fear out of his mind. Jimmy was right; the Deacon would eat his own grandmother! A cold, heartless fish!

All right, what would the Deacon do?

Again he heard his teacher's voice inside his head, an answer Matson had once given to a question put by another classmate: "There wasn't anything I could do, so I took a nap."

Rod squirmed around, rested his hand on "Colonel Bowie" and tried to take a nap. The unholy chorus made it almost impossible, but he did decide that the stobor in his tree—or was it the next tree?—did not seem to be coming closer. Not that it could come much closer without breathing on his neck, but at least it did not seem disposed to attack.

After a long time he fell into restless sleep, sleep that was no improvement, for he dreamed that he had a ring of sobbing, ululating stobor around him, staring at him, waiting for him to move. But he was trussed up tight and could not move.

The worst of it was that every time he turned his head to see what a stobor looked like it would fade back into the dark, giving him just a hint of red eyes, long teeth.

He woke with an icy shock, tried to sit up, found himself restrained by his chest strap, forced himself to lie back. What was it? What had happened?

In his suddenly-awakened state it took time to realize what had happened: the noise had stopped. He could not hear the cry of a single stobor, near or far. Rod found it more disturbing than their clamor, since a noisy stobor advertised its location whereas a silent one could be anywhere—why, the nearest one could now be sitting on the branch behind his head. He twisted his head around, pulled the insect netting off his face to see better. But it was too dark; stobor might be queued up three abreast for all he could tell.

Nevertheless the silence was a great relief. Rod felt himself relax as he listened to the other night sounds, noises that seemed almost friendly after that devils'

53

choir. He decided that it must be almost morning and that we would do well to stay awake.

Presently he was asleep.

He awoke with the certainty that someone was looking at him. When he realized where he was and that it was still dark, he decided that it was a dream. He stirred, looked around, and tried to go back to sleep.

Something *was* looking at him!

His eyes, made sensitive by darkness, saw the thing as a vague shape on the branch at his foot. Black on black, he could not make out its outline—but two faintly luminous eyes stared unwinkingly back into his.

"—nothing I could do, so I took a nap." Rod did not take a nap. For a time measured in eons he and the thing in the tree locked eyes. Rod tightened his grip on his knife and held still, tried to quell the noise of his pounding heart, tried to figure out how he could fight back from a hammock. The beast did not move, made no sound; it simply stared and seemed prepared to do it all night.

When the ordeal had gone on so long that Rod felt a mounting impulse to shout and get it over, the creature moved with light scratching sounds toward the trunk and was gone. Rod could feel the branch shift; he judged that the beast must weigh as much as he did.

Again he resolved to stay awake. Wasn't it getting less dark? He tried to tell himself so, but he still could not see his own fingers. He decided to count to ten thousand and bring on the dawn.

Something large went down the tree very fast, followed at once by another, and still a third. They did not stop at Rod's bedroom but went straight down the trunk. Rod put his knife back and uttered, "Noisy neighbors! You'd think this was Emigrants' Gap." He waited but the frantic procession never came back.

He was awakened by sunlight in his face. It made him sneeze; he tried to sit up, was caught by his safety belt, became wide awake and regretted it. His nose was stopped up, his eyes burned, his mouth tasted like a ditch, his teeth were slimy, and his back ached. When he moved to ease it he found that his legs ached, too—

54

and his arms—and his head. His neck refused to turn to the right.

Nevertheless he felt happy that the long night was gone. His surroundings were no longer terrifying, but almost idyllic. So high up that he could not see the ground he was still well below the roof of the jungle and could not see sky; he floated in a leafy cloud. The morning ray that brushed his face was alone, so thoroughly did trees shut out the sky.

This reminded him that he had to mark the direction of sunrise. Hmmm . . . not too simple. Would he be able to see the sun from the floor of the jungle? Maybe he should climb down quickly, get out in the open, and mark the direction while the sun was still low. But he noticed that the shaft which had wakened him was framed by a limb notch of another forest giant about fifteen meters away. Very well, that tree was "east" of his tree; he could line them up again when he reached the ground.

Getting out of his hammock was almost as hard as getting in; sore muscles resented the effort. At last he was balanced precariously on one limb. He crawled to the trunk, pulled himself painfully erect and, steadied by the trunk, took half-hearted setting-up exercises to work the knots out. Everything loosened up but his neck, which still had a crick like a toothache.

He ate and drank sitting on the limb with his back to the trunk. He kept no special lookout, rationalizing that night feeders would be bedded down and day feeders would hardly be prowling the tree tops—not big ones, anyway; they would be on the ground, stalking herbivores. The truth was that his green hide-away looked too peaceful to be dangerous.

He continued to sit after he finished eating, considered drinking more of his precious water, even considered crawling back into his hammock. Despite the longest night he had ever had he was bone tired and the day was already hot and sleepy and humid; why not stretch out? His only purpose was to survive; how better than by sleeping and thereby saving food and water?

He might have done so had he known what time it was. His watch told him that it was five minutes before twelve, but he could not make up his mind whether that was noon on Sunday or midnight coming into Monday. He was sure that this planet spun much more slowly than did Mother Earth; the night before had been at least as long as a full Earth day.

Therefore the test had been going on at least twenty-six hours and possibly thirty-eight—and recall could be any time after forty-eight hours. Why, it might be today, before sunset, and here he was in fine shape, still alive, still with food and water he could trust.

He felt good about it. What did a stobor have that a man did not have more of and better? Aside from a loud voice, he added.

But the exit gate might be as much as twenty kilometers "east" of where he had come in; therefore it behooved him to reach quickly a point ten kilometers east of where he had come in; he would lay money that that would land him within a kilometer or two of the exit. Move along, hole up, and wait—why, he might sleep at home tonight, after a hot bath!

He started unlashing his hammock while reminding himself that he must keep track of hours between sunrise and sunset today in order to estimate the length of the local day. Then he thought no more about it as he had trouble folding the hammock. It had to be packed carefully to fit into a pocket of his vest pack. The filmy stuff should have been spread on a table, but where he was the largest, flattest area was the palm of his hand.

But he got it done, lumpy but packed, and started down. He paused on the lowest branch, looked around. The oversized and hungry thing that had chased him up the tree did not seem to be around, but the undergrowth was too dense for him to be sure. He made a note that he must, all day long and every day, keep a climbable tree in mind not too far away; a few seconds woolgathering might use up his luck.

Okay, now for orientation— Let's see, there was the tree he had used to mark "east." Or was it? Could it be that one over there? He realized that he did not know and swore at himself for not checking it by compass. The truth was that he had forgotten that he was carrying a compass. He got it out now, but it told him nothing, since east by compass bore no necessary relation to direction of sunrise on this planet. The rays of the primary did not penetrate where he was; the forest was bathed by a dim religious light unmarked by shadows.

Well, the clearing could not be far away. He would just have to check. He descended by climbing spurs, dropped to spongy ground, and headed the way it should be. He counted his paces while keeping an eye peeled for hostiles.

One hundred paces later he turned back, retracing his own spoor. He found "his" tree; this time he examined it. There was where he had come down; he could see his prints. Which side had he gone up? There should be spur marks.

He found them . . . and was amazed at his own feat; they started high as his head. "I must have hit that trunk like a cat!" But it showed the direction from which he had come; five minutes later he was at the edge of the open country he had crossed the day before.

The sun made shadows here, which straightened him out and he checked by compass. By luck, east was "east" and he need only follow his compass. It took him back into the forest.

He traveled standing up. The belly sneak which he had used the day before was not needed here; he depended on moving noiselessly, using cover, and keeping an eye out behind as well as in front. He zigzagged in order to stay close to trees neither too big nor too small but corrected his course frequently by compass.

One part of his mind counted paces. At fifteen hundred broken-country steps to a kilometer Rod figured that fifteen thousand should bring him to his best-guess location for the exit gate, where he planned to set up housekeeping until recall.

But, even with part of his mind counting paces and watching a compass and a much larger part watching for carnivores, snakes, and other hazards, Rod still could enjoy the day and place. He was over his jitters of the night before, feeling good and rather cocky. Even though he tried to be fully alert, the place did not feel dangerous now—stobor or no stobor.

It was, he decided, jungle of semi-rainforest type, not dense enough to require chopping one's way. It was interlaced with game paths but he avoided these on the assumption that carnivores might lie waiting for lunch to come down the path—Rod had no wish to volunteer.

The place seemed thick with game, mostly of antelope type in many sizes and shapes. They were hard to spot; they faded into the bush with natural camouflage, but the glimpses he got convinced him that they were plentiful. He avoided them as he was not hunting and was aware that even a vegetarian could be dangerous with hooves and horns in self or herd defense.

The world above was inhabited, too, with birds and climbers. He spotted families of what looked like monkeys and speculated that this world would probably have developed its own race of humanoids. He wondered again what planet it was? Terrestrial to several decimal places it certainly seemed to be—except for the inconveniently long day—and probably one just opened, or it would be swarming with colonists. It would be a premium planet certainly; that clearing he had come through yesterday would make good farm land once it was burned off. Maybe he would come back some day and help clean out the stobor.

In the meantime he watched where he put his hands and feet, never walked under a low branch without checking it, and tried to make his eyes and ears as efficient as a rabbit's. He understood now what his sister had meant about how being unarmed makes a person careful, and realized also how little chance he would have to use a gun if he let himself be surprised.

It was this hyperacuteness that made him decide that he was being stalked.

At first it was just uneasiness, then it became a conviction. Several times he waited by a tree, stood frozen and listened; twice he did a sneak through bushes and doubled back on his tracks. But whatever it was seemed as good as he was at silent movement and taking cover and (he had to admit) a notch better.

He thought about taking to the trees and outwaiting it. But his wish to reach his objective outweighed his caution; he convinced himself that he would be safer if he pushed on. He continued to pay special attention to his rear, but after a while he decided that he was no longer being followed.

When he had covered, by his estimate, four kilometers, he began to smell water. He came to a ravine which sliced across his route. Game tracks led him to think it might lead down to a watering place, just the sort of danger area he wished to avoid, so Rod crossed quickly and went down the shoulder of the ravine instead. It led to a bank overlooking water; he could hear the stream before he reached it.

He took to the bushes and moved on his belly to a point where he could peer out from cover. He was about ten meters higher than the water. The ground dropped off on his right as well as in front; there the ravine joined the stream and an eddy pool formed the watering place he had expected. No animals were in sight but there was plenty of sign; a mud flat was chewed with hoof marks.

But he had no intention of drinking where it was easy; it would be too easy to die there. What troubled him was that he must cross the stream to reach the probable recall area. It was a small river or wide brook, not too wide to swim, probably not too deep to wade if he picked his spot. But he would not do either one unless forced—and not then without testing the water by chucking a lure into it . . . a freshly killed animal. The streams near his home were safe, but a tropical stream must be assumed to have local versions of alligator, piranha, or even worse.

The stream was too wide to cross through the tree tops. He lay still and considered the problem, then decided that he would work his way upstream and hope that it would narrow, or split into two smaller streams which he could tackle one at a time.

It was the last thing he thought about for some time.

When Rod regained consciousness it was quickly; a jackal-like creature was sniffing at him. Rod lashed out with one hand and reached for his knife with the other. The dog brute backed away, snarling, then disappeared in the leaves.

His knife was gone! The realization brought him groggily alert; he sat up. It made his head swim and hurt. He felt it and his fingers came away bloody. Further gingerly investigation showed a big and very tender swelling on the back of his skull, hair matted with blood, and failed to tell him whether or not his skull was fractured. He gave no thanks that he had been left alive; he was sure that the blow had been intended to kill.

But not only his knife was gone. He was naked, save for his shorts. Gone were his precious water, his vest pack with rations and a dozen other invaluable articles —his antibiotics, his salt, his compass, his climbers, his matches, his hammock . . . everything.

His first feeling of sick dismay was replaced by anger. Losing food and gear was no more than to be expected, since he had been such a fool as to forget his rear while he looked at the stream—but taking the watch his father had given him, that was stealing; he would make somebody pay for that!

His anger made him feel better. It was not until then that he noticed that the bandage on his left shin was undisturbed.

He felt it. Sure enough! Whoever it was who had hijacked him had not considered a bandage worth stealing; Rod unwrapped it and cradled Lady Macbeth in his hand.

Somebody was going to be sorry.

4

Savage

ROD WALKER WAS CROUCHING ON A TREE LIMB. HE HAD not moved for two hours, he might not move for as long a time. In a clearing near him a small herd of yearling bachelor buck were cropping grass; if one came close enough Rod intended to dine on buck. He was very hungry.

He was thirsty, too, not having drunk that day. Besides that, he was slightly feverish. Three long, imperfectly healed scratches on his left arm accounted for the fever, but Rod paid fever and scratches no attention —he was alive; he planned to stay alive.

A buck moved closer to him; Rod became quiveringly alert. But the little buck tossed his head, looked at the branch, and moved away. He did not appear to see Rod; perhaps his mother had taught him to be careful of overhanging branches—or perhaps a hundred thousand generations of harsh survival had printed it in his genes.

Rod swore under his breath and lay still. One of them was bound to make a mistake eventually; then he would eat. It had been days since he had thought about anything but food . . . food and how to keep his skin intact, how to drink without laying himself open to ambush, how to sleep without waking up in a fellow-denizen's belly.

The healing wounds on his arm marked how expensive his tuition had been. He had let himself get too far from a tree once too often, had not even had time to draw his knife. Instead he had made an impossible leap and had chinned himself with the wounded arm. The thing that had clawed him he believed to be the same sort as the creature that had treed him the day of his arrival; furthermore he believed it to be a lion. He had a theory about that, but had not yet been able to act on it.

He was gaunt almost to emaciation and had lost track of time. He realized that the time limit of the survival test had probably—almost certainly—passed, but he did not know how long he had lain in the crotch of a tree, waiting for his arm to heal, nor exactly how long it had been since he had come down, forced by thirst and hunger. He supposed that the recall signal had probably been given during one of his unconscious periods, but he did not worry nor even think about it. He was no longer interested in survival tests; he was interested in survival.

Despite his weakened condition his chances were better now than when he had arrived. He was becoming sophisticated, no longer afraid of things he had been afraid of, most acutely wary of others which had seemed harmless. The creatures with the ungodly voices which

61

he had dubbed "stobor" no longer fretted him; he had seen one, had disturbed it by accident in daylight and it had given voice. It was not as big as his hand, and reminded him of a horned lizard except that it had the habits of a tree toad. Its one talent was its voice; it could blow up a bladder at its neck to three times its own size, then give out with that amazing, frightening sob.

But that was all it could do.

Rod had guessed that it was a love call, then had filed the matter. He still called them "stobor."

He had learned about a forest vine much like a morning glory, but its leaves carried a sting worse than that of a nettle, toxic and producing numbness. Another vine had large grape-like fruits, deliciously tempting and pleasant to the palate; Rod had learned the hard way that they were a powerful purgative.

He knew, from his own narrow brushes and from kills left half-eaten on the ground, that there were carnivores around even though he had never had a good look at one. So far as he knew there were no carnivorous tree-climbers large enough to tackle a man, but he could not be certain; he slept with one eye open.

The behavior of this herd caused him to suspect that there must be carnivores that hunted as he was now hunting, even though he had had the good fortune not to tangle with one. The little buck had wandered all over the clearing, passed close by lesser trees, yet no one of them had grazed under the tree Rod was in.

Steady, boy . . . here comes one. Rod felt the grip of "Lady Macbeth," got ready to drop onto the graceful little creature as it passed under. But five meters away it hesitated, seemed to realize that it was straying from its mates, and started to turn.

Rod let fly.

He could hear the meaty *tunk!* as blade bit into muscle; he could see the hilt firm against the shoulder of the buck. He dropped to the ground, hit running and moved in to finish the kill.

The buck whipped its head up, turned and fled. Rod dived, did not touch it. When he rolled to his feet the clearing was empty. His mind was filled with bitter thoughts; he had promised himself never to throw his knife when there was any possibility of not being able to recover it, but he did not let regrets slow him; he got to work on the tracking problem.

Rod had been taught the first law of hunting sportsmanship, that a wounded animal must always be tracked down and finished, not left to suffer and die slowly. But there was no trace of "sportsmanship" in his present conduct; he undertook to track the buck because he intended to eat it, and—much more urgently—because he had to recover that knife in order to stay alive.

The buck had not bled at once and its tracks were mixed up with hundreds of other tracks. Rod returned three times to the clearing and started over before he picked up the first blood spoor. After that it was easier but he was far behind now and the stampeded buck moved much faster than he could track. His quarry stayed with the herd until it stopped in a new pasture a half kilometer away. Rod stopped still in cover and looked them over. His quarry did not seem to be among them.

But blood sign led in among them; he followed it and they stampeded again. He had trouble picking it up; when he did he found that it led into brush instead of following the herd. This made it easier and harder—easier because he no longer had to sort one spoor from many, harder because pushing through the brush was hard in itself and much more dangerous, since he must never forget that he himself was hunted as well as hunter, and lastly because the signs were so much harder to spot there. But it cheered him up, knowing that only a weakened animal would leave the herd and try to hide. He expected to find it down before long.

But the beast did not drop; it seemed to have a will to live as strong as his own. He followed it endlessly and was beginning to wonder what he would do if it grew dark before the buck gave up. He *had* to have that knife.

He suddenly saw that there were two spoors.

Something had stepped beside a fresh, split-hooved track of the little antelope; something had stepped on a drop of blood. Quivering, his subconscious "bush radar" at full power, Rod moved silently forward. He found new marks again . . . a man!

The print of a shod human foot—and so wild had he become that it gave him no feeling of relief; it made him more wary than ever.

Twenty minutes later he found them, the human and the buck. The buck was down, having died or perhaps been finished off by the second stalker. The human, whom Rod judged to be a boy somewhat younger and smaller than himself, was kneeling over it, slicing its belly open. Rod faded back into the bush. From there he watched and thought. The other hunter seemed much preoccupied with the kill . . . and that tree hung over the place where the butchering was going on—

A few minutes later Rod was again on a branch, without a knife but with a long thorn held in his teeth. He looked down, saw that his rival was almost under him, and transferred the thorn to his right hand. Then he waited.

The hunter below him laid the knife aside and bent to turn the carcass. Rod dropped.

He felt body armor which had been concealed by his victim's shirt. Instantly he transferred his attention to the bare neck, pushing the thorn firmly against vertebrae. "Hold still or you've had it!"

The body under him suddenly quit struggling.

"That's better," Rod said approvingly. "Cry pax?"

No answer. Rod jabbed the thorn again. "I'm not playing games," he said harshly. "I'm giving you one chance to stay alive. Cry pax and mean it, and we'll both eat. Give me any trouble and you'll never eat again. It doesn't make the least difference."

There was a moment's hesitation, then a muffled voice said, "Pax."

Keeping the thorn pressed against his prisoner's neck, Rod reached out for the knife which had been used to gut the buck. It was, he saw, his own Lady Macbeth. He sheathed it, felt around under the body he rested on, found another where he expected it, pulled it and kept it in his hand. He chucked away the thorn and stood up. "You can get up."

The youngster got up and faced him sullenly. "Give me my knife."

"Later . . . if you are a good boy."

"I said 'Pax.' "

"So you did. Turn around, I want to make sure you don't have a gun on you."

"I left—I've nothing but my knife. Give it to me."

"Left it where?"

The kid did not answer. Rod said, "Okay, turn around," and threatened with the borrowed knife. He was obeyed. Rod quickly patted all the likely hiding places, confirmed that the youngster was wearing armor under clothes and over the entire torso. Rod himself was dressed only in tan, scratches, torn and filthy shorts, and a few scars. "Don't you find that junk pretty hot in this weather?" he asked cheerfully. "Okay, you can turn around. Keep your distance."

The youngster turned around, still with a very sour expression. "What's your name, bud?"

"Uh, Jack."

"Jack what? Mine's Rod Walker."

"Jack Daudet."

"What school, Jack?"

"Ponce de León Institute."

"Mine's Patrick Henry High School."

"*Matson's* class?"

"The Deacon himself."

"I've heard of him." Jack seemed impressed.

"Who hasn't? Look, let's quit jawing; we'll have the whole county around our ears. Let's eat. You keep watch that way; I'll keep watch behind you."

"Then give me my knife. I need it to eat."

"Not so fast. I'll cut you off a hunk or two. Special Waldorf service."

Rod continued the incision Jack had started, carried it on up and laid the hide back from the right shoulder, hacked off a couple of large chunks of lean. He tossed one to Jack, hunkered down and gnawed his own piece while keeping sharp lookout. "You keeping your eyes peeled?" he asked.

"Sure."

Rod tore off a rubbery mouthful of warm meat. "Jack, how did they let a runt like you take the test? You aren't old enough."

"I'll bet I'm as old as you are!"

"I doubt it."

"Well . . . I'm qualified."

"You don't look it."

"I'm *here,* I'm alive."

Rod grinned. "You've made your point. I'll shut up." Once his portion was resting comfortably inside, Rod got up, split the skull and dug out the brains. "Want a handful?"

"Sure."

Rod passed over a fair division of the dessert. Jack accepted it, hesitated, then blurted out, "Want some salt?"

"Salt! You've got *salt?"*

Jack appeared to regret the indiscretion. "Some. Go easy on it."

Rod held out his handful. "Put some on. Whatever you can spare."

Jack produced a pocket shaker from between shirt and armor, sprinkled a little on Rod's portion, then shrugged and made it liberal. "Didn't you bring salt along?"

"Me?" Rod answered, tearing his eyes from the mouth-watering sight. "Oh, sure! But— Well, I had an accident." He decided that there was no use admitting that he had been caught off guard.

Jack put the shaker firmly out of sight. They munched quietly, each watching half their surroundings. After a while Rod said softly, "Jackal behind you, Jack."

"Nothing else?"

"No. But it's time we whacked up the meat and got out of here; we're attracting attention. How much can you use?"

"Uh, a haunch and a chunk of liver. I can't carry any more."

"And you can't eat more before it spoils, anyway." Rod started butchering the hind quarters. He cut a slice of hide from the belly, used it to sling his share around his neck. "Well, so long, kid. Here's your knife. Thanks for the salt."

"Oh, that's all right."

"Tasted mighty good. Well, keep your eyes open."

"Same to you. Good luck."

Rod stood still. Then he said almost reluctantly, "Uh, Jack, you wouldn't want to team up, would you?" He regretted it as soon as he said it, remembering how easily he had surprised the kid.

Jack chewed a lip. "Well . . . I don't know."

Rod felt affronted. "What's the matter? Afraid of me?" Didn't the kid see that Rod was doing him a favor?

"Oh, no! You're all right, I guess."

Rod had an unpleasant suspicion. "You think I'm trying to get a share of your salt, don't you?"

"Huh? Not at all. Look, I'll divvy some salt with you."

"I wouldn't touch it! I just thought—" Rod stopped. He had been thinking that they had both missed recall; it looked like a long pull.

"I didn't mean to make you mad, Rod. You're right. We ought to team."

"Don't put yourself out! I can get along."

"I'll bet you can. But let's team up. Is it a deal?"

"Well . . . Shake."

Once the contract was made Rod assumed leadership. There was no discussion; he simply did so and Jack let it stand. "You lead off," Rod ordered, "and I'll cover our rear."

"Okay. Where are we heading?"

"That high ground downstream. There are good trees there, better for all night than around here. I want us to have time to settle in before dark—so a quick sneak and no talking."

Jack hesitated. "Okay. Are you dead set on spending the night in a tree?"

Rod curled his lip. "Want to spend it on the ground? How did you stay alive this long?"

"I spent a couple of nights in trees," Jack answered mildly. "But I've got a better place now, maybe."

"Huh? What sort?"

"A sort of a cave."

Rod thought about it. Caves could be death traps. But the prospect of being able to stretch out swayed him. "Won't hurt to look, if it's not too far."

"It's not far."

5

The Nova

JACK'S HIDEAWAY WAS IN A BLUFF OVERLOOKING THE stream by which Rod had been robbed. At this point the bluffs walled a pocket valley and the stream meandered between low banks cut in an alluvial field between the bluffs. The cave was formed by an overhang of limestone which roofed a room water-carved from shale in one bluff. The wall below it was too sheer to climb; the overhanging limestone protected it above and the stream curved in sharply almost to the foot of the bluff. The only way to reach it was to descend the bluff farther upstream to the field edging the creek, then make a climbing traverse of the shale bank where it was somewhat less steep just upstream of the cave.

They slanted cautiously up the shale, squeezed under an overhang at the top, and stepped out on a hard slaty floor. The room was open on one side and fairly long and deep, but it squeezed in to a waist-high crawl space; only at the edge was there room to stand up. Jack grabbed some gravel, threw it into the dark hole, waited with knife ready. "Nobody home, I guess." They dropped to hands and knees, crawled inside. "How do you like it?"

"It's swell . . . provided we stand watches. Something could come up the way we did. You've been lucky."

"Maybe," Jack felt around in the gloom, dragged out dry branches of thorn bush, blocked the pathway, jamming them under the overhang. "That's my alarm."

"It wouldn't stop anything that got a whiff of you and really wanted to come in."

"No. But I would wake up and let it have some

rocks in the face. I keep a stack over there. I've got a couple of scare-flares, too."

"I thought— Didn't you say you had a gun?"

"I didn't say, but I do. But I don't believe in shooting when you can't see."

"It looks all right. In fact it looks good. I guess I did myself a favor when I teamed with you." Rod looked around. "You've had a *fire!*"

"I've risked it a couple of times, in daylight. I get so tired of raw meat."

Rod sighed deeply. "I know. Say, do you suppose?"

"It's almost dark. I've never lighted one when it could show. How about roast liver for breakfast, instead? With salt?"

Rod's mouth watered. "You're right, Jack. I do want to get a drink before it is too dark, though. How about coming along and we cover each other?"

"No need. There's a skin back there. Help yourself."

Rod congratulated himself on having teamed with a perfect housekeeper. The skin was of a small animal, not identifiable when distended with water. Jack had scraped the hide but it was uncured and decidedly unsavory. Rod was not aware that the water tasted bad; he drank deeply, wiped his mouth with his hand and felt at peace.

They did not sleep at once, but sat in the dark and compared notes. Jack's class had come through one day earlier, but with the same instructions. Jack agreed that recall was long overdue.

"I suppose I missed it while I was off my head," Rod commented. "I don't know how long I was foggy . . . I guess I didn't miss dying by much."

"That's not it, Rod."

"Why not?"

"I've been okay and keeping track of the time. There never was any recall."

"You're sure?"

"How could I miss? The siren can be heard for twenty kilometers, they use a smoke flare by day and a searchlight at night, and the law says they have to keep it up at least a week unless everybody returns . . . which certainly did not happen this time."

"Maybe we are out of range. Matter of fact—well, I don't know about you, but I'm lost. I admit it."

"I'm not. I'm about four kilometers from where they let my class through; I could show you the spot. Rod, let's face it; something has gone wrong. There is no way of telling how long we are going to be here." Jack added quietly, "That's why I thought it was a good idea to team."

Rod chewed it over, decided it was time to haul out his theory. "Me, too."

"Yes. Solo is actually safer, for a few days. But if we are stuck here indefinitely, then—"

"Not what I meant, Jack."

"Huh?"

"Do you know what planet this is?"

"No. I've thought about it, of course. It has to be one of the new list and it is compatible with—"

"I *know* what one it is."

"Huh? Which one?"

"It's Earth. Terra herself."

There was a long silence. At last Jack said, "Rod, are you all right? Are you still feverish?"

"I'm fine, now that I've got a full belly and a big drink of water. Look, Jack, I know it sounds silly, but you just listen and I'll add it up. We're on Earth and I think I know about where, too. I don't think they meant to sound recall; they meant us to figure out where we are . . . and walk out. It's a twist Deacon Matson would love."

"But—"

"Keep quiet, can't you? Yapping like a girl. Terrestrial planet, right?"

"Yes, but—"

"Stow it and let me talk. G-type star. Planetary rotation same as Earth."

"But it's not!"

"I made the same mistake. The first night I thought was a week long. But the truth was I was scared out of my skin and that made it seem endless. Now I know better. The rotation matches."

"No, it doesn't. My watch shows it to be about twenty-ty-six hours."

70

"You had better have your watch fixed when we get back. You banged it against a tree or something."

"But— Oh, go ahead. Keep talking; it's your tape."

"You'll see. Flora compatible. Fauna compatible. I know how they did it and why and where they put us. It's an economy measure."

"A what?"

"Economy. Too many people complaining about school taxes being too high. Of course, keeping an interstellar gate open is expensive and uranium doesn't grow on trees. I see their point. But Deacon Matson says it is false economy. He says, sure, it's expensive— but that the only thing more expensive than a properly trained explorer or pioneer leader is an improperly trained dead one.

"He told us after class one day," Rod went on, "that the penny-pinchers wanted to run the practices and tests in selected areas on Earth, but the Deacon claims that the essence of survival in the Outlands is the skill to cope with the unknown. He said that if tests were held on Earth, the candidates would just study up on terrestrial environments. He said any Boy Scout could learn the six basic Earth environments and how to beat them out of books . . . but that it was criminal to call that survival training and then dump a man in an un-Earthly environment on his first professional assignment. He said that it was as ridiculous as just teaching a kid to play chess and then send him him out to fight a duel."

"He's right," Jack answered. "Commander Benboe talks the same way."

"Sure he's right. He swore that if they went ahead with this policy this would be the last year he would teach. But they pulled a gimmick on him."

"How?"

"It's a good one. What the Deacon forgot is that any environment is as unknown as any other if you don't have the slightest idea where you are. So they rigged it so that we could not know. First they shot us to Luna; the Moon gates are always open and that doesn't cost anything extra. Of course that made us think we were in for a long jump. Besides, it confused us; we wouldn't know we were being dumped back into the gravity field

71

we had left—for that was what they did next; they shoved us back on Earth. Where? Africa, I'd say. I think they used the Luna Link to jump us to Witwatersrand Gate outside Johannesburg and there they were all set with a matched-in temporary link to drop us into the bush. Tshaka Memorial Park or some other primitive preserve, on a guess. Everything matches. A wide variety of antelope-type game, carnivores to feed on them —I've seen a couple of lions and—"

"You *have?*"

"Well, they will do for lions until I get a chance to skin one. But they threw in other dodges to confuse us, too. The sky would give the show away, particularly if we got a look at Luna. So they've hung an overcast over us. You can bet there are cloud generators not far away. Then they threw us one more curve. Were you warned against 'stobor'?"

"Yes."

"See any?"

"Well, I'm not sure what stobor are."

"Neither am I. Nor any of us, I'll bet. 'Stobor' is the bogeyman, chucked in to keep our pretty little heads busy. There aren't any 'stobor' on Terra so naturally we must be somewhere else. Even a suspicious character like me would be misled by that. In fact, I was. I even picked out something I didn't recognize and called it that, just as they meant me to do."

"You make it sound logical, Rod."

"Because it *is* logical. Once you realize that this is Earth—" He patted the floor of the cave. "—but that they have been trying to keep us from knowing it, everything falls into place. Now here is what we do. I was going to tackle it alone, as soon as I could—I haven't been able to move around much on account of this bad arm—but I decided to take you along, before you got hurt. Here's my plan. I think this is Africa, but it might be South America, or anywhere in the tropics. It does not matter, because we simply follow this creek downstream, keeping our eyes open because there really are hazards; you can get just as dead here as in the Outlands. It may take a week, or a month, but one day we'll come to a bridge. We'll follow the road it serves until somebody happens along. Once in town we'll check in with the authorities and get them to flip us home . . . and we get our solo test certificates. Simple."

"You make it sound too simple," Jack said slowly.

"Oh, we'll have our troubles. But we can do it, now that we know what to do. I didn't want to bring this up before, but do you have salt enough to cure a few kilos of meat? If we did not have to hunt every day, we could travel faster. Or maybe you brought some Kwik-Kure?"

"I did, but—"

"Good!"

"Wait a minute, Rod. That won't do."

"Huh? We're a team, aren't we?"

"Take it easy. Look, Rod, everything you said is logical, but—"

"No 'buts' about it."

"It's logical . . . but it's *all wrong!*"

"Huh? Now, listen, Jack—"

"*You* listen. You've done all the talking so far."

"But— Well, all right, say your say."

"You said that the sky would give it away, so they threw an overcast over the area."

"Yes. That's what they must have done, nights at least. They wouldn't risk natural weather; it might give the show away."

"What I'm trying to tell you is that it *did* give the show away. It hasn't been overcast every night, though maybe you were in deep forest and missed the few times it has been clear. But I've seen the night sky, Rod. I've seen stars."

"So? Well?"

"They aren't *our* stars, Rod. I'm sorry."

Rod chewed his lip. "You probably don't know southern constellations very well?" he suggested.

"I knew the Southern Cross before I could read. These aren't our stars, Rod; I know. There is a pentagon of bright stars above where the sun sets; there is nothing like that to be seen from Earth. And besides, anybody would recognize Luna, if it was there."

Rod tried to remember what phase the Moon should be in. He gave up, as he had only a vague notion of elapsed time. "Maybe the Moon was down?"

"Not a chance. I didn't see our Moon, Rod, but I

73

saw *moons* . . . two of them, little ones and moving fast, like the moons of Mars."

"You don't mean this is *Mars?*" Rod said scornfully.

"Think I'm crazy? Anyhow, the stars from Mars are exactly like the stars from Earth. Rod, what are we jawing about? It was beginning to clear when the sun went down; let's crawl out and have a look. Maybe you'll believe your eyes."

Rod shut up and followed Jack. From inside nothing was visible but dark trees across the stream, but from the edge of the shelf part of the sky could be seen. Rod looked up and blinked.

"Mind the edge," Jack warned softly.

Rod did not answer. Framed by the ledge above him and by tree tops across the stream was a pattern of six stars, a lopsided pentagon with a star in its center. The six stars were as bright and unmistakable as the seven stars of Earth's Big Dipper . . . nor did it take a degree in astrography to know that this constellation had never been seen from Terra.

Rod stared while the hard convictions he had formed fell in ruins. He felt lost and alone. The tree across the way seemed frightening. He turned to Jack, his cocky sophistication gone. "You've convinced me," he said dully. "What do we do now?"

Jack did not answer.

"Well?" Rod insisted. "No good standing here."

"Rod," Jack answered, "that star in the middle of the Pentagon—it wasn't there before."

"Huh? You probably don't remember."

"No, no, I'm sure! Rod, you know what? We're seeing a *nova.*"

Rod was unable to arouse the pure joy of scientific discovery; his mind was muddled with reorganizing his personal universe. A mere stellar explosion meant nothing. "Probably one of your moonlets."

"Not a chance. The moons are big enough to show disks. It's a nova; it has to be. What amazing luck to see one!"

"I don't see anything lucky about it," Rod answered moodily. "It doesn't mean anything to us. It's probably a hundred light-years away, maybe more."

"Yes, but doesn't it thrill you?"

"No." He stooped down and went inside. Jack took another look, then followed.

There was silence, moody on Rod's part. At last Jack said, "Think I'll turn in."

"I just can't see," Rod answered irrelevantly, "how I could be so wrong. It was a logical certainty."

"Forget it," Jack advised. "My analytics instructors says that all logic is mere tautology. She says it is impossible to learn anything through logic that you did not already know."

"Then what use is logic?" Rod demanded.

"Ask me an easy one. Look, partner, I'm dead for sleep; I want to turn in."

"All right. But, Jack, if this isn't Africa—and I've got to admit it isn't—what do we do? They've gone off and *left* us."

"Do? We do what we've been doing. Eat, sleep, stay alive. This is a listed planet; if we just keep breathing, someday somebody will show up. It might be just a power breakdown; they may pick us tomorrow."

"In that case, then—"

"In that case, let's shut up and go to sleep."

6

"I Think He Is Dead"

ROD WAS AWAKENED BY HEAVENLY ODORS. HE ROLLED over, blinked at light streaming under the overhang, managed by great effort to put himself back into the matrix of the day before. Jack, he saw, was squatting by a tiny fire on the edge of the shelf; the wonderful fragrance came from toasting liver.

Rod got to his knees, discovering that he was slightly stiff from having fought dream stobor in his sleep.

These nightmare stobor were bug-eyed monsters fit for a planet suddenly strange and threatening. Nevertheless he had had a fine night's sleep and his spirits could not be daunted in the presence of the tantalizing aroma drifting in.

Jack looked up. "I thought you were going to sleep all day. Brush your teeth, comb your hair, take a quick shower, and get on out here. Breakfast is ready." Jack looked him over again. "Better shave, too."

Rod grinned and ran his hand over his chin. "You're jealous of my manly beard, youngster. Wait a year or two and you'll find out what a nuisance it is. Shaving, the common cold, and taxes . . . my old man says those are the three eternal problems the race is never going to lick." Rod felt a twinge at the thought of his parents, a stirring of conscience that he had not thought of them in he could not remember how long. "Can I help, pal?"

"Sit down and grab the salt. This piece is for you."

"Let's split it."

"Eat and don't argue. I'll fix me some." Rod accepted the charred and smoky chunk, tossed it in his hands and blew on it. He looked around for salt. Jack was slicing a second piece; Rod's eyes passed over the operation—then whipped back.

The knife Jack was using was "Colonel Bowie."

The realization was accompanied by action; Rod's hand darted out and caught Jack's wrist in an anger-hard grip. "You stole my knife!"

Jack did not move. "Rod . . . have you gone crazy?"

"You slugged me and stole my knife."

Jack made no attempt to fight, nor even to struggle. "You aren't awake yet, Rod. Your knife is on your belt. This is another knife . . . mine."

Rod did not bother to look down. "The one I'm wearing is Lady Macbeth. I mean the knife you're using, Colonel Bowie—*my* knife."

"Let go my wrist."

"Drop it!"

"Rod . . . you can probably make me drop this knife. You're bigger and you've got the jump on me. But yesterday you teamed with me. You're busting that team right now. If you don't let go right away, the team is broken. Then you'll have to kill me . . . because if you

76

don't, I'll trail you. I'll keep on trailing you until I find you asleep. Then you've had it."

They faced each other across the little fire, eyes locked. Rod breathed hard and tried to think. The evidence was against Jack. But had this little runt tracked him, slugged him, stolen everything he had? It looked like it.

Yet it did not *feel* like it. He told himself that he could handle the kid if his story did not ring true. He let go Jack's wrist. "All right," he said angrily, "tell me how you got my knife."

Jack went on slicing liver. "It's not much of a story . . . and I don't know that it is *your* knife. But it was not mine to start with—you've seen mine. I use this one as a kitchen knife. Its balance is wrong."

"Colonel Bowie! Balanced wrong? That's the best throwing knife you ever saw!"

"Do you want to hear this? I ran across this hombre in the bush, just as the jackals were getting to him. I don't know what got him—stobor, maybe; he was pretty well clawed and half eaten. He wasn't one of my class, for his face wasn't marked and I could tell. He was carrying a Thunderbolt and—"

"Wait a minute. A Thunderbolt gun?"

"I said so, didn't I? I guess he tried to use it and had no luck. Anyhow, I took what I could use—this knife and a couple of other things; I'll show you. I left the Thunderbolt; the power pack was exhausted and it was junk."

"Jack, look at me. You're not lying?"

Jack shrugged. "I can take you to the spot. There might not be anything left of him, but the Thunderbolt ought to be there."

Rod stuck out his hand. "I'm sorry. I jumped to conclusions."

Jack looked at his hand, did not shake it. "I don't think you are much of a team mate. We had better call it quits." The knife flipped over, landed at Rod's toes. "Take your toadsticker and be on your way."

Rod did not pick up the knife. "Don't get sore, Jack. I made an honest mistake."

"It was a mistake, all right. You didn't trust me and I'm not likely to trust you again. You can't build a team on that." Jack hesitated. "Finish your breakfast and shove off. It's better than way."

"Jack, I truly am sorry. I apologize. But it was a mistake anybody could make—you haven't heard my side of the story."

"You didn't wait to hear *my* story!"

"So I was wrong, I *said* I was wrong." Rod hurriedly told how he had been stripped of his survival gear. "—so naturally, when I saw Colonel Bowie, I assumed that you must have jumped me. That's logical, isn't it?" Jack did not answer; Rod persisted: "Well? Isn't it?"

Jack said slowly, "You used 'logic' again. What you call 'logic.' Rod, you use the stuff the way some people use dope. Why don't you use your head, instead?"

Rod flushed and kept still. Jack went on, "If I had swiped your knife, would I have let you see it? For that matter, would I have teamed with you?"

"No, I guess not. Jack, I jumped at a conclusion and lost my temper."

"Commander Benboe says," Jack answered bleakly, "that losing your temper and jumping at conclusions is a one-way ticket to the cemetery."

Rod looked sheepish. "Deacon Matson talks the same way."

"Maybe they're right. So let's not do it again, huh? Every dog gets one bite, but only one."

Rod looked up, saw Jack's dirty paw stuck out at him. "You mean we're partners again?"

"Shake. I think we had better be; we don't have much choice." They solemnly shook hands. Then Rod picked up Colonel Bowie, looked at it longingly, and handed it hilt first to Jack.

"I guess it's yours, after all."

"Huh? Oh, no. I'm glad you've got it back."

"No," Rod insisted. "You came by it fair and square."

"Don't be silly, Rod. I've got 'Bluebeard'; that's the knife for me."

"It's yours. I've got Lady Macbeth."

Jack frowned. "We're partners, right?"

"Huh? Sure."

"So we share everything. Bluebeard belongs just as

78

much to you as to me. And Colonel Bowie belongs to both of us. But you are used to it, so it's best for the team for you to wear it. Does that appeal to your lop-sided sense of logic?"

"Well . . ."

"So shut up and eat your breakfast. Shall I toast you another slice? That one is cold."

Rod picked up the scorched chunk of liver, brushed dirt and ashes from it. "This is all right."

"Throw it in the stream and have a hot piece. Liver won't keep anyhow."

Comfortably stuffed, and warmed by companionship, Rod stretched out on the shelf after breakfast and stared at the sky. Jack put out the fire and tossed the remnants of their meal downstream. Something broke water and snapped at the liver even as it struck. Jack turned to Rod. "Well, what do we do today?"

"Mmm . . . what we've got on hand ought to be fit to eat tomorrow morning. We don't need to make a kill today."

"I hunt every second day, usually, since I found this place. Second-day meat is better than first, but by the third . . . phewy!"

"Sure. Well, what do you want to do?"

"Well, let's see. First I'd like to buy a tall, thick chocolate malted milk—or maybe a fruit salad. Both. I'd eat those—"

"Stop it, you're breaking my heart!"

"Then I'd have a hot bath and get all dressed up and flip out to Hollywood and see a couple of good shows. That superspectacle that Dirk Manleigh is starring in and then a good adventure show. After that I'd have another malted milk . . . strawberry, this time, and then—"

"*Shut up!*"

"You asked me what I wanted to do."

"Yes, but I expected you to stick to possibilities."

"Then why didn't you say so? Is that 'logical'? I thought you always used logic?"

"Say, lay off, will you? I apologized."

"Yeah, you apologized," Jack admitted darkly. "But I've got some mad I haven't used up yet "

79

"Well! Are you the sort of pal who keeps raking up the past?"

"Only when you least expect it. Seriously, Rod, I think we ought to hunt today."

"But you agreed we didn't need to. It's wrong, and dangerous besides, to make a kill you don't need."

"I think we ought to hunt people."

Rod pulled his ear. "Say that again."

"We ought to spend the day hunting people."

"Huh? Well, anything for fun I always say. What do we do when we find them? Scalp them, or just shout 'Beaver!'?"

"Scalping is more definite. Rod, how long will we be here?"

"Huh? All we know is that something has gone seriously cockeyed with the recall schedule. You say we've been here three weeks. I would say it was longer but you have kept a notch calendar and I haven't. Therefore . . ." He stopped.

"Therefore what?"

"Therefore nothing. They might have had some technical trouble, which they may clear up and recall us this morning. Deacon Matson and his fun-loving colleagues might have thought it was cute to double the period and not mention it. The Dalai Lama might have bombed the whiskers off the rest of the world and the Gates may be radioactive ruins. Or maybe the three-headed serpent men of the Lesser Magellanic Cloud have landed and have the situation well in hand—for them. When you haven't data, guessing is illogical. We might be here forever."

Jack nodded. "That's my point."

"Which point? We know we may be marooned; that's obvious."

"Rod, a two-man team is just right for a few weeks. But suppose this runs into months? Suppose one of us breaks a leg? Or even if we don't, how long is that thornbush alarm going to work? We ought to wall off that path and make this spot accessible only by rope ladder, with somebody here all the time to let the ladder down. We ought to locate a salt lick and think about curing hides and things like that—that water skin I

80

made is getting high already. For a long pull we ought to have at least four people."

Rod scratched his gaunt ribs thoughtfully. "I know. I thought about it last night, after you jerked the rug out from under my optimistic theory. But I was waiting for you to bring it up."

"Why?"

"This is your cave. You've got all the fancy equipment, a gun and pills and other stuff I haven't seen. You've got salt. All I've got is a knife—two knives now, thanks to you. I'd look sweet suggesting that you share four ways."

"We're a team, Rod."

"Mmm . . . yes. And we both figure the team would be strengthened with a couple of recruits. Well, how many people are there out there?" He gestured at the wall of green across the creek.

"My class put through seventeen boys and eleven girls. Commander Denboe told us there would be four classes in the same test area."

"That's more than the Deacon bothered to tell us. However, my class put through about twenty."

Jack looked thoughtful. "Around a hundred people, probably."

"Not counting casualties."

"Not counting casualties. Maybe two-thirds boys, one-third girls. Plenty of choice, if we can find them."

"No girls on this team, Jack."

"What have you got against girls?"

"Me? Nothing at all. Girls are swell on picnics, they are just right on long winter evenings. I'm one of the most enthusiastic supporters of the female race. But for a hitch like this, they are pure poison."

Jack did not say anything. Rod went on, "Use your head, brother. You get some pretty little darling on this team and we'll have more grief inside than stobor, or such, can give us from outside. Quarrels and petty jealousies and maybe a couple of boys knifing each other. It will be tough enough without that trouble."

"Well," Jack answered thoughtfully, "suppose the first one we locate is a girl? What are you going to do? Tip your hat and say, 'It's a fine day, ma'am. Now drop dead and don't bother me.?'"

Rod drew a pentagon in the ashes, put a star in the middle, then rubbed it out. "I don't know," he said slowly. "Let's hope we get our team working before we meet any. And let's hope they set up their own teams."

"I think we ought to have a policy."

"I'm clean out of policies. You would just accuse me of trying to be logical. Got any ideas about how to find anybody?"

"Maybe. Somebody has been hunting upstream from here."

"So? Know who it is?"

"I've seen him only at a distance. Nobody from my class. Half a head shorter than you are, light hair, pink skin—and a bad sunburn. Sound familiar?"

"Could be anybody," Rod answered, thinking fretfully that the description did sound familiar. "Shall we see if we can pick up some sign of him?"

"I can put him in your lap. But I'm not sure we want him."

"Why not? If he's lasted this long, he must be competent."

"Frankly, I don't see how he has. He's noisy when he moves and he has been living in one tree for the past week."

"Not necessarily bad technique."

"It is when you drop your bones and leavings out of the tree. It was jackals sniffing around that tipped me off to where he was living."

"Hmm . . . well, if we don't like him, we don't have to invite him."

"True."

Before they set out Jack dug around in the gloomy cave and produced a climbing line. "Rod, could this be yours?"

Rod looked it over. "It's just like the one I had. Why?"

"I got it the way I got Colonel Bowie, off the casualty. If it is not yours, at least it is a replacement." Jack got another, wrapped it around and over body armor. Rod suspected that Jack had slept in the armor, but he said nothing. If Jack considered such marginal protection more important than agility, that was Jack's business—each to his own methods, as the Deacon would say.

The tree stood in a semi-clearing but Jack brought Rod to it through bushes which came close to the trunk and made the final approach as a belly sneak. Jack pulled Rod's head over and whispered in his ear, "If we lie still for three or four hours, I'm betting that he will either come down or go up."

"Okay. You watch our rear."

For an hour nothing happened. Rod tried to ignore tiny flies that seemed to be all bite. Silently he shifted position to ward off stiffness and once had to kill a sneeze. At last he said, "Pssst!"

"Yeah, Rod?"

"Where those two big branches meet the trunk, could that be his nest?"

"Maybe."

"You see a hand sticking out?"

"Where? Uh, I think I see what you see. It might just be leaves."

"I think it's a hand and I think he is dead; it hasn't moved since we got here."

"Asleep?"

"Person asleep ordinarily doesn't hold still that long. I'm going up. Cover me. If that hand moves, yell."

"You ought not to risk it, Rod."

"You keep your eyes peeled." He crept forward.

The owner of the hand was Jimmy Throxton, as Rod had suspected since hearing the description. Jimmy was not dead, but he was unconscious and Rod could not rouse him.

Jim lay in an aerie half natural, half artificial; Rod could see that Jim had cut small branches and improved the triple crotch formed by two limbs and trunk. He lay cradled in this eagle's nest, one hand trailing out.

Getting him down was awkward; he weighed as much as Rod did. Rod put a sling under Jim's armpits and took a turn around a branch, checking the line by friction to lower him—but the hard part was getting Jim out of his musty bed without dropping him.

Halfway down the burden fouled and Jack had to

climb and free it. But with much sweat all three reached the ground and Jim was still breathing.

Rod had to carry him. Jack offered to take turns but the disparity in sizes was obvious; Rod said angrily for Jack to cover them, front, rear, all sides; Rod would be helpless if they had the luck to be surprised by one of the pseudo-lions.

The worst part was the climbing traverse over loose shale up to the cave. Rod was fagged from carrying the limp and heavy load more than a kilometer over rough ground; he had to rest before he could tackle it. When he did, Jack said anxiously, "Don't drop him in the drink! It won't be worthwhile fishing him out—I know."

"So do I. Don't give silly advice."

"Sorry."

Rod started up, as much worried for his own hide as for Jim's. He did not know what it was that lived in that stream; he did know that it was hungry. There was a bad time when he reached the spot where the jutting limestone made it necessary to stoop to reach the shelf. He got down as low as possible, attempted it, felt the burden on his back catch on the rock, started to slip.

Jack's hand steadied him and shoved him from behind. Then they were sprawled safe on the shelf and Rod gasped and tried to stop the trembling of his abused muscles.

They bedded Jimmy down and Jack took his pulse. "Fast and thready. I don't think he's going to make it."

"What medicines do you have?"

"Two of the neosulfas and verdomycin. But I don't know what to give him."

"Give him all three and pray."

"He might be allergic to one of them."

"He'll be more allergic to dying. I'll bet he's running six degrees of fever. Come on."

Rod supported Jim's shoulders, pinched his ear lobe, brought him partly out of coma. Between them they managed to get the capsules into Jim's mouth, got him to drink and wash them down. After that there was nothing they could do but let him rest.

They took turns watching him through the night. About dawn his fever broke, he roused and asked for water. Rod held him while Jack handled the waterskin. Jim drank deeply, then went back to sleep.

They never left him alone. Jack did the nursing and Rod hunted each day, trying to find items young and tender and suited to an invalid's palate. By the second day Jim, although weak and helpless, was able to talk without drifting off to sleep in the middle. Rod returned in the afternoon with the carcass of a small animal which seemed to be a clumsy cross between a cat and a rabbit. He encountered Jack heading down to fill the water skin. "Hi."

"Hi. I see you had luck. Say, Rod, go easy when you skin it. We need a new water bag. Is it cut much?"

"Not at all. I knocked it over with a rock."

"Good!"

"How's the patient?"

"Healthier by the minute. I'll be up shortly."

"Want me to cover you while you fill the skin?"

"I'll be careful. Go up to Jim."

Rod went up, laid his kill on the shelf, crawled inside. "Feeling better?"

"Swell. I'll wrestle you two falls out of three."

"Next week. Jack taking good care of you?"

"You bet. Say, Rod, I don't know how to thank you two. If it hadn't been for—"

"Then don't try. You don't owe me anything, ever. And Jack's my partner, so it's right with Jack."

"Jack is swell."

"Jack is a good boy. They don't come better. He and I really hit it off."

Jim looked surprised, opened his mouth, closed it suddenly. "What's the matter?" Rod asked. "Something bite you? Or are you feeling bad again?"

"What," Jim said slowly, "did you say about Jack?"

"Huh? I said they don't come any better. He and I team up like bacon and eggs. A number-one kid, that boy."

Jimmy Throxton looked at him. "Rod . . . were you born that stupid? Or did you have to study?"

"Huh?"

"Jack is a *girl*."

7

"I Should Have Baked a Cake"

THERE FOLLOWED A LONG SILENCE. "WELL," SAID JIM, "close your mouth before something flies in."

"Jimmy, you're still out of your head."

"I may be out of my head, but not so I can't tell a girl from a boy. When that day comes, I won't be sick; I'll be dead."

"But . . ."

Jim shrugged. "Ask her."

A shallow fell across the opening; Rod turned and saw Jack scrambling up to the shelf. "Fresh water, Jimmy!"

"Thanks, kid." Jim added to Rod, "Go on, dopy!"

Jack looked from one to the other. "Why the tableau? What are you staring for, Rod?"

"Jack," he said slowly, "what is your name?"

"Huh? Jack Daudet. I told you that."

"No, no! What's your full name, your legal name?"

Jack looked from Rod to Jimmy's grinning face and back again. "My full name is . . . Jacqueline Marie Daudet—if it's any business of yours. Want to make something of it?"

Rod took a deep breath. "Jacqueline," he said carefully, "I didn't know. I—"

"You weren't supposed to."

"I— Look, if I've said anything to offend you, I surely didn't mean to."

"You haven't said anything to offend me, you big stupid dear. Except about your knife."

"I didn't mean that."

"You mean about girls being poison? Well, did it ever occur to you that maybe boys are pure poison, too?

86

Under these circumstances? No, of course it didn't. But I don't mind your knowing now . . . now that there are three of us."

"But, Jacqueline—"

"Call me 'Jack,' please." She twisted her shoulders uncomfortably. "Now that you know, I won't have to wear this beetle case any longer. Turn your backs, both of you."

"Uh . . ." Rod turned his back. Jimmy rolled over, eyes to the wall.

In a few moments Jacqueline said, "Okay." Rod turned around. In shirt and trousers, without torso armor, her shoulders seemed narrower and she herself was slender now and pleasantly curved. She was scratching her ribs. "I haven't been able to scratch properly since I met you, Rod Walker," she said accusingly. "Sometimes I almost died."

"I didn't make you wear it."

"Suppose I hadn't? Would you have teamed with me?"

"Uh . . . well, it's like this. I . . ." He stopped.

"You see?" She suddenly looked worried. "We're still partners?"

"Huh? Oh, sure, sure!"

"Then shake on it again. This time we shake with Jimmy, too. Right, Jim?"

"You bet, Jack."

They made a three-cornered handshake. Jack pressed her left hand over the combined fists and said solemnly, "All for one!"

Rod drew Colonel Bowie with his left hand, laid the flat of the blade on the stacked hands. "And one for all!"

"Plus sales tax," Jimmy added. "Do we get it notarized?"

Jacqueline's eyes were swimming with tears. "Jimmy Throxton," she said fiercely, "someday I am going to make you take life seriously!"

"I take life seriously," he objected. "I just don't want life to take me seriously. When you're on borrowed time, you can't afford not to laugh."

"We're all on borrowed time," Rod answered him. "Shut up, Jimmy. You talk too much."

"Look who's preaching! The Decibel Kid himself."

"Well . . . you ought not to make fun of Jacqueline. She's done a lot for you."

"She has indeed!"

"Then——"

" 'Then' nothing!" Jacqueline said sharply. "My name is 'Jack,' Rod. Forget 'Jacqueline.' If either of you starts treating me with gallantry we'll have all those troubles you warned me about. 'Pure poison' was the expression you used, as I recall."

"But you can't reasonably expect——"

"Are you going to be 'logical' again? Let's be practical instead. Help me skin this beast and make a new water bag."

The following day Jimmy took over housekeeping and Jack and Rod started hunting together. Jim wanted to come along; he ran into a double veto. There was little advanage in hunting as a threesome whereas Jack and Rod paired off so well that a hunt was never hours of waiting, but merely a matter of finding game. Jack would drive and Rod would kill; they would pick their quarry from the fringe of a herd, Jack would sneak around and panic the animals, usually driving one into Rod's arms.

They still hunted with the knife, even though Jack's gun was a good choice for primitive survival, being an air gun that threw poisoned darts. Since the darts could be recovered and re-envenomed, it was a gun which would last almost indefinitely; she had chosen it for this reason over cartridge or energy guns.

Rod had admired it but decided against hunting with it. "The air pressure might bleed off and let you down."

"It never has. And you can pump it up again awfully fast."

"Mmm . . . yes. But if we use it, someday the last dart will be lost no matter how careful we are . . . and that might be the day we would need it bad. We may be here a long time, what do you say we save it?"

"You're the boss, Rod."

"No, I'm not. We all have equal say."

"Yes, you are. Jimmy and I agreed on that. Somebody has to boss."

Hunting took an hour or so every second day; they

88

spent most of daylight hours searching for another team mate, quartering the area and doing it systematically. Once they drove scavengers from a kill which seemed to have been butchered by knife; they followed a spoor from that and determined that it was a human spoor, but were forced by darkness to return to the cave. They tried to pick it up the next day, but it had rained hard in the night; they never found it.

Another time they found ashes of a fire, but Rod judged them to be at least two weeks old.

After a week of fruitless searching they returned one late afternoon. Jimmy looked up from the fire he had started. "How goes the census?"

"Don't ask," Rod answered, throwing himself down wearily. "What's for dinner?"

"Raw buck, roast buck, and burned buck. I tried baking some of it in wet clay. It didn't work out too well, but I've got some awfully good baked clay for dessert."

"Thanks. If that is the word."

"Jim," Jack said, "we ought to try to bake pots with that clay."

"I did. Big crack in my first effort. But I'll get the hang of it. Look, children," he went on, "has it ever occurred to your bright little minds that you might be going about this the wrong way?"

"What's wrong with it?" Rod demanded.

"Nothing . . . if it is exercise you are after. You are hurrying and scurrying over the countryside, getting in a sweat and nowhere else. Maybe it would be better to sit back and let them come to you."

"How?"

"Send up a smoke signal."

"We've discussed that. We don't want just anybody and we don't want to advertise where we live. We want people who will strengthen the team."

"That is what the engineers call a self-defeating criterion. The superior woodsman you want is just the laddy you will never find by hunting for him. *He* may find *you,* as you go tramping noisily through the brush, kicking rocks and stepping on twigs and scaring the birds. He may shadow you to see what you are up to. But *you* won't find *him.*"

"Rod, there is something to that," Jack said.

"We found *you* easily enough," Rod said to Jim. "Maybe you aren't the high type we need."

"I wasn't myself at the time," Jimmy answered blandly. "Wait till I get my strength back and my true nature will show. Ugh-Ugh, the ape man, that's me. Half Neanderthal and half sleek black leopard." He beat his chest and coughed.

"Are those the proportions? The Neanderthal strain seems dominant."

"Don't be disrespectful. Remember, you are my debtor."

"I think you read the backs of those cards. They are getting to be like waffles." When rescued, Jimmy had had on him a pack of playing cards, and had later explained that they were survival equipment.

"In the first place," he had said, "if I got lost I could sit down and play solitaire. Pretty soon somebody would come along and—"

"Tell you to play the black ten on the red jack. We've heard that one."

"Quiet, Rod. In the second place, Jack, I expected to team with old Stoneface here. I can always beat him at cribbage but he doesn't believe it. I figured that during the test I could win all his next year's allowance. Survival tactics."

Whatever his reasoning, Jimmy had had the cards. The three played a family game each evening at a million plutons a point. Jacqueline stayed more or less even but Rod owed Jimmy several hundred millions. They continued the discussion that evening over their game. Rod was still wary of advertising their hide-out.

"We might burn a smoke signal somewhere, though," he said thoughtfully. "Then keep watch from a safe spot. Cut 'em, Jim."

"Consider the relative risks—a five, just what I needed! If you put the fire far enough away to keep this place secret, then it means a trek back and forth at least twice a day. With all that running around you'll use up your luck; one day you won't come back. It's not that I'm fond of you, but it would bust up the game."

"Whose crib?"

"Jack's. But if we burn it close by and in sight, then

90

we sit up here safe and snug. I'll have my back to the wall facing the path, with Jack's *phht* gun in my lap. If an unfriendly face sticks up—*blooie!* Long pig for dinner. But if we like them, we cut them into the game."

"Your count."

"Fifteen-six, fifteen-twelve, a pair, six for jacks and the right jack. That's going to cost you another million, my friend."

"One of those jacks is a queen," Rod said darkly.

"Sure enough? You know, it's getting too dark to play. Want to concede?"

They adopted Jim's scheme. It gave more time for cribbage and ran Rod's debt up into billions. The signal fire was kept burning on the shelf at the downstream end, the prevailing wind being such that smoke usually did not blow back into the cave—when the wind did shift it was unbearable; they were forced to flee, eyes streaming.

This happened three times in four days. Their advertising had roused no customers and they were all getting tired of dragging up dead wood for fuel and green branches for smoke. The third time they fled from smoke Jimmy said, "Rod, I give up. You win. This is not the way to do it."

"No!"

"Huh? Have a heart, chum. I can't live on smoke—no vitamins. Let's run up a flag instead. I'll contribute my shirt."

Rod thought about it. "We'll do that."

"Hey, wait a minute. I was speaking rhetorically. I'm the delicate type. I sunburn easily."

"You can take it easy and work up a tan. We'll use your shirt as a signal flag. But we'll keep the fire going, too. Not up on the shelf, but down there—on that mud flat, maybe."

"And have the smoke blow right back into our summer cottage."

"Well, farther downstream. We'll make a bigger fire and a column of smoke that can be seen a long way. The flag we will put up right over the cave."

"Thereby inviting eviction proceedings from large, hairy individuals with no feeling for property rights."

91

"We took that chance when we decided to use a smoke signal. Let's get busy."

Rod picked a tall tree on the bluff above. He climbed to where the trunk had thinned down so much that it would hardly take his weight, then spent a tedious hour topping it with his knife. He tied the sleeves of Jim's shirt to it, then worked down, cutting foliage away as he went. Presently the branches became too large to handle with his knife, but the stripped main stem stuck up for several meters; the shirt could be seen for a long distance up and down stream. The shirt caught the wind and billowed; Rod eyed it, tired but satisfied—it was unquestionably a signal flag.

Jimmy and Jacqueline had built a new smudge farther downstream, carrying fire from the shelf for the purpose. Jacqueline still had a few matches and Jim had a pocket torch almost fully charged but the realization that they were marooned caused them to be miserly. Rod went down and joined them. The smoke was enormously greater now that they were not limited in space, and fuel was easier to fetch.

Rod looked them over. Jacqueline's face, sweaty and none too clean to start with, was now black with smoke, while Jimmy's pink skin showed the soot even more. "A couple of pyromaniacs."

"You ordered smoke," Jimmy told him. "I plan to make the burning of Rome look like a bonfire. Fetch me a violin and a toga."

"Violins weren't invented then. Nero played a lyre."

"Let's not be small. We're getting a nice mushroom cloud effect, don't you think?"

"Come on, Rod," Jacqueline urged, wiping her face without improving it. "It's fun!" She dipped a green branch in the stream, threw it on the pyre. A thick cloud of smoke and steam concealed her. "More dry wood, Jimmy."

"Coming!"

Rod joined in, soon was as dirty and scorched as the other two and having more fun than he had had since the test started. When the sun dropped below the tree tops they at last quit trying to make the fire bigger and better and smokier and reluctantly headed up to their cave. Only then did Rod realize that he had forgotten to remain alert.

Oh well, he assured himself, dangerous animals would avoid a fire.

While they ate they could see the dying fire still sending up smoke. After dinner Jimmy got out his cards, tried to riffle the limp mass. "Anyone interested in a friendly game? The customary small stakes."

"I'm too tired," Rod answered. "Just chalk up my usual losses."

"That's not a sporting attitude. Why, you won a game just last week. How about you, Jack?"

Jacqueline started to answer; Rod suddenly motioned for silence. "Sssh! I heard something."

The other two froze and silently got out their knives. Rod put Colonel Bowie in his teeth and crawled out to the edge. The pathway was clear and the thorn barricade was undisturbed. He leaned out and looked around, trying to locate the sound.

"Ahoy below!" a voice called out, not loudly. Rod felt himself tense. He glanced back, saw Jimmy moving diagonally over to cover the pathway. Jacqueline had her dart gun and was hurriedly pumping it up.

Rod answered, "Who's there?"

There was a short silence. Then the voice answered, "Bob Baxter and Carmen Garcia. Who are you?"

Rod sighed with relief. "Rod Walker, Jimmy Throxton. And one other, not our class . . . Jack Daudet."

Baxter seemed to think this over. "Uh, can we join you? For tonight, at least?"

"Sure!"

"How can we get down there? Carmen can't climb very well; she's got a bad foot."

"You're right above us?"

"I think so. I can't see you."

"Stay there. I'll come up." Rod turned, grinned at the others. "Company for dinner! Get a fire going, Jim."

Jimmy clucked mournfully. "And hardly a thing in the house. I should have baked a cake."

By the time they returned Jimmy had roast meat waiting. Carmen's semi-crippled condition had delayed them. It was just a sprained ankle but it caused her to

93

crawl up the traverse on her hands, and progress to that point had been slow and painful.

When she realized that the stranger in the party was another woman she burst into tears. Jackie glared at the males, for no cause that Rod could see, then led her into the remote corner of the cave where she herself slept. There they whispered while Bob Baxter compared notes with Rod and Jim.

Bob and Carmen had had no unusual trouble until Carmen had hurt her ankle two days earlier . . . except for the obvious fact that something had gone wrong and they were stranded. "I lost my grip," he admitted, "when I realized that they weren't picking us up. But Carmen snapped me out of it. Carmen is a very practical kid."

"Girls are always the practical ones," Jimmy agreed. "Now take me—I'm the poetical type."

"Blank verse, I'd say," Rod suggested.

"Jealousy ill becomes you, Rod. Bob, old bean, can I interest you in another slice? Rare, or well carbonized?"

"Either way. We haven't had much to eat the last couple of days. Boy, does this taste good!"

"My own sauce," Jimmy said modestly. "I raise my own herbs, you know. First you melt a lump of butter slowly in a pan, then you—"

"Shut up, Jimmy. Bob, do you and Carmen want to team with us? As I see it, we can't count on ever getting back. Therefore we ought to make plans for the future."

"I think you are right."

"Rod is always right," Jimmy agreed. " 'Plans for the future—' Hmm, yes . . . Bob, do you and Carmen play cribbage?"

"No."

"Never mind. I'll teach you."

8

"Fish, or Cut Bait"

THE DECISION TO KEEP ON BURNING THE SMOKE SIGNAL and thereby to call in as many recruits as possible was never voted on; it formed itself. The next morning Rod intended to bring the matter up but Jimmy and Bob rebuilt the smoke fire from its embers while down to fetch fresh water. Rod let the accomplished fact stand; two girls drifted in separately that day.

Nor was there any formal contract to team nor any selection of a team captain; Rod continued to direct operations and Bob Baxter accepted the arrangement. Rod did not think about it as he was too busy. The problems of food, shelter, and safety for their growing population left him no time to worry about it.

The arrival of Bob and Carmen cleaned out the larder, it was necessary to hunt the next day. Bob Baxter offered to go, but Rod decided to take Jackie as usual. "You rest today. Don't let Carmen put her weight on that bad ankle and don't let Jimmy go down alone to tend the fire. He thinks he is well again but he is not."

"I see that."

Jack and Rod went out, made their kill quickly. But Rod failed to kill clean and when Jacqueline moved in to help finish the thrashing, wounded buck she was kicked in the ribs. She insisted that she was not hurt; nevertheless her side was sore the following morning and Bob Baxter expressed the opinion that she had cracked a rib.

In the meantime two new mouths to feed had been added, just as Rod found himself with three on the sick list. But one of the new mouths was a big, grinning one belonging to Caroline Mshiyeni; Rod picked her as his hunting partner.

Jackie looked sour. She got Rod aside and whispered, "You haven't any reason to do this to me. I can hunt. My side is all right, just a little stiff."

"It is, huh? So it slows you down when I need you. I can't chance it, Jack."

She glanced at Caroline, stuck out her lip and looked stubborn. Rod said urgently, "Jack, remember what I said about petty jealousies? So help me, you make trouble and I'll paddle you."

"You aren't big enough!"

"I'll get help. Now, look—are we partners?"

"Well, I *thought* so."

"Then be one and don't cause trouble."

She shrugged. "All right. Don't rub it in—I'll stay home."

"I want you to do more than that. Take that old bandage of mine—it's around somewhere—and let Bob Baxter strap your ribs."

"No!"

"Then let Carmen do it. They're both quack doctors, sort of." He raised his voice. "Ready, Carol?"

"Quiverin' and bristlin'."

Rod told Caroline how he and Jacqueline hunted, explained what he expected of her. They located, and avoided, two family herds; old bulls were tough and poor eating and attempting to kill anything but the bull was foolishly dangerous. About noon they found a yearling herd upwind; they split and placed themselves cross wind for the kill. Rod waited for Caroline to flush the game, drive it to him.

He continued to wait. He was getting fidgets when Caroline showed up, moving silently. She motioned for him to follow. He did so, hard put to keep up with her and still move quietly. Presently she stopped; he caught up and saw that she had already made a kill. He looked at it and fought down the anger he felt.

Caroline spoke. "Nice tender one, I think. Suit you, Rod?"

He nodded. "Couldn't be better. A clean kill, too. Carol?"

"Huh?"

"I think you are better at this than I am."

"Oh, shucks, it was just luck." She grinned and looked sheepish.

"I don't believe in luck. Any time you want to lead the hunt, let me know. But be darn sure you let me know."

She looked at his unsmiling face, said slowly, "By any chance are you bawling me out?"

"You could call it that. I'm saying that any time you want to lead the hunt, you tell me. Don't switch in the middle. Don't ever. I mean it."

"What's the matter with you, Rod? Getting your feelings hurt just because I got there first—that's silly!"

Rod sighed. "Maybe that's it. Or maybe I don't like having a girl take the kill away from me. But I'm dead sure about one thing: I don't like having a partner on a hunt who can't be depended on. Too many ways to get hurt. I'd rather hunt alone."

"Maybe I'd rather hunt alone! I don't need any help."

"I'm sure you don't. Let's forget it, huh, and get this carcass back to camp."

Caroline did not say anything while they butchered. When they had the waste trimmed away and were ready to pack as much as possible back to the others Rod said, "You lead off. I'll watch behind."

"Rod?"

"Huh?"

"I'm sorry."

"What? Oh, forget it."

"I won't ever do it again. Look, I'll tell everybody you made the kill."

He stopped and put a hand on her arm. "Why tell anybody anything? It's nobody's business how we organize our hunt as long as we bring home the meat."

"You're still angry with me."

"I never was angry," he lied. "I just don't want us to get each other crossed up."

"Roddie, I'll never cross you up again! Promise."

Girls stayed in the majority to the end of the week. The cave, comfortable for three, adequate for twice that number, was crowded for the number that was daily

97

accumulating. Rod decided to make it a girls' dormitory and moved the males out into the open on the field at the foot of the path up the shale. The spot was unprotected against weather and animals but it did guard the only access to the cave. Weather was no problem; protection against animals was set up as well as could be managed by organizing a night watch whose duty it was to keep fires burning between the bluff and the creek on the upstream side and in the bottleneck downstream.

Rod did not like the arrangements, but they were the best he could do at the time. He sent Bob Baxter and Roy Kilroy downstream to scout for caves and Caroline and Margery Chung upstream for the same purpose. Neither party was successful in the one-day limit he had imposed; the two girls brought back another straggler.

A group of four boys came in a week after Jim's shirt had been requisitioned; it brought the number up to twenty-five and shifted the balance to more boys than girls. The four newcomers could have been classed as men rather than boys, since they were two or three years older than the average. Three of the four classes in this survival-test area had been about to graduate from secondary schools; the fourth class, which included these four, came from Outlands Arts College of Teller University.

"Adult" is a slippery term. Some cultures have placed adult age as low as eleven years, others as high as thirty-five—and some have not recognized any such age as long as an ancestor remained alive. Rod did not think of these new arrivals as senior to him. There were already a few from Teller U. in the group, but Rod was only vaguely aware which ones they were—they fitted in. He was too busy with the snowballing problems of his growing colony to worry about their backgrounds on remote Terra.

The four were Jock McGowan, a brawny youth who seemed all hands and feet, his younger brother Bruce, and Chad Ames and Dick Burke. They had arrived late in the day and Rod had not had time to get acquainted, nor was there time the following morning, as a group of four girls and five boys poured in on them unexpectedly. This had increased his administrative problems almost to the breaking point; the cave would hardly sleep four more females. It was necessary to find, or build, more shelter.

Rod went over to the four young men lounging near the cooking fire. He squatted on his heels and asked, "Any of you know anything about building?"

He addressed them all, but the others waited for Jock McGowan to speak. "Some," Jock admitted, "I reckon I could build anything I wanted to."

"Nothing hard," Rod explained. "Just stone walls. Ever tried your hand at masonry?"

"Sure. What of it?"

"Well, here's the idea. We've got to have better living arrangements right away—we've got people pouring out of our ears. The first thing we are going to do is to throw a wall from the bluff to the creek across this flat area. After that we will build huts, but the first thing is a kraal to stop dangerous animals."

McGowan laughed. "That will be some wall. Have you seen this dingus that looks like an elongated cougar? One of those babies would go over your wall before you could say 'scat.'"

"I know about them," Rod admitted, "and I don't like them." He rubbed the long white scars on his left arm. "They probably could go over any wall we could build. So we'll rig a surprise for them." He picked up a twig and started drawing in the dirt. "We build the wall . . . and bring it around to here. Then, inside for about six meters, we set up sharpened poles. Anything comes over the wall splits its gut on the poles."

Jock McGowan looked at the diagram. "Futile."

"Silly," agreed his brother.

Rod flushed but answered, "Got a better idea?"

"That's beside the point."

"Well," Rod answered slowly, "unless somebody comes down with a better scheme, or unless we find really good caves, we've got to fortify this spot the best we can . . . so we'll do this. I'm going to set the girls to cutting and sharpening stakes. The rest of us will start on the wall. If we tear into it we ought to have a lot of it built before dark. Do you four want to work together? There will be one party collecting rock and another digging clay and making clay mortar. Take your choice."

Again three of them waited. Jock McGowan lay back and laced his hands under his head. "Sorry. I've got a date to hunt today."

Rod felt himself turning red. "We don't need a kill today," he said carefully.

"Nobody asked you, youngster."

Rod felt the cold tenseness he always felt in a hunt. He was uncomfortably aware that an audience had gathered. He tried to keep his voice steady and said, "Maybe I've made a mistake. I—"

"You have."

"I thought you four had teamed with the rest of us. Well?"

"Maybe. Maybe not."

"You'll have to fish or cut bait. If you join, you work like anybody else. If not—well, you're welcome to breakfast and stop in again some time. But be on your way. I won't have you lounging around while everybody else is working."

Jock McGowan sucked his teeth, dug at a crevice with his tongue. His hands were still locked back of his head. "What you don't understand, sonny boy, is that nobody gives the McGowans orders. Nobody. Right, Bruce?"

"Right, Jock."

"Right, Chad? Dick?"

The other two grunted approval. McGowan continued to stare up at the sky. "So," he said softly, "I go where I want to go and stay as long as I like. The question is not whether we are going to join up with you, but what ones I am going to let team with us. But not you, sonny boy; you are still wet behind your ears."

"Get up and get out of here!" Rod started to stand up. He was wearing Colonel Bowie, as always, but he did not reach for it. He began to straighten up from squatting.

Jock McGowan's eyes flicked toward his brother. Rod was hit low . . . and found himself flat on his face with his breath knocked out. He felt the sharp kiss of a knife against his ribs; he held still. Bruce called out, "How about it, Jock?"

Rod could not see Jock McGowan. But he heard him answer, "Just keep him there."

"Right, Jock."

Jock McGowan was wearing both gun and knife. Rod now heard him say, "Anybody want to dance? Any trouble out of the rest of you lugs?"

Rod still could not see Jock, but he could figure from the naked, startled expression of a dozen others that McGowan must have rolled to his feet and covered them with his gun. Everybody in camp carried knives; most had guns as well and Rod could see that Roy Kilroy was wearing his—although most guns were kept when not in use in the cave in a little arsenal which Carmen superintended.

But neither guns nor knives were of use; it had happened too fast, shifting from wordy wrangling to violence with no warning. Rod could see none of his special friends from where he was; those whom he could see did not seem disposed to risk death to rescue him.

Jock McGowan said briskly, "Chad—Dick—got 'em all covered?"

"Right, Skipper."

"Keep 'em that way while I take care of this cholo." His hairy legs appeared in front of Rod's face. "Pulled his teeth, Bruce?"

"Not yet."

"I'll do it. Roll over, sonny boy, and let me at your knife. Let him turn over, Bruce."

Bruce McGowan eased up on Rod and Jock bent down. As he reached for Rod's knife a tiny steel flower blossomed in Jock's side below his ribs. Rod heard nothing, not even the small sound it must have made when it struck. Jock straightened up with a shriek, clutched at his side.

Bruce yelled, "Jock! What's the matter?"

"They got me." He crumpled to the ground like loose clothing.

Rod still had a man with a knife on his back but the moment was enough; he rolled and grabbed in one violent movement and the situation was reversed, with Bruce's right wrist locked in Rod's fist, with Colonel Bowie threatening Bruce's face.

101

A loud contralto voice sang out, "Take it easy down there! We got you covered."

Rod glanced up. Caroline stood on the shelf at the top of the path to the cave, with a rifle at her shoulder. At the downstream end of the shelf Jacqueline sat with her little dart gun in her lap; she was frantically pumping up again. She raised it, drew a bead on some one past Rod's shoulder.

Rod called out, "Don't shoot!" He looked around. "Drop it, you two!"

Chad Ames and Dick Burke dropped their guns. Rod added, "Roy! Grant Cowper! Gather up their toys. Get their knives, too." He turned back to Bruce McGowan, pricked him under the chin. "Let's have your knife." Bruce turned it loose; Rod took it and got to his feet.

Everyone who had been up in the cave was swarming down, Caroline in the lead. Jock McGowan was writhing on the ground, face turned blue and gasping in the sort of paralysis induced by the poison used on darts. Bob Baxter hurried up, glanced at him, then said to Rod, "I'll take care of that cut in your ribs in a moment." He bent over Jock McGowan.

Caroline said indignantly, "You aren't going to try to save him?"

"Of course."

"Why? Let's chuck him in the stream."

Baxter glanced at Rod. Rod felt a strong urge to order Caroline's suggestion carried out. But he answered, "Do what you can for him, Bob. Where's Jack? Jack—you've got antidote for your darts, haven't you? Get it."

Jacqueline looked scornfully at the figure on the ground. "What for? He's not hurt."

"Huh?"

"Just a pin prick. A practice dart—that's all I keep in Betsey. My hunting darts are put away so that nobody can hurt themselves—and I didn't have time to get them." She prodded Jock with a toe. "He's not poisoned. He's scaring himself to death."

Caroline chortled and waved the rifle she carried. "And this one is empty. Not even a good club."

Baxter said to Jackie, "Are you sure? The reactions look typical."

"Sure I'm sure! See the mark on the end sticking out? A target dart."

Baxter leaned over his patient, started slapping his face. "Snap out of it, McGowan! Stand up. I want to get that dart out of you."

McGowan groaned and managed to stand. Baxter took the dart between thumb and forefinger, jerked it free, Jock yelled. Baxter slapped him again. "Don't you faint on me," he growled. "You're lucky. Let it drain and you'll be all right." He turned to Rod. "You're next."

"Huh? There's nothing the matter with *me*."

"That stuff on your ribs is paint, I suppose." He looked around. "Carmen, get my kit."

"I brought it down."

"Good. Rod, sit down and lean forward. This is going to hurt a little."

It did hurt. Rod tried to chat to avoid showing that he minded it. "Carol," he asked, "I don't see how you and Jackie worked out a plan so fast. That was smooth."

"Huh? We didn't work out a plan; we both just did what we could and did it fast." She turned to Jacqueline and gave her a clap on the shoulder that nearly knocked her over. "This kid is solid, Roddie, solid!"

Jacqueline recovered, looked pleased and tried not to show it. "Aw, Carol!"

"Anyway I thank you both."

"A pleasure. I wish that pea shooter had been loaded. Rod, what are you going to do with them?"

"Well . . . ummph!"

"Whoops!" said Baxter, behind him. "I said it was going to hurt. I had better put one more clip in. I'd like to put a dressing on that, but we can't, so you lay off heavy work for a while and sleep on your stomach."

"Unh!" said Rod

"That's the last. You can get up now. Take it easy and give it a chance to scab."

"I still think," Caroline insisted, "that we ought to make them swim the creek. We could make bets on whether or not any of 'em make it across."

"Carol, you're uncivilized."

103

"I never claimed to be civilized. But I know which end wags and which end bites."

Rod ignored her and went to look at the prisoners. Roy Kilroy had caused them to lie down one on top of the other; it rendered them undignified and helpless. "Let them sit up."

Kilroy and Grant Cowper had been guarding them. Cowper said, "You heard the Captain. Sit up." They unsnarled and sat up, looking glum.

Rod looked at Jock McGowan. "What do you think we ought to do with you?"

McGowan said nothing. The puncture in his side was oozing blood and he was pale. Rod said slowly, "Some think we ought to chuck you in the stream. That's the same as condemning you to death—but if we are going to, we ought to shoot you or hang you. I don't favor letting anybody be eaten alive. Should we hang you?"

Bruce McGowan blurted out, "We haven't done anything!"

"No. But you sure tried. You aren't safe to have around other people."

Somebody called out, "Oh, let's shoot them and get it over with!" Rod ignored it. Grant Cowper came close to Rod and said, "We ought to vote on this. They ought to have a trial."

Rod shook his head. "No." He went on to the prisoners, "I don't favor punishing you—this is personal. But we can't risk having you around either." He turned to Cowper. "Give them their knives."

"Rod? You're not going to fight them?"

"Of course not." He turned back. "You can have your knives; we're keeping your guns. When we turn you loose, head downstream and keep going. Keep going for at least a week. If you ever show your faces again, you won't get a chance to explain. Understand me?"

Jock McGowan nodded. Dick Burke gulped and said, "But turning us out with just knives is the same as killing us."

"Nonsense! No guns. And remember, if you turn back this way, even to hunt, it's once too many. There may be somebody trailing you—with a gun."

104

"Loaded this time!" added Caroline. "Hey, Roddie, I want that job. Can I? Please?"

"Shut up, Carol. Roy, you and Grant start them on their way."

As exiles and guards, plus sightseers, moved off they ran into Jimmy Throxton coming back into camp. He stopped and stared. "What's the procession? Rod . . . what have you done to your ribs, boy? Scratching yourself again?"

Several people tried to tell him at once. He got the gist of it and shook his head mournfully. "And there I was, good as gold, looking for pretty rocks for our garden wall. Every time there's a party people forget to ask *me*. Discrimination."

"Stow it, Jim. It's not funny."

"That's what I said. It's discrimination."

Rod got the group started on the wall with an hour or more of daylight wasted. He tried to work on the wall despite Bob Baxter's medical orders, but found that he was not up to it; not only was his wound painful but also he felt shaky with reaction.

Grant Cowper looking him up during the noon break. "Skipper, can I talk with you? Privately?"

Rod moved aside with him. "What's on your mind?"

"Mmm . . . Rod, you were lucky this morning. You know that, don't you? No offense intended."

"Sure, I know. What about it?"

"Uh, do you know *why* you had trouble?"

"What? Of course I know—now. I trusted somebody when I should not have."

Cowper shook his head. "Not at all. Rod, what do you know about theory of government?"

Rod looked surprised. "I've had the usual civics courses. Why?"

"I doubt if I've mentioned it, but the course I'm majoring in at Teller U. is colonial administration. One thing we study is how authority comes about in human society and how it is maintained. I'm not criticizing . . . but to be blunt, you almost lost your life because you've never studied such things."

Rod felt annoyed. "What are you driving at?"

"Take it easy. But the fact remains that you didn't have any authority. McGowan knew it and wouldn't

105

take orders. Everybody else knew it, too. When it came to a showdown, nobody knew whether to back you up or not. Because you don't have a milligram of real authority."

"Just a moment! Are you saying I'm not leader of this team?"

"You are *de facto* leader, no doubt about it. But you've never been elected to the job. That's your weakness."

Rod chewed this over. "I know," he said slowly. "It's just that we have been so confounded busy."

"Sure, I know. I'd be the last person to criticize. But a captain ought to be properly elected."

Rod sighed. "I meant to hold an election but I thought getting the wall built was more urgent. All right, let's call them together."

"Oh, you don't need to do it this minute."

"Why not? The sooner the better, apparently."

"Tonight, when it's too dark to work, is soon enough."

"Well . . . okay."

When they stopped for supper Rod announced that there woud be an organization and planning meeting. No one seemed surprised, although he himself had mentioned it to no one. He felt annoyed and had to remind himself that there was nothing secret about it; Grant had been under no obligation to keep it quiet. He set guards and fire tenders, then came back into the circle of firelight and called out, "Quiet, everybody! Let's get started. If you guys on watch can't hear, be sure to speak up." He hesitated. "We're going to hold an election. Somebody pointed out that I never have been elected captain of this survival team. Well, if any of you have your noses out of joint, I'm sorry. I was doing the best I could. But you are entitled to elect a captain. All right, any nominations?"

Jimmy Throxton shouted, "I nominate Rod Walker!"

Caroline's voice answered, "I second it! Move the nominations be closed."

Rod said hastily, "Carol, your motion is out of order."

"Why?"

Before he could answer Roy Kilroy spoke up. "Rod, can I have the floor a moment? Privileged question."

Rod turned, saw that Roy was squatting beside Grant Cowper. "Sure. State your question."

"Matter of procedure. The first thing is to elect a temporary chairman."

Rod thought quickly. "I guess you're right. Jimmy, your nomination is thrown out. Nominations for temporary chairman are in order."

"Rod Walker for temporary chairman!"

"Oh, shut up, Jimmy! I don't want to be temporary chairman."

Roy Kilroy was elected. He took the imaginary gavel and announcement, "The chair recognizes Brother Cowper for a statement of aims and purposes of this meeting."

Jimmy Throxton called out, "What do we want any speeches for? Let's elect Rod and go to bed. I'm tired —and I've got a two-hour watch coming up."

"Out of order. The chair recognizes Grant Cowper."

Cowper stood up. The firelight caught his handsome features and curly, short beard. Rod rubbed the scraggly growth on his own chin and wished that he looked like Cowper. The young man was dressed only in walking shorts and soft bush shoes but he carried himself with the easy dignity of a distinguished speaker before some important body. "Friends," he said, "brothers and sisters, we are gathered here tonight not to elect a survival-team captain, but to found a new nation."

He paused to let the idea sink in. "You know the situation we are in. We fervently hope to be rescued, none more so than I. I will even go so far as to say that I think we will be rescued . . . eventually. But we have no way of knowing, we have no data on which to base an intelligent guess, as to *when* we will be rescued.

"It might be tomorrow . . . it might be our descendants a thousand years from now." He said the last very solemnly.

"But when the main body of our great race reestablishes contact with us, it is up to us, this little group here tonight, whether they find a civilized society . . . or flea-bitten animals without language, without

107

arts, with the light of reason grown dim . . . or no survivors at all, nothing but bones picked clean."

"Not mine!" called out Caroline. Kilroy gave her a dirty look and called for order.

"Not yours, Caroline," Cowper agreed gravely. "Nor mine. Not any of us. Because tonight we will take the step that will keep this colony alive. We are poor in things; we will make what we need. We are rich in knowledge; among us we hold the basic knowledge of our great race. We must preserve it . . . we *will!*"

Caroline cut through Cowper's dramatic pause with a stage whisper. "Talks pretty, doesn't he? Maybe I'll marry him."

He did not try to fit this heckling into his speech. "What is the prime knowledge acquired by our race? That without which the rest is useless? What flame must we guard like vestal virgins?"

Some one called out, "Fire." Cowper shook his head. "Writing!"

"The decimal system."

"Atomics!"

"The wheel, of course."

"No, none of those. They are all important, but they are not the keystone. The greatest invention of mankind is government. It is also the hardest of all. More individualistic than cats, nevertheless we have learned to cooperate more efficiently than ants or bees or termites. Wilder, bloodier, and more deadly than sharks, we have learned to live together as peacefully as lambs. But these things are not easy. That is why that which we do tonight will decide our future . . . and perhaps the future of our children, our children's children, our descendants far into the womb of time. We are not picking a temporary survival leader; we are setting up a government. We must do it with care. We must pick a chief executive for our new nation, a mayor of our city-state. But we must draw up a constitution, sign articles binding us together. We must organize and plan."

"Hear, hear!"

"Bravo!"

"We must establish law, appoint judges, arrange for orderly administration of our code. Take for example, this morning—" Cowper turned to Rod and gave him a friendly smile. "Nothing personal, Rod, you understand that. I think you acted with wisdom and I was happy that you tempered justice with mercy. Yet no one could have criticized if you had yielded to your impulse and killed all four of those, uh . . . anti-social individuals. But justice should not be subject to the whims of a dictator. We can't stake our lives on your temper . . . good or bad. You see that, don't you?"

Rod did not answer. He felt that he was being accused of bad temper, of being a tyrant and dictator, of being a danger to the group. But he could not put his finger on it. Grant Cowper's remarks had been friendly . . . yet they felt intensely personal and critical.

Cowper insisted on an answer. "You do see that, Rod? Don't you? You don't want to continue to have absolute power over the lives and persons of our community? You don't want *that*? Do you?" He waited.

"Huh? Oh, yeah, sure! I mean, I agree with you."

"Good! I was sure you would understand. And I must say that *I* think you have done a very good job in getting us together. I don't agree with any who have criticized you. You were doing your best and we should let bygones be bygones." Cowper grinned that friendly grin and Rod felt as if he were being smothered with kisses.

Cowper turned to Kilroy. "That's all I have to say, Mr. Chairman." He flashed his grin and added as he sat down, "Sorry I talked so long, folks. I had to get it off my chest."

Kilroy clapped his hands once. "The chair will entertain nominations for— Hey, Grant, if we don't call it 'captain,' then what should we call it?"

"Mmm . . ." Cowper said judicially. " 'President' seems a little pompous. I think 'mayor' would be about right—mayor of our city-state, our village."

"The chair will entertain nominations for mayor."

"Hey!" demanded Jimmy Throxton. "Doesn't anybody else get to shoot off his face?"

"Out of order."

"No," Cowper objected, "I don't think you should rule Jimmy out of order, Roy. Anyone who has something to contribute should be encouraged to speak. We mustn't act hastily."

"Okay, Throxton, speak your piece."

"Oh, I didn't want to sound off. I just didn't like the squeeze play."

"All right, the chair stands corrected. Anybody else? If not, we will entertain—"

"One moment, Mr. Chairman!"

Rod saw that it was Arthur Nielsen, one of the Teller University group. He managed to look neat even in these circumstances but he had strayed into camp bereft of all equipment, without even a knife. He had been quite hungry.

Kilroy looked at him. "You want to talk, Waxie?"

"Nielsen is the name. Or Arthur. As you know. Yes."

"Okay. Keep it short."

"I shall keep it as short as circumstances permit. Fellow associates, we have here a unique opportunity, probably one which has not occurred before in history. As Cowper pointed out, we must proceed with care. But, already we have set out on the wrong foot. Our object should be to found the first truly scientific community. Yet what do I find? You are proposing to select an executive by counting noses! Leaders should not be chosen by popular whim; they should be determined by rigorous scientific criteria. Once selected, those leaders must have full scientific freedom to direct the bio-group in accordance with natural law, unhampered by such artificial anachronisms as statutes, constitutions, and courts of law. We have here an adequate supply of healthy females; we have the means to breed scientifically a new race, a super race, a race which, if I may say so—"

A handful of mud struck Nielsen in the chest; he stopped suddenly. "I saw who did that!" he said angrily. "Just the sort of nincompoop who always—"

"Order, order, please!" Kilroy shouted. "No mud-slinging, or I'll appoint a squad of sergeants-at-arms. Are you through, Waxie?"

"I was just getting started."

"Just a moment," put in Cowper. "Point of order Mr. Chairman. Arthur has a right to be heard. But I think he is speaking before the wrong body. We're going to have a constitutional committee, I'm sure. He should

110

present his arguments to them. Then, if we like them, we can adopt his ideas."

"You're right, Grant. Sit down, Waxie."

"Huh? I appeal!"

Roy Kilroy said briskly, "The chair has ruled this out of order at this time and the speaker has appealed to the house, a priority motion not debatable. All in favor of supporting the chair's ruling, which is for Waxie to shut up, make it known by saying 'Aye.' "

There was a shouted chorus of assent. "Opposed: 'No.' Sit down, Waxie."

Kilroy looked around. "Anybody else?"

"Yes."

"I can't see. Who is it?"

"Bill Kennedy, Ponce de Leon class. I don't agree with Nielsen except on one point: we are fiddling around with the wrong things. Sure, we need a group captain but, aside from whatever it takes to eat, we shouldn't think about anything but how to get back. I don't want a scientific society; I'd settle for a hot bath and decent food."

There was scattered applause. The chairman said, "I'd like a bath, too . . . and I'd fight anybody for a dish of cornflakes. But, Bill, how do you suggest that we go about it?"

"Huh? We set up a crash-priority project and build a gate. Everybody works on it."

There was silence, then several talked at once: "Crazy! No uranium."—"We might *find* uranium."—"Where do we get the tools? Shucks, I don't even have a screwdriver."—"But where are we?"—"It is just a matter of—"

"*Quiet!*" yelled Kilroy. "Bill, do you know how to build a gate?"

"No."

"I doubt if anybody does."

"That's a defeatist attitude. Surely some of you educated blokes from Teller have studied the subject. You should get together, pool what you know, and put us to work. Sure, it may take a long time. But that's what we ought to do."

Cowper said, "Just a minute, Roy. Bill, I don't dispute what you say; every idea should be explored. We're

111

bound to set up a planning committee. Maybe we had better elect a mayor, or a captain, or whatever you want to call him—and then dig into your scheme when we can discuss it in detail. I think it has merit and should be discussed at length. What do you think?"

"Why, sure, Grant. Let's get on with the election. I just didn't want that silly stuff about breeding a superman to be the last word."

"Mr. Chairman! I protest—"

"Shut up, Waxie. Are you ready with nominations for mayor? If there is no objection, the chair rules debate closed and will entertain nominations."

"I nominate Grant Cowper!"

"Second!"

"I second the nomination."

"Okay, I third it!"

"Let's make it unanimous! Question, question!"

Jimmy Throxton's voice cut through the shouting, "I NOMINATE ROD WALKER!"

Bob Baxter stood up. "Mr. Chairman?"

"Quiet, everybody. Mr. Baxter."

"I second Rod Walker."

"Okay. Two nominations, Grant Cowper and Rod Walker. Are there any more?"

There was a brief silence. Then Rod spoke up. "Just a second, Roy." He found that his voice was trembling and he took two deep breaths before he went on. "I don't want it. I've had all the grief I want for a while and I'd like a rest. Thanks anyhow, Bob. Thanks, Jimmy."

"Any further nominations?"

"Just a sec, Roy . . . point of personal privilege." Grant Cowper stood up. "Rod, I know how you feel. Nobody in his right mind seeks public office . . . except as a duty, willingness to serve. If you withdraw, I'm going to exercise the same privilege; I don't want the headaches any more than you do."

"Now wait a minute, Grant. You—"

"*You* wait a minute. I don't think either one of us should withdraw; we ought to perform any duty that is handed to us, just as we stand a night watch when it's our turn. But I think we ought to have more nominations." He looked around. "Since that mix-up this morn-

112

ing we have as many girls as men . . . yet both of the candidates are male. That's not right. Uh, Mr. Chairman, I nominate Caroline Mshiyeni."

"Huh? Hey, Grant, don't be silly. I'd look good as a lady mayoress, wouldn't I? Anyhow, I'm for Roddie."

"That's your privilege, Caroline. But you ought to let yourself be placed before the body, just like Rod and myself."

"Nobody's going to vote for *me!*"

"That's where you're wrong. I'm going to vote for you. But we still ought to have more candidates."

"Three nominations before the house," Kilroy announced. "Any more? If not, I declare the—"

"Mr. Chairman!"

"Huh? Okay, Waxie, you want to nominate somebody?"

"Yes."

"Who?"

"Me."

"You want to nominate *yourself?*"

"I certainly do. What's funny about that? I am running on a platform of strict scientific government. I want the rational minds in this group to have someone to vote for."

Kilroy looked puzzled. "I'm not sure that is correct parliamentary procedure. I'm afraid I'll have to over—"

"Never mind, never mind!" Caroline chortled. "*I* nominate him. But I'm going to vote for Roddie," she added.

Kilroy sighed. "Okay, four candidates. I guess we'll have to have a show of hands. We don't have anything for ballots."

Bob Baxter stood up. "Objection, Mr. Chairman. I call for a secret ballot. We can find some way to do it."

A way was found. Pebbles would signify Rod, a bare twig was a note for Cowper, a green leaf meant Caroline, while one of Jimmy's ceramic attempts was offered as a ballot box. "How about Nielsen?" Kilroy asked.

Jimmy spoke up. "Uh, maybe this would do: I made another pot the same time I made this one, only it busted. I'll get chunks of it and all the crackpots are votes for Waxie."

"Mr. Chairman, I resent the insinua—"

"Save it, Waxie. Pieces of baked clay for you, pebbles for Walker, twigs for Grant, leaves for Carol. Get your votes, folks, then file past and drop them in the ballot box. Shorty, you and Margery act as tellers."

The tellers solemnly counted the ballots by firelight. There were five votes for Rod, one for Nielsen, none for Caroline, and twenty-two for Cowper. Rod shook hands with Cowper and faded back into the darkness so that no one would see his face. Caroline looked at the results and said, "Hey, Grant! You promised to vote for me. What happened? Did you vote for yourself? Huh? How about that?"

Rod said nothing. He had voted for Cowper and was certain that the new mayor had not returned the compliment . . . he was sure who his five friends were. Dog take it!—he had seen it coming; why hadn't Grant let him bow out?

Grant ignored Caroline's comment. He briskly assumed the chair and said, "Thank you. Thank you all. I know you want to get to sleep, so I will limit myself tonight to appointing a few committees—"

Rod did not get to sleep at once. He told himself that there was no disgrace in losing an election—shucks, hadn't his old man lost the time he had run for community corporation board? He told himself, too, that trying to ride herd on those apes was enough to drive a man crazy and he was well out of it—he had never *wanted* the job! Nevertheless there was a lump in his middle and a deep sense of personal failure.

It seemed that he had just gone to sleep . . . his father was looking at him saying, "You know we are proud of you, son. Still, if you had had the foresight to—" when someone touched his arm.

He was awake, alert, and had Colonel Bowie out at once.

"Put away that toothpick," Jimmy whispered, "before you hurt somebody. Me, I mean."

"What's up?"

"I'm up, I've got the fire watch. You're about to be, because we are holding a session of the inner sanctum."

"Huh?"

"Shut up and come along. Keep quiet, people are asleep."

The inner sanctum turned out to be Jimmy, Caroline, Jacqueline, Bob Baxter, and Carmen Garcia. They gathered inside the ring of fire but as far from the sleepers as possible. Rod looked around at his friends. "What's this all about?"

"It's about this," Jimmy said seriously. "You're our Captain. And we like that election as much as I like a crooked deck of cards."

"That's right," agreed Caroline. "All that fancy talk!"

"Huh? Everybody got to talk. Everybody got to vote."

"Yes," agreed Baxter. "Yes . . . and no."

"It was all proper. I have no kick."

"I didn't expect you to kick, Rod. Nevertheless . . . well, I don't know how much politicking you've seen, Rod. I haven't seen much myself, except in church matters and we Quakers don't do things that way; we wait until the Spirit moves. But, despite all the rigamarole, that was a slick piece of railroading. This morning you would have been elected overwhelmingly; tonight you did not stand a chance."

"The point is," Jimmy put in, "do we stand for it?"

"What can we do?"

"What can we do? We don't have to stay here. We've still got our own group; we can walk out and find another place . . . a bigger cave maybe."

"Yes, sir!" agreed Caroline. "Right tonight."

Rod thought about it. The idea was tempting; they didn't need the others . . . guys like Nielsen—and Cowper. The discovery that his friends were loyal to him, loyal to the extent that they would consider exile rather than let him down choked him up. He turned to Jacqueline. "How about you, Jackie?"

"We're partners, Rod. Always."

"Bob—do you want to do this? You and Carmen?"

"Yes. Well . . ."

" 'Well' what?"

"Rod, we're sticking with you. This election is all very well—but you took us in when we needed it and teamed with us. We'll never forget it. Furthermore I think that you make a sounder team captain than Cowper is likely to make. But there is one thing."

"Yes."

"If you decide that we leave, Carmen and I will appreciate it if you put it off a day."

"Why?" demanded Caroline. "Now is the time."

"Well—they've set this up as a formal colony, a village with a mayor. Everybody knows that a regularly elected mayor can perform weddings."

"Oh!" said Caroline. "Pardon my big mouth."

"Carmen and I can take care of the religious end— it's not very complicated in our church. But, just in case we ever are rescued, we would like it better and our folks would like it if the civil requirements were all perfectly regular and legal. You see?"

Rod nodded. "I see."

"But if you say to leave tonight . . ."

"I don't," Rod answered with sudden decision. "We'll stay and get you two properly married. Then—"

"Then we all shove off in a shower of rice," Caroline finished.

"Then we'll see. Cowper may turn out to be a good mayor. We won't leave just because I lost an election." He looked around at their faces. "But . . . but I certainly do thank you. I—"

He could not go on. Carmen stepped forward and kissed him quickly. "Goodnight, Rod. Thanks."

9

"A Joyful Omen"

MAYOR COWPER GOT OFF TO A GOOD START. HE approved, took over, and embellished a suggestion that Carmen and Bob should have their own quarters. He suspended work on the wall and set the whole village to constructing a honeymoon cottage. Not until his deputy,

Roy Kilroy, reminded him did he send out hunting parties.

He worked hard himself, having set the wedding for that evening and having decreed that the building must be finished by sundown. Finished it was by vandalizing part of the wall to supply building stone when the supply ran short. Construction was necessarily simple since they had no tools, no mortar but clay mud, no way to cut timbers. It was a stone box as tall as a man and a couple of meters square, with a hole for a door. The roof was laid up from the heaviest poles that could be cut from a growth upstream of giant grass much like bamboo—the colonists simply called it "bamboo." This was thatched and plastered with mud; it sagged badly.

But it was a house and even had a door which could be closed—a woven grass mat stiffened with bamboo. It neither hinged nor locked but it filled the hole and could be held in place with a stone and a pole. The floor was clean sand covered with fresh broad leaves.

As a doghouse for a St. Bernard it would have been about right; as a dwelling for humans it was not much. But it was better than that which most human beings had enjoyed through the history and prehistory of the race. Bob and Carmen did not look at it critically.

When work was knocked off for lunch Rod self-consciously sat down near a group around Cowper. He had wrestled with his conscience for a long time in the night and had decided that the only thing to do was to eat sour grapes and pretend to like them. He could start by not avoiding Cowper.

Margery Chung was cook for the day; she cut Rod a chunk of scorched meat. He thanked her and started to gnaw it. Cowper was talking. Rod was not trying to overhear but there seemed to be no reason not to listen.

"—which is the only way we will get the necessary discipline into the group. I'm sure you agree." Cowper glanced up, caught Rod's eye, looked annoyed, then grinned. "Hello, Rod."

"Hi, Grant."

"Look, old man, we're having an executive committee meeting. Would you mind finding somewhere else to eat lunch?"

Rod stood up blushing. "Oh! Sure."

117

Cowper seemed to consider it. "Nothing private, of course—just getting things done. On second thought maybe you should sit in and give us your advice."

"Huh? Oh, no! I didn't know anything was going on." Rod started to move away.

Cowper did not insist. "Got to keep working, lots to do. See you later, then. Any time." He grinned and turned away.

Rod wandered off, feeling conspicuous. He heard himself hailed and turned gratefully, joined Jimmy Throxton. "Come outside the wall," Jimmy said quietly. "The Secret Six are having a picnic. Seen the happy couple?"

"You mean Carmen and Bob?"

"Know any other happy couples? Oh, there they are —staring hungrily at their future mansion. See you outside."

Rod went beyond the wall, found Jacqueline and Caroline sitting near the water and eating. From habit he glanced around, sizing up possible cover for carnivores and figuring escape routes back into the kraal, but his alertness was not conscious as there seemed no danger in the open so near other people. He joined the girls and sat down on a rock. "Hi, kids."

"Hello, Rod."

"H'lo, Roddie," Caroline seconded. " 'What news on the Rialto?"

"None, I guess. Say, did Grant appoint an executive committee last night?"

"He appointed about a thousand committees but no executive committee unless he did it after we adjourned. Why an executive committee? This gang needs one the way I need a bicycle."

"Who is on it, Rod?" asked Jacqueline.

Rod thought back and named the faces he had seen around Cowper. She looked thoughtful. "Those are his own special buddies from Teller U."

"Yes, I guess so."

"I don't like it," she answered.

"What's the harm?"

"Maybe none . . . maybe. It is about what we could expect. But I'd feel better if all the classes were on it, not just that older bunch. You know."

118

"Shucks, Jack, you've got to give him some leeway."

"I don't see why," put in Caroline. "That bunch you named are the same ones Hizzonor appointed as chairmen of the other committees. It's a tight little clique. You notice none of us unsavory characters got named to any important committee—I'm on waste disposal and camp sanitation, Jackie is on food preparation, and you aren't on any. You should have been on the constitution, codification, and organization committee, but he made himself chairman and left you out. Add it up."

Rod did not answer. Caroline went on, "I'll add it if you won't. First thing you know there will be a nominating committee. Then we'll find that only those of a certain age, say twenty-one, can hold office. Pretty soon that executive committee will turn into a senate (called something else, probably) with a veto that can be upset only by a three-quarters majority that we will never get. That's the way my Uncle Phil would have rigged it."

"Your Uncle Phil?"

"Boy, there was a politician! I never liked him—he had kissed so many babies his lips were puckered. I used to hide when he came into our house. But I'd like to put him up against Hizzonor. It'ud be a battle of dinosaurs. Look, Rod, they've got us roped and tied; I say we should fade out right after the wedding." She turned to Jacqueline. "Right, pardner?"

"Sure . . . if Rod says so."

"Well, I don't say so. Look, Carol, I don't like the situation. To tell the truth . . . well, I was pretty sour at being kicked out of the captaincy. But I can't let the rest of you pull out on that account. There aren't enough of us to form another colony, not safely."

"Why, Roddie, there are three times as many people still back in those trees as there are here in camp. This time we'll build up slowly and be choosy about whom we take. Six is a good start. We'll get by."

"Not six, Carol. Four."

"Huh? Six! We shook on it last night before Jimmy woke you."

Rod shook his head. "Carol, how can we expect Bob and Carmen to walk out . . . right after the rest have made them a wedding present of a house of their own?"

"Well . . . darn it, we'd build them another house!"

"They would go with us, Carol—but it's too much to ask."

"I think," Jacqueline said grudgingly, "that Rod has something, Carol."

The argument was ended by the appearance of Bob, Carmen, and Jimmy. They had been delayed, explained Jimmy, by the necessity of inspecting the house. "As if I didn't know every rock in it. Oh, my back!"

"I appreciate it, Jim," Carmen said softly. "I'll rub your back."

"Sold!" Jimmy lay face down.

"Hey!" protested Caroline. "I carried more rocks than he did. Mostly he stood around and bossed."

"Supervisory work is exceptionally tiring," Jimmy said smugly. "You get Bob to rub your back."

Neither got a back rub as Roy Kilroy called to them from the wall. "Hey! You down there—lunch hour is over. Let's get back to work."

"Sorry, Jimmy. Later." Carmen turned away.

Jimmy scrambled to his feet. "Bob, Carmen—don't go 'way yet. I want to say something."

They stopped. Rod waved to Kilroy. "With you in a moment!" He turned back to the others.

Jimmy seemed to have difficulty in choosing words. "Uh, Carmen . . . Bob. The future Baxters. You know we think a lot of you. We think it's swell that you are going to get married—every family ought to have a marriage. But . . . well, shopping isn't what it might be around here and we didn't know what to get you. So we talked it over and decided to give you this. It's from all of us. A wedding present." Jimmy jammed a hand in his pocket, hauled out his dirty, dog-eared playing cards and handed them to Carmen.

Bob Baxter looked startled. "Gosh, Jimmy, we can't take your cards—your *only* cards."

"I—we want you to have them."

"But—"

"Be quiet, Bob!" Carmen said and took the cards. "Thank you, Jimmy. Thank you very much. Thank you all." She looked around. "Our getting married isn't going to make any difference, you know. It's still one family. We'll expect you all . . . to come play cards . . .

120

at our house just as—" She stopped suddenly and started to cry, buried her head on Bob's shoulder. He patted it. Jimmy looked as if he wanted to cry and Rod felt nakedly embarrassed.

They started back, Carmen with an arm around Jimmy and the other around her betrothed. Rod hung back with the other two. "Did Jimmy," he whispered, "say anything to either of you about this?"

"No," Jacqueline answered.

"Not me," Caroline agreed. "I was going to give 'em my stew pan, but now I'll wait a day or two." Caroline's "bag of rocks" had turned out to contain an odd assortment for survival—among other things, a thin-page diary, a tiny mouth organ, and a half-litre sauce pan. She produced other unlikely but useful items from time to time. Why she had picked them and how she had managed to hang on to them after she discarded the bag were minor mysteries, but, as Deacon Matson had often told the class: "Each to his own methods. Survival is an art, not a science." It was undeniable that she had appeared at the cave healthy, well fed, and with her clothing surprisingly neat and clean in view of the month she had been on the land.

"They won't expect you to give up your stew pan, Caroline."

"I can't use it now that the crowd is so big, and they can set up housekeeping with it. Anyhow, I want to."

"I'm going to give her two needles and some thread. Bob made her leave her sewing kit behind in favor of medical supplies. But I'll wait a while, too."

"I haven't anything I can give them," Rod said miserably.

Jacqueline turned gentle eyes on him. "You can make them a water skin for their house, Rod," she said softly. "They would like that. We can use some of my Kwik-Kure so that it will last."

Rod cheered up at once. "Say, that's a swell idea!"

"We are gathered here," Grant Cowper said cheerfully, "to join these two people in the holy bonds of matrimony. I won't give the usual warning because we all know that no impediment exists to this union. In fact it is the finest thing that could happen to our little community, a joyful omen of things to come, a promise for the future, a guarantee that we are firmly resolved to keep the torch of civilization, now freshly lighted on this planet, forever burning in the future. It means that—"

Rod stopped listening. He was standing at the groom's right as best man. His duties had not been onerous but now he found that he had an overwhelming desire to sneeze. He worked his features around, then in desperation rubbed his upper lip violently and overcame it. He sighed silently and was glad for the first time that Grant Cowper had this responsibility. Grant seemed to know the right words and he did not.

The bride was attended by Caroline Mshiyeni. Both girls carried bouquets of a flame-colored wild bloom. Caroline was in shorts and shirt as usual and the bride was dressed in the conventional blue denim trousers and overshirt. Her hair was arranged *en brosse;* her scrubbed face shone in the firelight and she was radiantly beautiful.

"Who giveth this woman?"

Jimmy Throxton stepped forward and said hoarsely, "I do!"

"The ring, please."

Rod had it on his little finger; with considerable fumbling he got it off. It was a Ponce de Leon senior-class ring, borrowed from Bill Kennedy. He handed it to Cowper.

"Carmen Eleanora, do you take this man to be your lawfully wedded husband, to have and to hold, for better and for worse, in sickness and in health, till death do you part?"

"I do."

"Robert Edward, do you take this woman to be your lawfully wedded wife? Will you keep her and cherish her, cleaving unto her only, until death do you part?"

"I do. I mean, I will. Both."

"Take her hand in yours. Place the ring on her finger. Repeat after me—"

Rod's sneeze was coming back again; he missed part of it.

"—so, by authority vested in me as duly elected

Chief Magistrate of this sovereign community, I pronounce you man and wife! Kiss her, chum, before I beat you to it."

Carol and Jackie both were crying; Rod wondered what had gone wrong. He missed his turn at kissing the bride, but she turned to him presently, put an arm around his neck and kissed him. He found himself shaking hands with Bob very solemnly. "Well, I guess that does it. Don't forget you are supposed to carry her though the door."

"I won't forget."

"Well, you told me to remind you. Uh, may the Principle bless you both."

10

"I So Move"

THERE WAS NO MORE TALK OF LEAVING. EVEN CAROline dropped the subject.

But on other subjects talk was endless. Cowper held a town meeting every evening. These started with committee reports—the committee on food resources and natural conservation, the committees on artifacts and inventory, on waste disposal and camp sanitation, on exterior security, on human resources and labor allotment, on recruitment and immigration, on conservation of arts and sciences, on constitution, codification, and justice, on food preparation, on housing and city planning—

Cowper seemed to enjoy the endless talk and Rod was forced to admit that the others appeared to have a good time, too—he surprised himself by discovering that he too looked forward to the evenings. It was the village's social life, the only recreation. Each session

123

produced wordy battles, personal remarks and caustic criticisms; what was lacking in the gentlemanly formality found in older congresses was made up in spice. Rod liked to sprawl on the ground with his ear near Jimmy Throxton and listen to Jimmy's slanderous asides about the intelligence, motives, and ancestry of each speaker. He waited for Caroline's disorderly heckling.

But Caroline was less inclined to heckle now; Cowper had appointed her Historian on discovering that she owned a diary and could take shorthand. "It is extremely important," he informed her in the presence of the village, "that we have a full record of these pioneer days for posterity. You've been writing in your diary every day?"

"Sure. That's what it's for."

"Good! From here on it will be an official account. I want you to record the important events of each day."

"All right. It doesn't make the tiniest bit of difference, I do anyhow."

"Yes, yes, but in greater detail. I want you to record our proceedings, too. Historians will treasure this document, Carol."

"I'll bet!"

Cowper seemed lost in thought. "How many blank leaves left in your diary?"

"Couple of hundred, maybe."

"Good! That solves a problem I had been wondering about. Uh, we will have to requisition half of that supply for official use—public notices, committee transactions, and the like. You know."

Caroline looked wide-eyed. "That's a lot of paper, isn't it? You had better send two or three big husky boys to carry it."

Cowper looked puzzled. "You're joking."

"Better make it *four* big huskies. I could probably manage three . . . and somebody is likely to get hurt."

"Now, see here, Caroline, it is just a temporary requisition, in the public interest. Long before you need all of your diary we will devise other writing materials."

"Go ahead and devise! That's *my* diary."

Caroline sat near Cowper, diary in her lap and style in her hand, taking notes. Each evening she opened proceedings by reading the minutes of the previous

124

meeting. Rod asked her if she took down the endless debates.

"Goodness no!"

"I wondered. It seemed to me that you would run out of paper. Your minutes are certainly complete."

She chuckled. "Roddie, want to know what I really write down? Promise not to tell."

"Of course I won't."

"When I 'read the minutes' I just reach back in my mind and recall what the gabble was the night before—I've got an awfully good memory. But what I actually dirty the paper with . . . well, here—" She took her diary from a pocket. "Here's last night: 'Hizzoner called us to disorder at half-past burping time. The committee on cats and dogs reported. No cats, no dogs. The shortage was discussed. We adjourned and went to sleep, those who weren't already.' "

Rod grinned. "A good thing Grant doesn't know shorthand."

"Of course, if anything *real* happens, I put it down. But not the talk, talk, talk."

Caroline was not adamant about not sharing her supply of paper when needed. A marriage certificate, drawn up in officialese by Howard Goldstein, a Teller law student, was prepared for the Baxters and signed by Cowper, the couple themselves, and Rod and Caroline as witnesses. Caroline decorated it with flowers and turtle doves before delivering it.

There were others who seemed to feel that the new government was long on talk and short on results. Among them was Bob Baxter, but the Quaker couple did not attend most of the meetings. But when Cowper had been in office a week, Shorty Dumont took the floor after the endless committee reports:

"Mr. Chairman!"

"Can you hold it, Shorty? I have announcements to make before we get on to new business."

"This is still about committee reports. When does the committee on our constitution report?"

"Why, I made the report myself."

"You said that a revised draft was being prepared and the report would be delayed. That's no report. What I want to know is: when do we get a permanent set-up? When do we stop floating in air, getting along from day to day on 'temporary executive notices'?"

Cowper flushed. "Do you object to my executive decisions?"

"Won't say that I do, won't say that I don't. But Rod was let out and you were put in on the argument that we needed constitutional government, not a dictatorship. That's why I voted for you. All right, where's our laws? When do we vote on them?"

"You must understand," Cowper answered carefully, "that drawing up a constitution is not done overnight. Many considerations are involved."

"Sure, sure—but it's time we had some notion of what sort of a constitution you are cooking up. How about a bill of rights? Have you drawn up one?"

"All in due time."

"Why wait? For a starter let's adopt the Virginia Bill of Rights as article one. I so move."

"You're out of order. Anyhow we don't even have a copy of it."

"Don't let that bother you; I know it by heart. You ready, Carol? Take this down . . ."

"Never mind," Caroline answered. "I know it, too. I'm writing it."

"You see? These things aren't any mystery, Grant; most of us could quote it. So let's quit stalling."

Somebody yelled, "Whoopee! That's telling him, Shorty. I second the motion."

Cowper shouted for order. He went on, "This is not the time nor the place. When the committee reports, you will find that all proper democratic freedoms and safeguards have been included—modified only by the stern necessities of our hazardous position." He flashed his smile. "Now let's get on with business. I have an announcement about hunting parties. Hereafter each hunting party will be expected to—"

Dumont was still standing. "I said no more stalling, Grant. You argued that what we needed was laws, not a captain's whim. You've been throwing your weight around quite a while now and I don't see any laws. What are your duties? How much authority do you have? Are you both the high and the low justice? Or do the rest of us have rights?"

126

"Shut up and sit down!"

"How long is your term of office?"

Cowper made an effort to control himself. "Shorty, if you have suggestions on such things, you must take them up with the committee."

"Oh, slush! Give me a straight answer."

"You are out of order."

"I am *not* out of order. I'm insisting that the committee on drawing up a constitution tell us what they are doing. I won't surrender the floor until I get an answer. This is a town meeting and I have as much right to talk as anybody."

Cowper turned red. "I wouldn't be too sure," he said ominously. "Just how old are you, Shorty?"

Dumont stared at him. "Oh, so *that's* it? And the cat is out of the bag!" He glanced around. "I see quite a few here who are younger than I am. See what he's driving at, folks? Second-class citizens. He's going to stick an age limit in that so-called constitution. Aren't you, Grant? Look me in the eye and deny it."

"Roy! Dave! Grab him and bring him to order."

Rod had been listening closely; the show was better than usual. Jimmy had been adding his usual flippant commentary. Now Jimmy whispered, "That tears it. Do we choose up sides or do we fade back and watch the fun?"

Before he could answer Shorty made it clear that he needed no immediate help. He set his feet wide and snapped, "Touch me and somebody gets hurt!" He did not reach for any weapon but his attitude showed that he was willing to fight.

He went on, "Grant, I've got one thing to say, then I'll shut up." He turned and spoke to all. "You can see that we don't have any rights and we don't know where we stand—but we are already organized like a straitjacket. Committees for this, committees for that—and what good has it done? Are we better off than we were before all these half-baked committees were appointed? The wall is still unfinished, the camp is dirtier than ever, and nobody knows what he is supposed to do. Why, we even let the signal fire go out yesterday. When a roof leaks, you don't appoint a committee; you fix the leak. I say give the job back to Rod, get rid of these silly

127

committees, and get on with fixing the leaks. Anybody with me? Make some noise!"

They made plenty of noise. The shouts may have come from less than half but Cowper could see that he was losing his grip on them. Roy Kilroy dropped behind Shorty Dumont and looked questioningly at Cowper; Jimmy jabbed Rod in the ribs and whispered, "Get set, boy."

But Cowper shook his head at Roy. "Shorty," he said quietly, "are you through making your speech?"

"That wasn't a speech, that was a motion. And you had better not tell me it's out of order."

"I did not understand your motion. State it."

"You understood it. I'm moving that we get rid of you and put Rod back in."

Kilroy interrupted. "Hey, Grant, he can't do that. That's not according to—"

"Hold it, Roy. Shorty, your motion is not in order."

"I thought you would say that!"

"And it is really two motions. But I'm not going to bother with trifles. You say people don't like the way I'm doing things, so we'll find out." He went on briskly, "Is there a second to the motion?"

"Second!"

"I second it."

"Moved and seconded. The motion is to recall me and put Rod in office. Any remarks?"

A dozen people tried to speak. Rod got the floor by outshouting the others. "Mr. Chairman, *Mr. Chairman!* Privileged question!"

"The chair recognizes Rod Walker."

"Point of personal privilege. I have a statement to make."

"Well? Go ahead."

"Look, Grant, I didn't know Shorty planned to do this. Tell him, Shorty."

"That's right."

"Okay, okay," Cowper said sourly. "Any other remarks? Don't yell, just stick up your hands."

"I'm not through," insisted Rod.

"Well?"

"I not only did not know, I'm not for it. Shorty, I want you to withdraw your motion."

128

"No!"

"I think you should. Grant has only had a week; you can't expect miracles in that time—I *know;* I've had grief enough with this bunch of wild men. You may not like the things he's done—I don't myself, a lot of them. That's to be expected. But if you let that be an excuse to run him out of office, then sure as daylight this gang will break up."

"I'm not busting it up—he is! He may be older than I am but if he thinks that makes the least difference when it comes to having a say—well . . . he'd better think twice. I'm warning him. You hear that, Grant?"

"I heard it. You misunderstood me."

"Like fun I did!"

"Shorty," Rod persisted, "will you drop this idea? I'm asking you *please.*"

Shorty Dumont looked stubborn. Rod looked helplessly at Cowper, shrugged and sat down. Cowper turned away and growled, "Any more debate? You back there . . . Agnes? You've got the floor."

Jimmy whispered, "Why did you pull a stunt like that, Rod? Nobility doesn't suit you."

"I wasn't being noble. I knew what I was doing," Rod answered in low tones.

"You messed up your chances to be re-elected."

"Stow it." Rod listened; it appeared that Agnes Fries had more than one grievance. "Jim?"

"Huh?"

"Jump to your feet and move to adjourn."

"What? Ruin this when it's getting good? There is going to be some hair pulled . . . I hope."

"Don't argue; do it!—or I'll bang your heads together."

"Oh, all right. Spoilsport." Jimmy got reluctantly to his feet, took a breath and shouted, "I move we adjourn!"

Rod bounced to his feet. "SECOND THE MOTION!"

Cowper barely glanced at them. "Out of order. Sit down."

"It is *not* out of order," Rod said loudly. "A motion to adjourn is always in order, it takes precedence, and it cannot be debated. I call for the question."

"I never recognized you. This recall motion is going to be voted on if it is the last thing I do." Cowper's face was tense with anger. "Are you through, Agnes? Or do you want to discuss my table manners, too?"

"You *can't* refuse a motion to adjourn," Rod insisted "Question! Put the question."

Several took up the shout, drowning out Agnes Fries, preventing Cowper from recognizing another speaker. Boos and catcalls rounded out the tumult.

Cowper held up both hands for silence, then called out, "It has been moved and seconded that we adjourn. Those in favor say, 'Aye.' "

"*AYE!!*"

"Opposed?"

"No," said Jimmy.

"The meeting is adjourned." Cowper strode out of the circle of firelight.

Shorty Dumont came over, planted himself in front of Rod and looked up. "A fine sort of a pal you turned out to be!" He spat on the ground and stomped off.

"Yeah," agreed Jimmy, "what gives? Schizophrenia? Your nurse drop you on your head? That noble stuff in the right doses might have put us back in business. But you didn't know when to stop."

Jacqueline had approached while Jimmy was speaking. "I wasn't pulling any tricks," Rod insisted. "I meant what I said. Kick a captain out when he's had only a few days to show himself and you'll bust us up into a dozen little groups. *I* wouldn't be able to hold them together. Nobody could."

"Bosh! Jackie, tell the man."

She frowned. "Jimmy, you're sweet, but you're not bright."

"*Et tu,* Jackie?"

"Never mind, Jackie will take care of you. A good job, Rod. By tomorrow everybody will realize it. Some of them are a little stirred up tonight."

"What I don't see," Rod said thoughtfully, "is what got Shorty stirred up in the first place?"

"Hadn't you heard? Maybe it was while you were out hunting. I didn't see it, but he got into a row with Roy, then Grant bawled him out in front of everybody. I

130

think Shorty is self-conscious about his height," she said seriously. "He doesn't like to take orders."

"Does anybody?"

The next day Grant Cowper acted as if nothing had happened. But his manner had more of King Log and less of King Stork. Late in the afternoon he looked up Rod. "Walker? Can you spare me a few minutes?"

"Why not?"

"Let's go where we can talk." Grant led him to a spot out of earshot. They sat on the ground and Rod waited. Cowper seemed to have difficulty in finding words.

Finally he said, "Rod, I think I can depend on you." He threw in his grin, but it looked forced.

"Why?" asked Rod.

"Well . . . the way you behaved last night."

"So? Don't bank on it, I didn't do it for you." Rod paused, then added, "Let's get this straight. I don't like you."

For once Cowper did not grin. "That makes it mutual. I don't like you a little bit. But we've got to get along . . . and I think I can trust you."

"Maybe."

"I'll risk it."

"I agree with every one of Shorty's gripes. I just didn't agree with his solution."

Cowper gave a wry smile unlike his usual expression. For an instant Rod found himself almost liking him. "The sad part is that I agree with his gripes myself."

"Huh?"

"Rod, you probably think I'm a stupid jerk but the fact is I do know quite a bit about theory of government. The hard part is to apply it in a . . . a transitional period like this. We've got fifty people here and not a one with any practical experience in government—not even myself. But every single one considers himself an expert. Take that bill-of-rights motion; I couldn't let that stand. I know enough about such things to know that the rights and duties needed for a co-operative colony like this can't be taken over word for word from an agrarian democracy, and they are still different from those necessary for an industrial republic." He looked worried. "It is true that we had considered limiting the franchise."

"You do and they'll toss you in the creek!"

"I know. That's one reason why the law committee hasn't made a report. Another reason is—well, confound it, how can you work out things like a constitution when you practically haven't any writing paper? It's exasperating. But about the franchise: the oldest one of us is around twenty-two and the youngest is about sixteen. The worst of it is that the youngest are the most precocious, geniuses or near-geniuses." Cowper looked up. "I don't mean you."

"Oh, no," Rod said hastily. "I'm no genius!"

"You're not sixteen, either. These brilliant brats worry me. 'Bush lawyers,' every blessed one, with always a smart answer and no sense. We thought with an age limit—a reasonable one—the older heads could act as ballast while they grow up. But it won't work."

"No. It won't."

"But what am I to *do*? That order about hunting teams not being mixed—that wasn't aimed at teams like you and Carol, but she thought it was and gave me the very deuce. I was just trying to take care of these kids. Confound it, I wish they were all old enough to marry and settle down—the Baxters don't give me trouble."

"I wouldn't worry. In a year or so ninety per cent of the colony will be married."

"I hope so! Say . . . are *you* thinking about it?"

"Me?" Rod was startled. "Farthest thing from my mind."

"Um? I thought— Never mind; I didn't get you out here to ask about your private affairs. What Shorty had to say was hard to swallow—but I'm going to make some changes. I'm abolishing most of the committees."

"So?"

"Yes. Blast them, they don't *do* anything; they just produce reports. I'm going to make one girl boss cook —and one man boss hunter. I want you to be chief of police."

"Huh? Why in Ned do you want a chief of police?"

"Well . . . somebody has to see that orders are carried out. You know, camp sanitation and such. Somebody has to keep the signal smoking—we haven't accounted for thirty-seven people, aside from known dead. Somebody has to assign the night watch and check on it. The kids run hog wild if you don't watch them. You are the one to do it."

"Why?"

"Well . . . let's be practical, Rod. I've got a following and so have you. We'll have less trouble if everybody sees that we two stand together. It's for the good of the community."

Rod realized, as clearly as Grant did, that the group had to pull together. But Cowper was asking him to shore up his shaky administration, and Rod not only resented him but thought that Cowper was all talk and no results.

It was not just the unfinished wall, he told himself, but a dozen things. Somebody ought to search for a salt lick, every day. There ought to be a steady hunt for edible roots and berries and things, too—he, for one, was tired of an all-meat diet. Sure, you could stay healthy if you didn't stick just to lean meat, but who wanted to eat nothing but meat, maybe for a lifetime? And there were those stinking hides . . . Grant had ordered every kill skinned, brought back for use.

"What are you going to do with those green hides?" he asked suddenly.

"Huh? Why?"

"They stink. If you put me in charge, I'm going to chuck them in the creek."

"But we're going to need them. Half of us are in rags now."

"But we're not short on hides; tanning is what we need. Those hides won't sun-cure this weather."

"We haven't got tannin. Don't be silly, Rod."

"Then send somebody out to chew bark till they find some. You can't mistake the puckery taste. And get rid of those hides!"

"If I do, will you take the job?"

"Maybe. You said, 'See that orders are carried out.' Whose orders? Yours? Or Kilroy's?"

"Well, both. Roy is my deputy."

Rod shook his head. "No, thanks. You've got him, so

133

you don't need me. Too many generals, not enough privates."

"But, Rod, I *do* need you. Roy doesn't get along with the younger kids. He rubs them the wrong way."

"He rubs me the wrong way, too. Nothing doing, Grant. Besides, I don't like the title anyhow. It's silly."

"Pick your own. Captain of the Guard . . . City Manager. I don't care what you call it; I want you to take over the night guard and see that things run smoothly around camp—and keep an eye on the younger kids. You can do it and it's your duty."

"What will you be doing?"

"I've got to whip this code of laws into shape. I've got to think about long-range planning. Heavens, Rod, I've got a thousand things on my mind. I can't stop to settle a quarrel just because some kid has been teasing the cook. Shorty was right; we can't wait. When I give an order I want a law to back it and not have to take lip from some young snotty. But I can't do it all, I need help."

Cowper put it on grounds impossible to refuse, nevertheless . . . "What about Kilroy?"

"Eh? Confound it, Rod, you can't ask me to kick out somebody else to make room for *you*."

"I'm not *asking* for the job!" Rod hesitated. He needed to say that it was a matter of stubborn pride to him to back up the man who had beaten him, it was that more than any public-spiritedness. He could not phrase it, but he did know that Cowper and Kilroy were not the same case.

"I won't pull Kilroy's chestnuts out of the fire. Grant, I'll stooge for you; you were elected. But I won't stooge for a stooge."

"Rod, be reasonable! If you got an order from Roy, it would be *my* order. He would simply be carrying it out."

Rod stood up. "No deal."

Cowper got angrily to his feet and strode away.

There was no meeting that night, for the first time. Rod was about to visit the Baxters when Cowper called him aside. "You win. I've made Roy chief hunter."

"Huh?"

"You take over as City Manager, or Queen of the May, or whatever you like. Nobody has set the night watch. So get busy."

"Wait a minute! I never said I would take the job."

"You made it plain that the only thing in your way was Roy. Okay, you get your orders directly from me."

Rod hesitated. Cowper looked at him scornfully and said, "So you can't co-operate even when you have it all your own way?"

"Not that, but—"

"No 'buts.' Do you take the job? A straight answer: yes, or no."

"Uh . . . yes."

"Okay." Cowper frowned and added, "I almost wish you had turned it down."

"That makes two of us."

Rod started to set the guard and found that every boy he approached was convinced that he had had more than his share of watches. Since the exterior security committee had kept no records—indeed, had had no way to—it was impossible to find out who was right and who was shirking. "Stow it!" he told one. "Starting tomorrow we'll have an alphabetical list, straight rotation. I'll post it even if we have to scratch it on a rock." He began to realize that there was truth in what Grant had said about the difficulty of getting along without writing paper.

"Why don't you put your pal Baxter on watch?"

"Because the Mayor gave him two weeks honeymoon, as you know. Shut up the guff. Charlie will be your relief; make sure you know where he sleeps."

"I think I'll get married. I could use two weeks of loafing."

"I'll give you five to one you can't find a girl that far out of her mind. You're on from midnight to two."

Most of them accepted the inevitable once they were assured of a square deal in the future, but Peewee Schneider, barely sixteen and youngest in the community, stood on his "rights"—he had stood a watch the night before, he did not rate another for at least three nights, and nobody could most colorfully make him.

Rod told Peewee that he would either stand his watch, or Rod would slap his ears loose—and then he would still stand his watch. To which he added that if he heard Peewee use that sort of language around camp again he would wash Peewee's mouth out with soap.

Schneider shifted the argument. "Yah! Where are you going to find soap?"

"Until we get some, I'll use sand. You spread that word, Peewee: no more rough language around camp. We're going to be civilized if it kills us. Four to six, then, and show Kenny where you sleep." As he left Rod made a mental note that they should collect wood ashes and fat; while he had only a vague idea of how to make soap probably someone knew how . . . and soap was needed for other purposes than curbing foul-mouthed pip-squeaks. He had felt a yearning lately to be able to stand upwind of himself . . . he had long ago thrown away his socks.

Rod got little sleep. Everytime he woke he got up and inspected the guard, and twice he was awakened by watchmen who thought they saw something prowling outside the circle of firelight. Rod was not sure, although it did seem once that he could make out a large, long shape drifting past in the darkness. He stayed up a while each time, another gun in case the prowler risked the wall or the fires in the gap. He felt great temptation to shoot at the prowling shadows, but suppressed it. To carry the attack to the enemy would be to squander their scanty ammunition without making a dent in the dangerous beasts around them. There were prowlers every night; they had to live with it.

He was tired and cranky the next morning and wanted to slip away after breakfast and grab a nap in the cave. He had not slept after four in the morning, but had checked on Peewee Schneider at frequent intervals. But there was too much to do; he promised himself a nap later and sought out Cowper instead. "Two or three things on my mind, Grant."

"Spill it."

"Any reason not to put girls on watch?"

"Eh? I don't think it's a good idea."

"Why not? These girls don't scream at a mouse. Every one of them stayed alive by her own efforts at

136

least a month before she joined up here. Ever seen Caroline in action?"

"Mmm . . . no."

"You should. It's a treat. Sudden death in both hands, and eyes in the back of her head. If she were on watch, I would sleep easy. How many men do we have now?"

"Uh, twenty-seven, with the three that came in yesterday."

"All right, out of twenty-seven who doesn't stand watch?"

"Why, everybody takes his turn."

"You?"

"Eh? Isn't that carrying it pretty far? I don't expect *you* to take a watch; you run it and check on the others."

"That's two off. Roy Kilroy?"

"Uh, look, Rod, you had better figure that he is a department head as chief hunter and therefore exempt. You know why—no use looking for trouble."

"I know, all right. Bob Baxter is off duty, too."

"Until next week."

"But this is this week. The committee cut the watch down to one at a time; I'm going to boost it to two again. Besides that I want a sergeant of the guard each night. He will be on all night and sleep all next day . . . then I don't want to put him on for a couple of days. You see where that leaves me? I need twelve watch-standers every night; I have less than twenty to draw from."

Cowper looked worried. "The committee didn't think we had to have more than one guard at a time."

"Committee be hanged!" Rod scratched his scars and thought about shapes in the dark. "Do you want me to run this the way I think it has to be run? Or shall I just go through the motions?"

"Well . . ."

"One man alone either gets jittery and starts seeing shadows—or he dopes off and is useless. I had to wake one last night—I won't tell you who; I scared him out of his pants; he won't do it again. I say we need a real guard, strong enough in case of trouble to handle things while the camp has time to wake up. But if you want it

137

your way, why not relieve me and put somebody else in?"

"No, no, you keep it. Do what you think necessary."

"Okay, I'm putting the girls on. Bob and Carmen, too. And *you*."

"Huh?"

"And me. And Roy Kilroy. Everybody. That's the only way you will get people to serve without griping; that way you will convince them that it is serious, a first obligation, even ahead of hunting."

Cowper picked at a hangnail, "Do you honestly think I should stand watch? And you?"

"I do. It would boost morale seven hundred per cent. Besides that, it would be a good thing, uh, politically."

Cowper glanced up, did not smile. "You've convinced me. Let me know when it's my turn."

"Another thing. Last night there was barely wood to keep two fires going."

"Your problem. Use anybody not on the day's hunting or cooking details."

"I will. You'll hear some beefs. Boss, those were minor items; now I come to the major one. Last night I took a fresh look at this spot. I don't like it, not as a permanent camp. We've been lucky."

"Eh? Why?"

"This place is almost undefendable. We've got a stretch over fifty meters long between shale and water on the upstream side. Downstream isn't bad, because we build a fire in the bottleneck. But upstream we have walled off less than half and we need a lot more stakes behind the wall. Look," Rod added, pointing, "you could drive an army through there—and last night I had only two little bitty fires. We ought to finish that wall."

"We will."

"But we ought to make a real drive to find a better place. This is makeshift at best. Before you took over I was trying to find more caves—but I didn't have time to explore very far. Ever been to Mesa Verde?"

"In Colorado? No."

"Cliff dwellings, you've seen pictures. Maybe somewhere up or down stream—more likely down—we will find pockets like those at Mesa Verde where we can build homes for the whole colony. You ought to send a

138

team out for two weeks or more, searching. I volunteer for it."

"Maybe. But you can't go; I need you."

"In a week I'll have this guard duty lined up so that it will run itself. Bob Baxter can relieve me; they respect him. Uh . . ." He thought for a moment. Jackie? Jimmy? "I'll team with Carol."

"Rod, I told you I want you here. But are you and Caroline planning to marry?"

"Huh? What gave you that notion?"

"Then you can't team with her in any case. We are trying to re-introduce amenities around here."

"Now see here, Cowper!"

"Forget it."

"Unh . . . all right. But the first thing—the very first —is to finish that wall. I want to put everybody to work right away."

"Mmm . . ." Cowper said. "I'm sorry. You can't."

"Why not?"

"Because we are going to build a house today. Bill Kennedy and Sue Briggs are getting married tonight."

"Huh? I hadn't heard."

"I guess you are the first to hear. They told me about it privately, at breakfast."

Rod was not surprised, as Bill and Sue preferred each other's company. "Look, do they have to get married tonight? That wall is urgent, Grant; I'm telling you."

"Don't be so intense, Rod. You can get along a night or two with bigger fires. Remember, there are human values more important than material values."

11

The Beach of Bones

"*July 29*—BILL AND SUE GOT MARRIED TONIGHT.
Hizzoner never looked lovelier. He made a mighty pretty
service out of it—I cried and so did the other girls. If
that boy could *do* the way he can talk! I played Men-
delssohn's Wedding March on my harmonica with tears
running down my nose and gumming up the reeds—
that's a touch I wanted to put into darling Carmen's
wedding but I couldn't resist being bridesmaid. The
groom got stuck carrying his lady fair over the thres-
hold of their 'house'—if I may call it that—and had to
put her down and shove her in ahead of him. The ceiling is lower than it ought to be which is why he got
stuck, because we ran out of rock and Roddie raised
Cain when we started to use part of the wall. Hizzoner
was leading the assault on the wall and both of them
got red in the face and shouted at each other. But Hizzoner backed down after Roddie got him aside and said
something—Bill was pretty sore at Roddie but Bob
sweet-talked him and offered to swap houses and Roddie promised Bill that we would take the roof off and
bring the walls up higher as soon as the wall is finished.
That might not be as soon as he thinks, though—
usable rock is getting hard to find. I've broken all my
nails trying to pry out pieces we could use. But I agree
with Roddie that we ought to finish that wall and I
sleep a lot sounder now that he is running the watch
and I'll sleep sounder yet when that wall is tight and the
pin-cushion back of it finished. Of course we girls sleep
down at the safe end but who wants to wake up and
find a couple of our boys missing? It is not as if we had
them to spare, bless their silly little hearts. Nothing like

a man around the house, Mother always said, to give a home that lived-in look.

"*July 30*—I'm not going to write in this unless something happens. Hizzoner talks about making papyrus like the Egyptians but I'll believe it when I see it.

"*Aug 5*—I was sergeant of the guard last night and Roddie was awake practically all night. I turned in after breakfast and slept until late afternoon—when I woke up there was Roddie, red-eyed and cross, yelling for more rocks and more firewood. Sometimes Roddie is a little hard to take.

"*Aug 9*—the salt lick Alice found is closer than the one Shorty found last week, but not as good.

"*Aug 11*—Jackie finally made up her mind to marry Jim and I think Roddie is flabbergasted—but I could have told him a month ago. Roddie is stupid about such things. I see another house & wall crisis coming and Roddie will get a split personality because he will want Jimmy and Jacqueline to have a house right away and the only decent stone within reach is built into the wall.

"*Aug 15*—Jimmy and Jackie, Agnes and Curt, were married today in a beautiful double ceremony. The Throxtons have the Baxter house temporarily and the Pulvermachers have the Kennedy's doll house while we partition the cave into two sets of married quarters and a storeroom.

"*Sep 1*—the roots I dug up didn't poison me, so I served a mess of them tonight. The shield from power pack of that Thunderbolt gun we salvaged—Johann's, it must have been—made a big enough boiler to cook a little helping for everybody. The taste was odd, maybe because Agnes had been making soap in it—it wasn't very good soap, either. I'm going to call these things yams because they look like yams although they taste more like parsnips. There are a lot of them around. Tomorrow I'm going to try boiling them with greens, a strip of side meat, and plenty of salt. Yum, yum! I'm going to bake them in ashes, too.

"*Sep 16*—Chad Ames and Dick Burke showed up with their tails tucked in; Hizzoner got soft-hearted and let them stay. They say Jock McGowan is crazy. I can believe it.

"*Sep 28*—Philip Schneider died today, hunting. Roy carried him in, but he was badly clawed and lost a lot of blood and was D.O.A. Roy resigned as boss hunter and Hizzoner appointed Cliff. Roy is broken up about it and nobody blames him. The Lord giveth and the Lord taketh away. Blessed be the Name of the Lord.

"*Oct 7*—I've decided to marry M.

"*Oct 10*—seems I was mistaken—M. is going to marry Margery Chung. Well, they are nice kids and if we ever get out of this I'll be glad I'm single since I want to buck for a commission in the Amazons. Note: be a little more standoffish, Caroline. Well, *try!*

"*Oct 20*—Carmen????

"*Oct 21*—Yes.

"*Nov 1*—well Glory be! I'm the new *City Manager*. Little Carol, the girl with two left feet. Just a couple of weeks, temporary and acting while Roddie is away, but say 'sir' when you speak to me. Hizzoner finally let Roddie make the down-river survey he has been yipping about, accompanying it with a slough of advice and injunctions that Roddie will pay no attention to once he is out of sight—if I know Roddie. It's a two-man team and Roddie picked Roy as his teamer. They left this morning.

"*Nov 5*—being City Manager is not all marshmallow sundae. I wish Roddie would get back.

"*Nov 11*—Hizzoner wants me to copy off in here the 'report of the artifacts committee'! Mick Mahmud has been keeping it in his head which strikes me as a good place. But Hizzoner has been very jumpy since Roddie and Roy left, so I guess I will humor him—here it is:

"12 spare knives (besides one each for everybody)

"53 firearms and guns of other sorts—but only about half of them with even one charge left.

"6 Testaments

"2 Peace of the Flame

"1 Koran

"1 Book of Mormon

"1 Oxford Book of English Verse, Centennial Edition

"1 steel bow and 3 hunting arrows

"1 boiler made from a wave shield and quite a bit of metal and plastic junk (worth its weight in uranium, I admit) from the Thunderbolt Jackie salvaged.

"1 stew pan (Carmen's)

"1 pack playing cards with the nine of hearts missing

"13 matches, any number of pocket flamers no longer working, and 27 burning glasses

"1 small hand ax

"565 meters climbing line, some of it chopped up for other uses

"91 fishhooks (and no fish fit to eat!)

"61 pocket compasses, some of them broken

"19 watches that still run (4 of them adjusted to our day)

"2 bars of scented soap that Theo has been hoarding

"2 boxes Kwik-Kure and part of a box of Tan-Fast

"Several kilos of oddments that I suppose we will find a use for but I won't list. Mick has a mind like a pack rat.

"Lots of things we have made and can make more of —pots, bows and arrows, hide scrapers, a stone-age mortar & pestle we can grind seeds on if you don't mind grit in your teeth, etc. Hizzoner says the Oxford Verse is the most valuable thing we have and I agree, but not for his reasons. He wants me to cover all the margins with shorthand, recording all special knowledge that any of us have—everything from math to pig-raising. Cliff says go ahead as long as we don't deface the verses. I don't see when I'm going to find time. I've hardly been out of the settlement since Roddie left and sleep is something I just hear about.

"*Nov 13*—only two more days. 'For this relief, much thanks . . .'

"*Nov 16*—I didn't think they would be on time.

"*Nov 21*—We finally adopted our constitution and basic code today, the first town meeting we've had in weeks. It covers the flyleaves of two Testaments, Bob's and Georgia's. If anybody wants to refer to it, which I doubt, that's where to look.

"*Nov 29*—Jimmy says old Rod is too tough to kill. I hope he's right. Why, oh, why didn't I twist Hizzoner's arm and make him let me go?

"*Dec 15*—there's no use kidding ourselves any longer.

"*Dec 21*—the Throxtons and Baxters and myself and Grant gathered privately in the Baxter house to-night and Grant recited the service for the dead. Bob said a prayer for both of them and then we sat quietly for a long time, Quaker fashion. Roddie always re-minded me of my brother Rickie, so I privately asked Mother to take care of him, and Roy, too—Mother had a lap big enough for three, any time.
"Grant hasn't made a public announcement; officially they are just 'overdue.'

"*Dec 25*—Christmas"

Rod and Roy traveled light and fast downstream, taking turns leading and covering. Each carried a few kilos of salt meat but they expected to eat off the land. In addition to game they now knew of many edible fruits and berries and nuts; the forest was a free cafe-teria to those who knew it. They carried no water since they expected to follow the stream. But they continued to treat the water with respect; in addition to ichthyo-saurs that sometimes pulled down a drinking buck there were bloodthirsty little fish that took very small bites— but they traveled in schools and could strip an animal to bones in minutes.

Rod carried both Lady Macbeth and Colonel Bowie; Roy Kilroy carried his Occam's Razor and a knife borrowed from Carmen Baxter. Roy had a climbing rope wrapped around his waist. Each had a hand gun strapped to his hip but these were for extremity; one gun had only three charges. But Roy carried Jacqueline Throxton's air pistol, with freshly envenomed darts; they expected it to save hours of hunting, save time for travel.

Three days downstream they found a small cave, found living in it a forlorn colony of five girls. They powwowed, then headed on down as the girls started upstream to find the settlement. The girls had told them of a place farther down where the creek could be crossed. They found it, a wide rocky shallows with natural stepping stones . . . then wasted two days on the far side before crossing back.

By the seventh morning they had found no cave other than one the girls had occupied. Rod said to Roy, "Today makes a week. Grant said to be back in two weeks."

"That's what the man said. Yes, sir!"

"No results."

"Nope. None."

"We ought to start back."

Roy did not answer. Rod said querulously, "Well, what do you think?"

Kilroy was lying down, watching the local equivalent of an ant. He seemed in no hurry to do anything else. Finally he answered, "Rod, you are bossing this party. Upstream, downstream—just tell me."

"Oh, go soak your head."

"On the other hand, a bush lawyer like Shorty might question Grant's authority to tell us to return at a given time. He might use words like 'free citizen' and 'sovereign autonomy.' Maybe he's got something—this neighborhood looks awfully far 'West of the Pecos.' "

"Well . . . we could stretch it a day, at least. We won't be taking that side trip going back."

"Obviously. Now, if I were leading the party—but I'm not."

"Cut the double talk! I asked for advice."

"Well, I say we are here to find caves, not to keep a schedule."

Rod quit frowning. "Up off your belly. Let's go."

They headed downstream.

The terrain changed from forest valley to canyon country as the stream cut through a plateau. Game became harder to find and they used some of their salt meat. Two days later they came to the first of a series of bluffs carved eons earlier into convolutions, pockets, blank dark eyes. "This looks like it."

"Yes," agreed Roy. He looked around. "It might be even better farther down."

"It might be."

They went on.

In time the stream widened out, there were no more caves, and the canyons gave way to a broad savannah, treeless except along the banks of the river. Rod sniffed. "I smell salt."

"You ought to. There's ocean over there somewhere."

"I don't think so." They went on.

They avoided the high grass, kept always near the trees. The colonists had listed more than a dozen predators large enough to endanger a man, from a leonine creature twice as long as the biggest African lion down to a vicious little scaly thing which was dangerous if cornered. It was generally agreed that the leonine monster was the "stobor" they had been warned against, although a minority favored a smaller carnivore which was faster, trickier, and more likely to attack a man.

One carnivore was not considered for the honor. It was no larger than a jack rabbit, had an oversize head, a big jaw, front legs larger than hind, and no tail. It was known as "dopy joe" from the silly golliwog expression it had and its clumsy, slow movements when disturbed. It was believed to live by waiting at burrows of field rodents for supper to come out. Its skin cured readily and made a good water bag. Grassy fields such as this savannah often were thick with them.

They camped in a grove of trees by the water. Rod said, "Shall I waste a match, or do it the hard way?"

146

"Suit yourself. I'll knock over something for dinner."

"Watch yourself. Don't go into the grass."

"I'll work the edges. Cautious Kilroy they call me, around the insurance companies."

Rod counted his three matches, hoping there would be four, then started making fire by friction. He had just succeeded, delayed by moss that was not as dry as it should have been, when Roy returned and dropped a small carcass. "The durnedest thing happened."

The kill was a dopy joe; Rod looked at it with distaste. "Was that the best you could do? They taste like kerosene."

"Wait till I tell you. I wasn't hunting him; he was hunting *me*."

"Don't kid me!"

"Truth. I had to kill him to keep him from snapping my ankles. So I brought him in."

Rod looked at the small creature. "Never heard the like. Must be insanity in his family."

"Probably." Roy started skinning it.

Next morning they reached the sea, a glassy body untouched by tide, unruffled by wind. It was extremely briny and its shore was crusted with salt. They concluded that it was probably a dead sea, not a true ocean. But their attention was not held by the body of water. Stretching away along the shore apparently to the horizon were millions on heaping millions of whitened bones. Rod stared. "Where did they all come from?"

Roy whistled softly. "Search me. But if we could sell them at five pence a metric ton, we'd be millionaires."

"Billionaires, you mean."

"Let's not be fussy." They walked out along the beach, forgetting to be cautious, held by the amazing sight. There were ancient bones, cracked by sun and sea, new bones with gristle clinging, big bones of the giant antelope the colonists never hunted, tiny bones of little buck no larger than terriers, bones without number of all sorts. But there were no carcasses.

They inspected the shore for a couple of kilometers, awed by the mystery. When they turned they knew that they were turning back not just to camp but to head home. This was as far as they could go.

On the trip out they had not explored the caves. On

their way back Rod decided that they should try to pick the best place for the colony, figuring game, water supply, and most importantly, shelter and ease of defense.

They were searching a series of arched galleries water-carved in sandstone cliff. The shelf of the lowest gallery was six or seven meters above the sloping stand of soil below. The canyon dropped rapidly here; Rod could visualize a flume from upstream, bringing running water right to the caves . . . not right away, but when they had time to devise tools and cope with the problems. Someday, someday—but in the meantime here was plenty of room for the colony in a spot which almost defended itself. Not to mention, he added, being in out of the rain.

Roy was the better Alpinist; he inched up, flat to the rock, reached the shelf and threw down his line to Rod —snaked him up quickly. Rod got an arm over the edge, scrambled to his knees, stood up—and gasped, "What the deuce!"

"That," said Roy, "is why I kept quiet. I thought you would think I was crazy."

"I think we both are." Rod stared around. Filling the depth of the gallery, not seen from below, was terrace on terrace of cliff dwellings.

They were not inhabited, nor had they ever been by men. Openings which must have been doors were no higher than a man's knee, not wide enough for shoulders. But it was clear that they were dwellings, not merely formations carved by water. There were series of rooms arranged in half a dozen low stories from floor to ceiling of the gallery. The material was a concrete of dried mud, an adobe, used with wood.

But there was nothing to suggest what had built them. Roy started to stick his head into an opening; Rod shouted, "Hey! Don't do that!"

"Why not? It's abandoned."

"You don't know what might be inside. Snakes, maybe."

"There are no snakes. Nobody's ever seen one."

"No . . . but take it easy."

"I wish I had a torch light."

"I wish I had eight beautiful dancing girls and a

148

Cadillac copter. Be careful. I don't want to walk back alone."

They lunched in the gallery and considered the matter. "Of course they were intelligent," Roy declared. "We may find them elsewhere. Maybe really civilized now—these look like ancient ruins."

"Not necessarily intelligent," Rod argued. "Bees make more complicated homes."

"Bees don't combine mud and wood the way these people did. Look at that lintel."

"Birds do. I'll concede that they were bird-brained, no more."

"Rod, you won't look at the evidence."

"Where are their artifacts? Show me one ash tray marked 'Made in Jersey City.' "

"I might find some if you weren't so jumpy."

"All in time. Anyhow, the fact that *they* found it safe shows that we can live here."

"Maybe. What killed them? Or why did they go away?"

They searched two galleries after lunch, found more dwellings. The dwellers had apparently formed a very large community. The fourth gallery they explored was almost empty, containing a beginning of a hive in one corner. Rod looked it over. "We can use this. It may not be the best, but we can move the gang in and then find the best at our leisure."

"We're heading back?"

"Uh, in the morning. This is a good place to sleep and tomorrow we'll travel from 'can' to 'can't'—I wonder what's up there?" Rod was looking at a secondary shelf inside the main arch.

Roy eyed it. "I'll let you know in a moment."

"Don't bother. It's almost straight up. We'll build ladders for spots like that."

"My mother was a human fly, my father was a mountain goat. Watch me."

The shelf was not much higher than his head. Roy had a hand over—when a piece of rock crumbled away. He did not fall far.

Rod ran to him. "You all right, boy?"

Roy grunted, "I guess so," then started to get up. He yelped.

"What's the matter?"

"My right leg. I think . . . ow! I think it's broken."

Rod examined the break, then went down to cut splints. With a piece of the line Roy carried, used economically, for he needed most of it as a ladder, he bound the leg, padding it with leaves. It was a simple break of the tibia, with no danger of infection.

They argued the whole time. "Of course you will," Roy was saying. "Leave me a fresh kill and what salt meat there is. You can figure some way to leave water."

"Come back and find your chawed bones!"

"Not at all. Nothing can get at me. If you hustle, you can make it in three days."

"Four, or five more likely. Six days to lead a party back. Then you want to go back in a stretcher? How would you like to be helpless when a stobor jumps us?"

"But I wouldn't go back. The gang would be moving down here."

"Suppose they do? Eleven days, more likely twelve— Roy, you didn't just bang your shin; you banged your head, too."

The stay in the gallery while Roy's leg repaired was not difficult nor dangerous; it was merely tedious. Rod would have liked to explore all the caves, but the first time he was away longer than Roy thought necessary to make a kill Rod returned to find his patient almost hysterical. He had let his imagination run away, visioning Rod as dead and thinking about his own death, helpless, while he starved or died of thirst. After that Rod left him only to gather food and water. The gallery was safe from all dangers; no watch was necessary, fire was needed only for cooking. The weather was getting warmer and the daily rains dropped off.

They discussed everything from girls to what the colony needed, what could have caused the disaster that had stranded them, what they would have to eat if they could have what they wanted, and back to girls again. They did not discuss the possibility of rescue; they took it for granted that they were there to stay. They slept much of the time and often did nothing, in animal-like torpor.

Roy wanted to start back as soon as Rod removed

the splints, but it took him only seconds to discover that he no longer knew how to walk. He exercised for days, then grew sulky when Rod still insisted that he was not able to travel; the accumulated irritations of invalidism spewed out in the only quarrel they had on the trip.

Rod grew as angry as he was, threw Roy's climbing rope at him and shouted, "Go ahead! See how far you get on that gimp leg!"

Five minutes later Rod was arranging a sling, half dragging Roy, white and trembling and thoroughly subdued, back up onto the shelf. Thereafter they spent ten days getting Roy's muscles into shape, then started back.

Shorty Dumont was the first one they ran into as they approached the settlement. His jaw dropped and he looked scared, then he ran to greet them, ran back to alert those in camp. "Hey, everybody! They're *back!*"

Caroline heard the shout, outdistanced the others in great flying leaps, kissed and hugged them both. "Hi, Carol," Rod said. "What are you bawling about?"

"Oh, Roddie, you bad, *bad* boy!"

12

"It Won't Work, Rod"

IN THE MIDST OF JUBILATION ROD HAD TIME TO NOTICE many changes. There were more than a dozen new buildings, including two long shedlike affairs of bamboo and mud. One new hut was of sunbaked brick; it had windows. Where the cooking fire had been was a barbecue pit and by it a Dutch oven. Near it a stream of water spilled out of bamboo pipe, splashed through a rawhide net, fell into a rock bowl, and was led away to

151

the creek . . . he hardly knew whether to be pleased or irked at this anticipation of his own notion.

He caught impressions piecemeal, as their triumphal entry was interrupted by hugs, kisses, and bone-jarring slaps on the back, combined with questions piled on questions. "No, no trouble—except that Roy got mad and busted his leg . . . yeah, sure, we found what we went after; wait till you *see* . . . no . . . yes . . . Jackie! . . . Hi, Bob!—it's good to see you, too, boy! Where's Carmen . . . Hi, Grant!"

Cowper was grinning widely, white teeth splitting his beard. Rod noticed with great surprise that the man looked *old*—why, shucks, Grant wasn't more than twenty-two, twenty-three at the most. Where did he pick up those lines?

"Rod, old boy! I don't know whether to have you two thrown in the hoosegow or decorate your brows with laurel."

"We got held up."

"So it seems. Well, there is more rejoicing for the strayed lamb than for the ninety and nine. Come on up to the city hall."

"The what?"

Cowper looked sheepish. "They call it that, so I do. Better than 'Number Ten, Downing Street' which it started off with. It's just the hut where I sleep—it doesn't belong to me," he added. "When they elect somebody else, I'll sleep in bachelor hall." Grant led them toward a little building apart from the others and facing the cooking area.

The wall was gone.

Rod suddenly realized what looked strange about the upstream end of the settlement; the wall was gone completely and in its place was a thornbush barricade. He opened his mouth to make a savage comment—then realized that it really did not matter. Why kick up a row when the colony would be moving to the canyon of the Dwellers? They would never need walls again; they would be up high at night, with their ladders pulled up after them. He picked another subject.

"Grant, how in the world did you guys get the inner partitions out of those bamboo pipes?"

"Eh? Nothing to it. You tie a knife with rawhide to a

152

thinner bamboo pole, then reach in and whittle. All it takes is patience. Waxie worked it out. But you haven't seen anything yet. We're going to have *iron.*"

"Huh?"

"We've got ore; now we are experimenting. But I do wish we could locate a seam of coal. Say, you didn't spot any, did you?"

Dinner was a feast, a *luau,* a celebration to make the weddings look pale. Rod was given a real plate to eat on—unglazed, lopsided, ungraceful, but a plate. As he took out Colonel Bowie, Margery Chung Kinksi put a wooden spoon in his hand. "We don't have enough to go around, but the guests of honor rate them tonight." Rod looked at it curiously. It felt odd in his hand.

Dinner consisted of boiled greens, some root vegetables new to him, and a properly baked haunch served in thin slices. Roy and Rod were served little unleavened cakes like tortillas. No one else had them, but Rod decided that it was polite not to comment on that. Instead he made a fuss over eating bread again.

Margery dimpled. "We'll have plenty of bread some day. Maybe next year."

There were tart little fruits for dessert, plus a bland, tasteless sort which resembled a dwarf banana with seeds. Rod ate too much.

Grant called them to order and announced that he was going to ask the travelers to tell what they had experienced. "Let them get it all told—then they won't have to tell it seventy times over. Come on, Rod. Let's see your ugly face."

"Ah, let Roy. He talks better than I do."

"Take turns. When your voice wears out, Roy can take over."

Between them they told it all, interrupting and supplementing each other. The colonists were awed by the beach of a billion bones, still more interested in the ruins of the Dwellers. "Rod and I are still arguing," Roy told them. "I say that it was a civilization. He says that it could be just instinct. He's crazy with the heat; the Dwellers were *people.* Not humans, of course, but people."

"Then where are they now?"

Roy shrugged. "Where are the Selenites, Dora? What became of the Mithrans?"

"Roy is a romanticist," Rod objected. "But you'll be able to form your own opinions when we get there."

"That's right, Rod," Roy agreed.

"That covers everything," Rod went on. "The rest was just waiting while Roy's leg healed. But it brings up the main subject. How quickly can we move? Grant, is there any reason not to start at once? Shouldn't we break camp tomorrow and start trekking? I've been studying it—how to make the move, I mean—and I would say to send out an advance party at daybreak. Roy or I can lead it. We go downstream an easy day's journey, pick a spot, make a kill, and have fire and food ready when the rest arrive. We do it again the next day. I think we can be safe and snug in the caves in five days."

"Dibs on the advance party!"

"Me, too!"

There were other shouts but Rod could not help but realize that the response was not what he had expected. Jimmy did not volunteer and Caroline merely looked thoughtful. The Baxters he could not see; they were in shadow.

He turned to Cowper. "Well, Grant? Do you have a better idea?"

"Rod," Grant said slowly, "your plan is okay ... but you've missed a point."

"Yes?"

"Why do you assume that we are going to move?"

"Huh? Why, that's what we were sent for! To find a better place to live. We found it—you could hold those caves against an army. What's the hitch? Of *course* we move!"

Cowper examined his nails. "Rod, don't get sore. I don't see it and I doubt if other people do. I'm not saying the spot you and Roy found is not good. It may be better than here—the way this place used to be. But we are doing all right here—and we've got a lot of time and effort invested. Why move?"

"Why, I told you. The caves are safe, completely safe. This spot is exposed ... it's *dangerous.*"

"Maybe. Rod, in the whole time we've been here,

154

nobody has been hurt inside camp. We'll put it to a vote, but you can't expect us to abandon our houses and everything we have worked for to avoid a danger that may be imaginary."

"Imaginary? Do you think that a stobor couldn't jump that crummy barricade?" Rod demanded, pointing.

"I think a stobor would get a chest full of pointed stakes if he tried it," Grant answered soberly. "That 'crummy barricade' is a highly efficient defense. Take a better look in the morning."

"Where we were you wouldn't need it. You wouldn't need a night watch. Shucks, you wouldn't need houses. Those caves are better than the best house here!"

"Probably. But, Rod, you haven't seen all we've done, how much we would have to abandon. Let's look it over in the daylight, fellow, and then talk."

"Well . . . no, Grant, there is only one issue: the caves are safe; this place isn't. I call for a vote."

"Easy now. This isn't a town meeting. It's a party in your honor. Let's not spoil it."

"Well . . . I'm sorry. But we're all here; let's vote."

"No." Cowper stood up. "There will be a town meeting on Friday as usual. Goodnight, Rod. Goodnight, Roy. We're awfully glad you're back. Goodnight all."

The party gradually fell apart. Only a few of the younger boys seemed to want to discuss the proposed move. Bob Baxter came over, put a hand on Rod and said, "See you in the morning, Rod. Bless you." He left before Rod could get away from a boy who was talking to him.

Jimmy Throxton stayed, as did Caroline. When he got the chance Rod said, "Jimmy? Where do you stand?"

"Me? You know me, pal. Look, I sent Jackie to bed; she wasn't feeling well. But she told me to tell you that we were back of you a hundred per cent, always."

"Thanks. I feel better."

"See you in the morning? I want to check on Jackie."

"Sure. Sleep tight."

He was finally left with Caroline. "Roddie? Want to inspect the guard with me? You'll do it after tonight, but we figured you could use a night with no worries."

"Wait a minute. Carol . . . you've been acting funny."

"Me? Why, Roddie!"

"Well, maybe not. What do you think of the move? I didn't hear you pitching in."

She looked away. "Roddie," she said, "if it was just me, I'd say start tomorrow. I'd be on the advance party."

"Good! What's got into these people? Grant has them buffaloed but I can't see why." He scratched his head. "I'm tempted to make up my own party—you, me, Jimmy and Jack, the Baxters, Roy, the few who were rarin' to go tonight, and anybody else with sense enough to pound sand."

She sighed. "It won't work, Roddie."

"Huh? Why not?"

"I'll go. Some of the youngsters would go for the fun of it. Jimmy and Jack would go if you insisted . . . but they would beg off if you made it easy for them. The Baxters should not and I doubt if Bob would consent. Carmen isn't really up to such a trip."

13

Unkillable

THE MATTER NEVER CAME TO A VOTE. LONG BEFORE Friday Rod knew how a vote would go—about fifty against him, less than half that for him, with his friends voting with him through loyalty rather than conviction . . . or possibly against him in a showdown.

He made an appeal in private to Cowper. "Grant, you've got me licked. Even Roy is sticking with you now. But you could swing them around."

"I doubt it. What you don't see, Rod, is that we have

156

taken root. You may have found a better place . . . but it's too late to change. After all, you picked this spot."

"Not exactly, it . . . well, it just sort of happened."

"Lots of things in life just sort of happen. You make the best of them."

"That's what I'm *trying* to do! Grant, admitted that the move is hard; we could manage it. Set up way stations with easy jumps, send our biggest huskies back for what we don't want to abandon. Shucks, we could move a person on a litter if we had to—using enough guards."

"If the town votes it, I'll be for it. But I won't try to argue them into it. Look, Rod, you've got this fixed idea that this spot is dangerously exposed. The facts don't support you. On the other hand see what we have. Running water from upstream, waste disposal downstream, quarters comfortable and adequate for the climate. Salt—do you have salt there?"

"We didn't look for it—but it would be easy to bring it from the seashore."

"We've got it closer here. We've got prospects of metal. You haven't seen that ore outcropping yet, have you? We're better equipped every day; our standard of living is going up. We have a colony nobody need be ashamed of and we did it with bare hands; we were never meant to be a colony. Why throw up what we have gained to squat in caves like savages?"

Rod sighed. "Grant, this bank may be flooded in the rainy season—aside from its poor protection now."

"It doesn't look it to me, but if so, we'll see it in time. Right now we are going into the dry season. So let's talk it over a few months from now."

Rod gave up. He refused to resume as "City Manager" nor would Caroline keep it when Rod turned it down. Bill Kennedy was appointed and Rod went to work under Cliff as a hunter, slept in the big shed upstream with the bachelors, and took his turn at night watch. The watch had been reduced to one man, whose duty was simply to tend fires. There was talk of cutting out the night fires, as fuel was no longer easy to find nearby and many seemed satisfied that the thorn barrier was enough.

Rod kept his mouth shut and stayed alert at night.

Game continued to be plentiful but became skittish.

157

Buck did not come out of cover the way they had in rainy weather; it was necessary to search and drive them out. Carnivores seemed to have became scarcer. But the first real indication of peculiar seasonal habits of native fauna came from a very minor carnivore. Mick Mahmud returned to camp with a badly chewed foot; Bob Baxter patched him up and asked about it.

"You wouldn't believe it."

"Try me."

"Well, it was just a dopy joe. I paid no attention to it, of course. Next thing I knew I was flat on my back and trying to shake it loose. He did all that to me before I got a knife into him. Then I had to cut his jaws loose."

"Lucky you didn't bleed to death."

When Rod heard Mick's story, he told Roy. Having had one experience with a dopy joe turned aggressive, Roy took it seriously and had Cliff warn all hands to watch out; they seemed to have turned nasty.

Three days later the migration of animals started.

At first it was just a drifting which appeared aimless except that it was always downstream. Animals had long since ceased to use the watering place above the settlement and buck rarely appeared in the little valley; now they began drifting into it, would find themselves baffled by the thorn fence, and would scramble out. Nor was it confined to antelope types; wingless birds with great "false faces," rodents, rooters, types nameless to humans, all joined the migration. One of the monstrous leonine predators they called stobor approached the barricade in broad daylight, looked at it, lashed his tail, then clawed his way up the bluff and headed downstream again.

Cliff called off his hunting parties; there was no need to hunt when game walked into camp.

Rod found himself more edgy than usual that night as it grew dark. He left his seat near the barbecue pit and went over to Jimmy and Jacqueline. "What's the matter with this place? It's spooky."

Jimmy twitched his shoulders. "I feel it. Maybe it's the funny way the animals are acting. Say, did you hear they killed a joe inside camp?"

"I know what it is," Jacqueline said suddenly. "No 'Grand Opera.' "

"Grand Opera" was Jimmy's name for the creatures with the awful noises, the ones which had turned Rod's first night into a siege of terror. They serenaded every evening for the first hour of darkness. Rod's mind had long since blanked them out, heeded them no more than chorusing cicadas. He had not consciously heard them for weeks.

Now they failed to wail on time; it upset him.

He grinned sheepishly. "That's it, Jack. Funny how you get used to a thing. Do you suppose they are on strike?"

"More likely a death in the family," Jimmy answered. "They'll be back in voice tomorrow."

Rod had trouble getting to sleep. When the night watch gave an alarm he was up and out of bachelors' barracks at once, Colonel Bowie in hand. "What's up?"

Arthur Nielsen had the watch. "It's all right now," he answered nervously. "A big buffalo buck crashed the fence. And this got through." He indicated the carcass of a dopy joe.

"You're bleeding."

"Just a nip."

Others gathered around. Cowper pushed through, sized the situation and said, "Waxie, get that cut attended to. Bill . . . where's Bill? Bill, put somebody else on watch. And let's get that gap fixed as soon as it's light."

It was greying in the east. Margery suggested, "We might as well stay up and have breakfast. I'll get the fire going." She left to borrow flame from a watch fire.

Rod peered through the damaged barricade. A big buck was down on the far side and seemed to have at least six dopy joes clinging to it. Cliff was there and said quietly, "See a way to get at them?"

"Only with a gun."

"We can't waste ammo on that."

"No." Rod thought about it, then went to a pile of bamboo poles, cut for building. He selected a stout one a head shorter than himself, sat down and began to bind Lady Macbeth to it with rawhide, forming a crude pike spear.

159

Caroline came over and squatted down. "What are you doing?"

"Making a joe-killer."

She watched him. "I'm going to make me one," she said suddenly and jumped up.

By daylight the animals were in full flight downstream as if chased by forest fire. As the creek had shrunk with the dry season a miniature beach, from a meter to a couple of meters wide, had been exposed below the bank on which the town had grown. The thorn kraal had been extended to cover the gap, but the excited animals crushed through this weak point and now streamed along the water past the camp.

After a futile effort no attempt was made to turn them back. They were pouring into the valley; they had to go somewhere, and the route between water and bank made a safety valve. It kept them from shoving the barricade aside by sheer mass. The smallest animals came through it anyhow, kept going, paid no attention to humans.

Rod stayed at the barricade, ate breakfast standing up. He had killed six joes since dawn while Caroline's score was still higher. Others were making knives into spears and joining them. The dopy joes were not coming through in great numbers; most of them continued to chase buck along the lower route past camp. Those who did seep through were speared; meeting them with a knife gave away too much advantage.

Cowper and Kennedy, inspecting defenses, stopped by Rod; they looked worried. "Rod," said Grant, "how long is this going to last?"

"How should I know? When we run out of animals. It looks like—get him, Shorty! It looks as if the joes were driving the others, but I don't think they are. I think they've *all* gone crazy."

"But what would cause that?" demanded Kennedy.

"Don't ask me. But I think I know where all those bones on that beach came from. But don't ask why. Why does a chicken cross the road? Why do lemmings do what they do? What makes a plague of locusts? Behind you! *Jump!*"

Kennedy jumped, Rod finished off a joe, and they went on talking. "Better detail somebody to chuck these into the water, Bill, before they stink. Look, Grant, we're okay now, but I know what I would do."

"What? Move to your caves? Rod, you were right—but it's too late."

"No, no! That's spilt milk; forget it. The thing that scares me are these mean little devils. They are no longer dopy; they are fast as can be and nasty . . . and they can slide through the fence. We can handle them now—but how about when it gets dark? We've got to have a solid line of fire inside the fence and along the bank. Fire is one thing they can't go through . . . I hope."

"That'll take a lot of wood." Grant looked through the barricade and frowned.

"You bet it will. But it will get us through the night. See here, give me the ax and six men with spears. I'll lead the party."

Kennedy shook his head. "It's my job."

"No, Bill," Cowper said firmly. "I'll lead it. You stay here and take care of the town."

Before the day was over Cowper took two parties out and Bill and Rod led one each. They tried to pick lulls in the spate of animals but Bill's party was caught on the bluff above, where it had been cutting wood and throwing it down past the cave. They were treed for two hours. The little valley had been cleaned out of dead wood months since; it was necessary to go into the forest above to find wood that would burn.

Cliff Pawley, hunter-in-chief, led a fifth party in the late afternoon, immediately broke the handle of the little ax. They returned with what they could gather with knives. While they were away one of the giant buck they called buffalo stampeded off the bluff, fell into camp, broke its neck. Four dopy joes were clinging to it. They were easy to kill as they would not let go.

Jimmy and Rod were on pike duty at the barricade. Jimmy glanced back at where a couple of girls were disposing of the carcasses. "Rod," he said thoughtfully, "we got it wrong. *Those* are stobor . . . the *real* stobor."

"Huh?"

"The big babies we've been calling that aren't 'stobor.' *These* things are what the Deacon warned us against."

"Well . . . I don't care what you call them as long as they're dead. On your toes, boy; here they come again."

Cowper ordered fires laid just before dark and was studying how to arrange one stretch so as not to endanger the flume when the matter was settled; the structure quivered and water ceased to flow. Upstream something had crashed into it and broken the flimsy pipe line.

The town had long since abandoned waterskins. Now they were caught with only a few litres in a pot used by the cooks, but it was a hardship rather than a danger; the urgent need was to get a ring of fire around them. There had already been half a dozen casualties—no deaths but bites and slashings, almost all from the little carnivores contemptuously known as dopy joes. The community's pool of antiseptics, depleted by months of use and utterly irreplaceable, had sunk so low that Rob Baxter used it only on major wounds.

When fuel had been stretched ready to burn in a long arc inside the barricade and down the bank to where it curved back under the cave, the results of a hard day's work looked small; the stockpile was not much greater than the amount already spread out. Bill Kennedy looked at it. "It won't last the night, Grant."

"It's *got* to, Bill. Light it."

"If we pulled back from the fence and the bank, then cut over to the bluff— What do you think?"

Cowper tried to figure what might be saved by the change. "It's not much shorter. Uh, don't light the downstream end unless they start curving back in on us. But let's move; it's getting dark." He hurried to the cooking fire, got a brand and started setting the chain of fire. Kennedy helped and soon the townsite was surrounded on the exposed sides by blaze. Cowper chucked his torch into the fire and said, "Bill, better split the men into two watches and get the women up into the cave—they can crowd in somehow."

"You'll have trouble getting thirty-odd women in there, Grant."

"They can sit up all night. But send them up. Yes, and the wounded men, too."

"Can do." Kennedy started passing the word. Caroline came storming up, spear in hand.

162

"Grant, what's this nonsense about the girls having to go up to the cave? If you think you're going to cut me out of the fun you had better think again!"

Cowper looked at her wearily. "Carol, I haven't time to monkey. Shut your face and do as you are told."

Caroline opened her mouth, closed it, and did as she was told. Bob Baxter claimed Cowper's attention; Rod noticed that he looked very upset. "Grant? You ordered all the women up to the cave?"

"Yes."

"I'm sorry but Carmen can't."

"You'll have to carry her. She is the one I had most on my mind when I decided on the move."

"But—" Baxter stopped and urged Grant away from the others. He spoke insistently but quietly. Grant shook his head.

"It's not safe, Grant," Baxter went on, raising his voice. "I don't dare risk it. The interval is nineteen minutes now."

"Well . . . all right. Leave a couple of women with her. Use Caroline, will you? That'll keep her out of my hair."

"Okay." Baxter hurried away.

Kennedy took the first watch with a dozen men spread out along the fire line; Rod was on the second watch commanded by Cliff Pawley. He went to the Baxter house to find out how Carmen was doing, was told to beat it by Agnes. He then went to the bachelors' shed and tried to sleep.

He was awakened by yells, in time to see one of the leonine monsters at least five meters long go bounding through the camp and disappear downstream. It had jumped the barrier, the stakes behind it, and the fire behind that, all in one leap.

Rod called out, "Anybody hurt?"

Shorty Dumont answered. "No. It didn't even stop to wave." Shorty was bleeding from a slash in his left calf; he seemed unaware of it. Rod crawled back inside, tried again to sleep.

He was awakened again by the building shaking. He hurried out. "What's up?"

"That you, Rod? I didn't know anybody was inside. Give me a hand; we're going to burn it." The voice was

Baxter's; he was prying at a corner post and cutting rawhide strips that held it.

Rod put his spear where it would not be stepped on, resheathed Colonel Bowie, and started to help. The building was bamboo and leaves, with a mud-and-thatch roof; most of it would burn. "How's Carmen?"

"Okay. Normal progress. I can do more good here. Besides they don't *want* me." Baxter brought the corner of the shed down with a crash, gathered a double armful of wreckage and hurried away. Rod picked up a load and followed him.

The reserve wood pile was gone; somebody was tearing the roof off the "city hall" and banging pieces on the ground to shake clay loose. The walls were sunbaked bricks, but the roof would burn. Rod came closer, saw that it was Cowper who was destroying this symbol of the sovereign community. He worked with the fury of anger. "Let me do that, Grant. Have you had any rest?"

"Huh? No."

"Better get some. It's going to be a long night. What time is it?"

"I don't know. Midnight, maybe." Fire blazed up and Cowper faced it, wiping his face with his hand. "Rod, take charge of the second watch and relieve Bill. Cliff got clawed and I sent him up."

"Okay. Burn everything that will burn—right?"

"Everything but the roof of the Baxter house. But don't use it up too fast; it's got to last till morning."

"Got it." Rod hurried to the fire line, found Kennedy. "Okay, Bill, I'll take over—Grant's orders. Get some sleep. Anything getting through?"

"Not much. And not far." Kennedy's spear was dark with blood in the firelight. "I'm not going to sleep, Rod. Find yourself a spot and help out."

Rod shook his head. "You're groggy. Beat it. Grant's orders."

"No!"

"Well . . . look, take your gang and tear down the old maids' shack. That'll give you a change, at least."

"Uh—all right." Kennedy left, almost staggering. There was a lull in the onrush of animals; Rod could see none beyond the barricade. It gave him time to sort out his crew, send away those who had been on duty since sunset, send for stragglers. He delegated Doug Sanders and Mick Mahmud as firetenders, passed the word that no one else was to put fuel on the fires.

He returned from his inspection to find Bob Baxter, spear in hand, holding his place at the center of the line. Rod put a hand on his shoulder. "The medical officer doesn't need to fight. We aren't that bad off."

Baxter shrugged. "I've got my kit, what there is left of it. This is where I use it."

"Haven't you enough worries?"

Baxter grinned wanly. "Better than walking the floor. Rod, they're stirring again. Hadn't we better build up the fires?"

"Mmm . . . not if we're going to make it last. I don't think they can come through that."

Baxter did not answer, as a joe came through at that instant. It ploughed through the smouldering fire and Baxter speared it. Rod cupped his hands and shouted, "Build up the fires! But go *easy*."

"Behind you, Rod!"

Rod jumped and whirled, got the little devil. "Where did that one come from? I didn't see it."

Before Bob could answer Caroline came running out of darkness. "Bob! Bob Baxter! I've got to find Bob Baxter!"

"Over here!" Rod called.

Baxter was hardly able to speak. "Is she—is she?" His face screwed up in anguish.

"No, no!" yelled Caroine. "She's all right, she's fine. *It's a girl!*"

Baxter quietly fainted, his spear falling to the ground. Caroline grabbed him and kept him from falling into the fire. He opened his eyes and said, "Sorry. You scared me. You're sure Carmen is all right?"

"Right as rain. The baby, too. About three kilos. Here, give me that sticker—Carmen wants you."

Baxter stumbled away and Caroline took his place. She grinned at Rod. "I feel *swell!* How's business, Roddie? Brisk? I feel like getting me eight or nine of these vermin."

Cowper came up a few minutes later. Caroline called out, "Grant, did you hear the good news?"

"Yes. I just came from there." He ignored Caroline's presence at the guard line but said to Rod, "We're making a stretcher out of pieces of the flume and they're going to haul Carmen up. Then they'll throw the stretcher down and you can burn it."

"Good."

"Agnes is taking the baby up. Rod, what's the very most we can crowd into the cave?"

"Gee!" Rod glanced up at the shelf. "They must be spilling off the edge now."

"I'm afraid so. But we've just *got* to pack them in. I want to send up all married men and the youngest boys. The bachelors will hold on here."

"I'm a bachelor!" Caroline interrupted.

Cowper ignored her. "As soon as Carmen is safe we'll do it—we can't keep fires going much longer." He turned away, headed up to the cave.

Caroline whistled softly. "Roddie, we're going to have fun."

"Not my idea of fun. Hold the fort, Carol. I've got to line things up." He moved down the line, telling each one to go or to stay.

Jimmy scowled at him. "I won't go, not as long as anybody stays. I couldn't look Jackie in the face."

"You'll button your lip and do as Grant says—or I'll give you a mouthful of teeth. Hear me?"

"I hear you. I don't like it."

"You don't have to like it, just do it. Seen Jackie? How is she?"

"I snuck up a while ago. She's all right, just queasy. But the news about Carmen makes her feel so good she doesn't care."

Rod used no age limit to determine who was expendable. With the elimination of married men, wounded, and all women he had little choice; he simply told those whom he considered too young or not too skilled that they were to leave when word was passed. It left him with half a dozen, plus himself, Cowper, and—possibly —Caroline. Trying to persuade Caroline was a task he had postponed.

He returned and found Cowper. "Carmen's gone up," Cowper told him. "You can send the others up now."

"Then we can burn the roof of the Baxter house."

"I tore it down while they were hoisting her." Cowper looked around. "Carol! Get on up."

She set her feet. "I won't!"

Rod said softly, "Carol, you heard him. Go up— *right now!*"

She scowled, stuck out her lip, then said, "All right for *you*, Roddie Walker!"—turned and fled up the path.

Rod cupped his hands and shouted, "All right, everybody! All hands up but those I told to stay. Hurry!"

About half of those leaving had started up when Agnes called down, "Hey! Take it slow! Somebody will get pushed over the edge if you don't quit shoving."

The queue stopped. Jimmy called out, "Everybody exhale. That'll do it."

Somebody called back, "Throw Jimmy off . . . *that* will do it." The line moved again, slowly. In ten minutes they accomplished the sardine packing problem of fitting nearly seventy people into a space comfortable for not more than a dozen. It could not even be standing room since a man could stand erect only on the outer shelf. The girls were shoved inside, sitting or squatting, jammed so that they hardly had air to breathe. The men farthest out could stand but were in danger of stepping off the edge in the dark, or of being elbowed off.

Grant said, "Watch things, Rod, while I have a look." He disappeared up the path, came back in a few minutes. "Crowded as the bottom of a sack," he said. "Here's the plan. They can scrunch back farther if they have to. It will be uncomfortable for the wounded and Carmen may have to sit up—she's lying down—but it can be done. When the fires die out, we'll shoehorn the rest in. With spears poking out under the overhang at the top of the path we ought to be able to hold out until daylight. Check me?"

"Sounds as good as can be managed."

"All right. When the time comes, you go up next to last, I go up last."

"Unh . . . I'll match you."

Cowper answered with surprising vulgarity and added, "I'm boss; I go last. We'll make the rounds and pile anything left on the fires, then gather them all here. You take the bank, I take the fence."

It did not take long to put the remnants on the fires,

then they gathered around the path and waited—Roy, Kenny, Doug, Dick, Charlie, Howard, and Rod and Grant. Another wave of senseless migration was rolling but the fires held it, bypassed it around by the water.

Rod grew stiff and shifted his spear to his left hand. The dying fires were only glowing coals in spots. He looked for signs of daylight in the east. Howard Goldstein said, "One broke through at the far end."

"Hold it, Goldie," Cowper said. "We won't bother it unless it comes here." Rod shifted his spear back to his right hand.

The wall of fire was now broken in many places. Not only could joes get through, but worse, it was hard to see them, so little light did the embers give off. Cowper turned to Rod and said, "All right, everybody up. You tally them." Then he shouted, "Bill! Agnes! Make room, I'm sending them up."

Rod threw a glance at the fence, then turned. "Okay, Kenny first. Doug next, don't crowd. Goldie and then Dick. Who's left? Roy—" He turned, uneasily aware that something had changed.

Grant was no longer behind him. Rod spotted him bending over a dying fire. "Hey, Grant!"

"Be right with you." Cowper selected a stick from the embers, waved it into flame. He hopped over the coals, picked his way through sharpened stakes, reached the thornbush barrier, shoved his torch into it. The dry branches flared up. He moved slowly away, picking his way through the stake trap.

"I'll help you!" Rod shouted. "I'll fire the other end."

Cowper turned and light from the burning thorn showed his stern, bearded face. "Stay back. Get the others up. That's an order!"

The movement upward had stopped. Rod snarled, "Get on up, you lunkheads! Move!" He jabbed with the butt of his spear, then turned around.

Cowper had set the fire in a new place. He straightened up, about to move farther down, suddenly turned and jumped over the dying line of fire. He stopped and jabbed at something in the darkness . . . then screamed.

"Grant!" Rod jumped down, ran toward him. But Grant was down before he reached him, down with a joe worrying each leg and more coming. Rod thrust at one, jerked his spear out, and jabbed at the other, trying not to stab Grant. He felt one grab his leg and wondered that it did not hurt.

Then it did hurt, terribly, and he realized that he was down and his spear was not in his hand. But his hand found his knife without asking; Colonel Bowie finished off the beast clamped to his ankle.

Everything seemed geared to nightmare slowness. Other figures were thrusting leisurely at shapes that hardly crawled. The thornbush, flaming high, gave him light to see and stab a dopy joe creeping toward him. He got it, rolled over and tried to get up.

He woke with daylight in his eyes, tried to move and discovered that his left leg hurt. He looked down and saw a compress of leaves wrapped with a neat hide bandage. He was in the cave and there were others lying parallel to him. He got to one elbow. "Say, what—"

"Sssh!" Sue Kennedy crawled over and knelt by him. "The baby is asleep."

"Oh . . ."

"I'm on nurse duty. Want anything?"

"I guess not. Uh, what did they name her?"

"Hope. Hope Roberta Baxter. A pretty name. I'll tell Caroline you are awake." She turned away.

Caroline came in, squatted and looked scornfully at his ankle. "That'll teach you to have a party and not invite *me*."

"I guess so. Carol, what's the situation?"

"Six on the sick list. About twice that many walking wounded. Those not hurt are gathering wood and cutting thorn. We fixed the ax."

"Yes, but . . . we're not having to fight them off?"

"Didn't Sue tell you? A few buck walking around as if they were dazed. That's all."

"They may start again."

"If they do, we'll be ready."

"Good." He tried to raise up. "Where's Grant? How bad was he hurt?"

She shook her head. "Grant didn't make it, Roddie."

"Huh?"

"Bob took off both legs at the knee and would have

taken off one arm, but he died while he was operating." She made a very final gesture. "In the creek."

Rod started to speak, turned his head and buried his face. Caroline put a hand on him. "Don't take it hard, Roddie. Bob shouldn't have tried to save him. Grant is better off."

Rod decided that Carol was right—no frozen limb banks on *this* planet. But it did not make him feel better. "We didn't appreciate him," he muttered.

"Stow it!" Caroline whispered fiercely. "He was a fool."

"Huh? Carol, I'm ashamed of you."

He was surprised to see tears rolling down her cheeks. "You *know* he was a fool, Roddie Walker. Most of us knew . . . but we loved him anyhow. I would 'uv *married* him, but he never asked me." She wiped at tears. "Have you seen the baby?"

"No."

Her face lit up. "I'll fetch her. She's beautiful."

"Sue said she was asleep."

"Well . . . all right. But what I came up for is this: what do you want us to do?"

"Huh?" He tried to think. Grant was dead. "Bill was his deputy. Is Bill laid up?"

"Didn't Sue tell you?"

"Tell me what?"

"You're the mayor. We elected you this morning. Bill and Roy and I are just trying to hold things together."

Rod felt dizzy. Caroline's face kept drawing back, then swooping in; he wondered if he were going to faint.

"—plenty of wood," she was saying, "and we'll have the kraal built by sundown. We don't need meat; Margery is butchering that big fellow that fell off the bluff and busted his neck. We can't trek out until you and Carmen and the others can walk, so we're trying to get the place back into shape temporarily. Is there anything you want us to do now?"

He considered it. "No. Not now."

"Okay. You're supposed to rest." She backed out, stood up. "I'll look in later." Rod eased his leg and turned over. After a while he quieted and went to sleep.

Sue brought broth in a bowl, held his head while he

170

drank, then fetched Hope Baxter and held her for him to see. Rod said the usual inanities, wondering if all new babies looked that way.

Then he thought for a long time.

Caroline showed up with Roy. "How's it going, Chief?" Roy said.

"Ready to bite a rattlesnake."

"That's a nasty foot, but it ought to heal. We boiled the leaves and Bob used sulfa."

"Feels all right. I don't seem feverish."

"Jimmy always said you were too mean to die," added Caroline. "Want anything, Roddie? Or to tell us anything?"

"Yes."

"What?"

"Get me out of here. Help me down the path."

Roy said hastily, "Hey, you can't do that. You're not in shape."

"Can't I? Either help, or get out of my way. And get everybody together. We're going to have a town meeting."

They looked at each other and walked out on him. He had made it to the squeeze at the top when Baxter showed up. "Now, Rod! Get back and lie down."

"Out of my way."

"Listen, boy, I don't like to get rough with a sick man. But I will if you make me."

"Bob . . . how bad is my ankle?"

"It's going to be all right . . . *if* you behave. If you don't well, have you ever seen gangrene? When it turns black and has that sweetish odor?"

"Quit trying to scare me. Is there any reason not to put a line under my arms and lower me?"

"Well . . ."

They used two lines and a third to keep his injured leg free, with Baxter supervising. They caught him at the bottom and carried him to the cooking space, laid him down. "Thanks," he grunted. "Everybody here who can get here?"

"I think so, Roddie. Shall I count?"

"Never mind. I understand you folks elected me cap—I mean 'mayor'—this morning?"

"That's right," agreed Kennedy.

171

"Uh, who else was up? How many votes did I get?"

"Huh? It was unanimous."

Rod sighed. "Thanks. I'm not sure I would have held still for it if I'd been here. I gathered something else. Do I understand that you expect me to take you down to the caves Roy and I found? Caroline said something . . ."

Roy looked surprised. "We didn't vote it, Rod, but that was the idea. After last night everybody knows we can't stay here."

Rod nodded. "I see. Are you all where I can see you? I've got something to say. I hear you adopted a constitution and things while Roy and I were away. I've never read them, so I don't know whether this is legal or not. But if I'm stuck with the job, I expect to run things. If somebody doesn't like what I do and we're both stubborn enough for a showdown, then you will vote. You back me up, or you turn me down and elect somebody else. Will that work? How about it, Goldie? You were on the law committee, weren't you?"

Howard Goldstein frowned. "You don't express it very well, Rod."

"Probably not. Well?"

"But what you have described is the parliamentary vote-of-confidence. That's the backbone of our constitution. We did it that way to keep it simple and still democratic. It was Grant's notion."

"I'm glad," Rod said soberly. "I'd hate to think that I had torn up Grant's laws after he worked so hard on them. I'll study them, I promise, first chance I get. But about moving to the caves—we'll have a vote of confidence right now."

Goldstein smiled. "I can tell you how it will come out. We're convinced."

Rod slapped the ground. "You don't understand! If you want to move, move . . . but get somebody else to lead you. Roy can do it. Or Cliff, or Bill. But if you leave it to me, no dirty little beasts, all teeth and no brains, are going to drive us out. We're *men* . . . and men don't *have* to be driven out, not by the likes of those. Grant paid for this land—and I say stay here and keep it for him!"

14

Civilization

The Honorable Roderick L. Walker, Mayor of
Cowpertown, Chief of State of the sovereign planet
GO-73901-II (Lima Catalog), Commander-in-Chief of
the Armed Forces, Chief Justice, and Defender of Freedoms, was taking his ease in front of the Mayor's
Palace. He was also scratching and wondering if he
should ask somebody to cut his hair again—he suspected lice . . . only this planet did not have lice.

His Chief of Government, Miss Caroline Beatrice
Mshiyeni, squatted in front of him. "Roddie, I've told
them and told them and told them . . . and it does no
good. That family makes more filth than everybody else
put together. You should have seen it this morning.
Garbage in front of their door . . . flies!"

"I saw it."

"Well, what do I do? If you would let me rough him
up a little. But you're too soft."

"I guess I am." Rod looked thoughtfully at a slab of
slate erected in the village square. It read:

To the Memory of
ULYSSES GRANT COWPER,
First Mayor
—who died for his city

The carving was not good; Rod had done it.

"Grant told me once," he added, "that government
was the art of getting along with people you don't like."

"Well, I sure don't like Bruce and Theo!"

"Neither do I. But Grant would have figured out a
way to keep them in line without getting rough."

173

"You figure it out, I can't. Roddie, you should never have let Bruce come back. That was bad enough. But when he married that little . . . well!"

"They were made for each other," Rod answered. "Nobody else would have married either of them."

"It's no joke. It's almost—*Hope!* Quit teasing Grantie!" She bounced up.

Miss Hope Roberta Baxter, sixteen months, and Master Grant Roderick Throxton, thirteen months, stopped what they were doing, which was, respectively, slapping and crying. Both were naked and very dirty. It was "clean" dirt; each child had been bathed by Caroline an hour earlier, and both were fat and healthy.

Hope turned up a beaming face. " '*Ood* babee!" she asserted.

"I *saw* you." Caroline upended her, gave her a spat that would not squash a fly, then picked up Grant Throxton.

"Give her to me," Rod said.

"You're welcome to her," Caroline said. She sat down with the boy in her lap and rocked him. "Poor baby! Show Auntie Carol where it hurts."

"You shouldn't talk like that. You'll make a sissy of him."

"Look who's talking! Wishy-Washy Walker."

Hope threw her arms around Rod, part way, and cooed, "Woddie!" adding a muddy kiss. He returned it. He considered her deplorably spoiled; nevertheless he contributed more than his share of spoiling.

"Sure," agreed Carol. "Everybody loves Uncle Roddie. He hands out the medals and Aunt Carol does the dirty work."

"Carol, I've been thinking."

"Warm day. Don't strain any delicate parts."

"About Bruce and Theo. I'll talk to them."

"Talk!"

"The only real punishment is one we never use— and I hope we never have to. Kicking people out, I mean. The McGowans do as they please because they don't think we would. But I would love to give them the old heave-ho . . . and if it comes to it, I'll make an issue of it before the town—either kick them out or I quit."

"They'd back you. Why, I bet he hasn't taken a bath this week!"

"I don't care whether they back me or not. I've ridden out seven confidence votes; someday I'll be lucky and retire. But the problem is to convince Bruce that I am willing to face the issue, for then I won't have to. Nobody is going to chance being turned out in the woods, not when they've got it soft here. But he's got to be convinced."

"Uh, maybe if he thought you were carrying a grudge about that slice in the ribs he gave you?"

"And maybe I am. But I can't let it be personal, Carol; I'm too stinkin' proud."

"Uh . . . Turn it around. Convince him that the town is chompin' at the bit—which isn't far wrong— and you are trying to restrain them."

"Um, that's closer. Yes, I think Grant would have gone for that. I'll think it over."

"Do that." She stood up. "I'm going to give these children another bath. I declare I don't know where they find so much dirt."

She swung away with a child on each hip, heading for the shower sheds. Rod watched her lazily. She was wearing a leather bandeau and a Maori grass skirt, long leaves scraped in a pattern, curled, and dried. It was a style much favored and Caroline wore it around town, although when she treated herself to a day's hunting she wore a leather breechclout such as the men wore.

The same leaf fibre could be retted and crushed, combed and spun, but the cloth as yet possessed by the colony was not even enough for baby clothes. Bill Kennedy had whittled a loom for Sue and it worked, but neither well nor fast and the width of cloth was under a half meter. Still, Rod mused, it was progress, it was civilization. They had come a long way.

The town was stobor-tight now. An adobe wall too high and sheer for any but the giant lions covered the upstream side and the bank, and any lion silly enough to jump it landed on a bed of stakes too wide now for even their mighty leaps—the awning under which Rod lolled was the hide of one that had made that mistake. The wall was pierced by stobor traps, narrow tunnels

175

just big enough for the vicious little beasts and which gave into deep pits, where they could chew on each other like Kilkenny cats—which they did.

It might have been easier to divert them around the town, but Rod wanted to kill them; he would not be content until their planet was rid of those vermin.

In the meantime the town was safe. Stobor continued to deserve the nickname "dopy joe" except during the dry season and then they did not become dangerous until the annual berserk migration—the last of which had passed without loss of blood; the colony's defenses worked, now that they understood what to defend against. Rod had required mothers and children to sit out the stampede in the cave; the rest sat up two nights and stayed on guard . . . but no blade was wet.

Rod thought sleepily that the next thing they needed was paper; Grant had been right . . . even a village was hard to run without writing paper. Besides, they must avoid losing the habit of writing. He wanted to follow up Grant's notion of recording every bit of knowledge the gang possessed. Take logarithms—logarithms might not be used for generations, but when it came time to log a couple of rhythms, then . . . he went to sleep.

"You busy, Chief?"

Rod looked up at Arthur Nielsen. "Just sleeping . . . a practice I heartily recommend on a warm Sabbath afternoon. What's up, Art? Are Shorty and Doug pushing the bellows alone?"

"No. Confounded plug came out and we lost our fire. The furnace is ruined." Nielsen sat down wearily. He was hot, very red in the face, and looked discouraged. He had a bad burn on a forearm but did not seem to know it. "Rod, what are we doing wrong? Riddle me that."

"Talk to one of the brains. If you didn't know more about it than I do, we'd swap jobs."

"I wasn't really asking. I know two things that are wrong. We can't build a big enough installation and we don't have coal. Rod, we've *got* to have coal; for cast iron or steel we need coal. Charcoal won't do for anything but spongy wrought iron."

"What do you expect to accomplish overnight, Art? Miracles? You are years ahead of what anybody could

176

ask. You've turned out metal, whether it's wrought iron or uranium. Since you made that spit for the barbecue pit, Margery thinks you are a genius."

"Yes, yes, we've made iron—but it ought to be lots better and more of it. This ore is wonderful . . . the real Lake Superior hematite. Nobody's seen such ore in commercial quantity on Terra in centuries. You ought to be able to breathe on it and make steel. And I could, too, if I had coal. We've got clay, we've got limestone, we've got this lovely ore—but I *can't* get a hot enough fire."

Rod was not fretted; the colony was getting metal as fast as needed. But Waxie was upset. "Want to knock off and search for coal?"

"Uh . . . no, I don't. I want to rebuild that furnace." Nielsen gave a bitter description of the furnace's origin, habits, and destination.

"Who knows most about geology?"

"Uh, I suppose I do."

"Who knows next most?"

"Why, Doug I guess."

"Let's send him out with a couple of boys to find coal. You can have Mick in his place on the bellows— no, wait a minute. How about Bruce?"

"Bruce? *He* won't work."

"Work him. If you work him so hard he runs away and forgets to come back, we won't miss him. Take him, Art, as a favor to me."

"Well . . . okay, if you say so."

"Good. You get one bonus out of losing your batch. You won't miss the dance tonight. Art, you shouldn't start a melt so late in the week; you need your day of rest . . . and so do Shorty and Doug."

"I know. But when it's ready to go I want to fire it off. Working the way we do is discouraging; before you can make anything you have to make the thing that makes it—and usually you have to make something else to make that. Futile!"

"You don't know what 'futile' means. Ask our 'Department of Agriculture.' Did you take a look at the farm before you came over the wall?"

"Well, we walked through it."

177

"Better not let Cliff catch you, or he'll scalp you. I might hold you for him."

"Humph! A lot of silly grass! Thousands of hectares around just like it."

"That's right. Some grass and a few rows of weeds. The pity is that Cliff will never live to see it anything else. Nor little Cliff. Nevertheless our great grandchildren will eat white bread, Art. But you yourself will live to build precision machinery—you know it can be done, which, as Bob Baxter says, is two-thirds of the battle. Cliff *can't* live long enough to eat a slice of light, tasty bread. It doesn't stop him."

"You should have been a preacher, Rod." Art stood up and sniffed himself. "I'd better get a bath, or the girls won't dance with me."

"I was just quoting. You've heard it before. Save me some soap."

Caroline hit two bars of *Arkansas Traveler,* Jimmy slapped his drum, and Roy called, "Square 'em up, folks!" He waited, then started in high, nasal tones:

"Honor y'r *part*ners!

"Honor y'r *cor*ners!

"Now *all* jump *up* and *when* y' come *down*—"

Rod was not dancing; the alternate set would be his turn. The colony formed eight squares, too many for a caller, a mouth organ, and a primitive drum all unassisted by amplifying equipment. So half of them babysat and gossiped while the other half danced. The caller and the orchestra were relieved at each intermission to dance the other sets.

Most of them had not known how to square-dance. Agnes Pulvermacher had put it over almost single-handed, in the face of kidding and resistance—training callers, training dancers, humming tunes to Caroline, cajoling Jimmy to carve and shrink a jungle drum. Now she had nine out of ten dancing.

Rod had not appreciated it at first (he was not familiar with the history of the Mormon pioneers) and had regarded it as a nuisance which interfered with work. Then he saw the colony, which had experienced a bad letdown after the loss in one night of all they had built,

178

an apathy he had not been able to lift—he saw this same colony begin to smile and joke and work hard simply from being exposed to music and dancing.

He decided to encourage it. He had trouble keeping time and could not carry a tune, but the bug caught him, too; he danced not well but with great enthusiasm.

The village eventually limited dances to Sabbath nights, weddings, and holidays—and made them "formal" . . . which meant that women wore grass skirts. Leather shorts, breechclouts, and slacks (those not long since cut up for rags) were not acceptable. Sue talked about making a real square dance dress as soon as she got far enough ahead in her weaving, and a cowboy shirt for her husband . . . but the needs of the colony made this a distant dream.

Music stopped, principals changed, Caroline tossed her mouth organ to Shorty, and came over, "Come on, Roddie, let's kick some dust."

"I asked Sue," he said hastily and truthfully. He was careful not to ask the same girl twice, never to pay marked attention to any female; he had promised himself long ago that the day he decided to marry should be the day he resigned and he was not finding it hard to stay married to his job. He liked to dance with Caroline; she was a popular partner—except for a tendency to swing her partner instead of letting him swing her—but he was careful not to spend much social time with her because she was his right hand, his alter ego.

Rod went over and offered his arm to Sue. He did not think about it; the stylized amenities of civilization were returning and the formal politenesses of the dance made them seem natural. He led her out and assisted in making a botch of *Texas Star*.

Later, tired, happy, and convinced that the others in his square had made the mistakes and he had straightened them out, Rod returned Sue to Bill, bowed and thanked him, and went back to the place that was always left for him. Margery and her assistants were passing out little brown somethings on wooden skewers. He accepted one. "Smells good, Marge. What are they?"

"Mock Nile birds. Smoked baby-buck bacon wrapped around hamburger. Salt and native sage, pan broiled. You'd better like it; it took us *hours*."

"Mmmm! I do! How about another?"

"Wait and see. Greedy."

"But I need more. I work hardest. I have to keep up my strength."

"That was *work* I saw you doing this afternoon?" She handed him another.

"I was planning. The old brain was buzzing away."

"I heard the buzzing. Pretty loud, when you lie on your back."

He snagged a third as she turned away, looked up to catch Jacqueline smiling; he winked and grinned.

"Happy, Rod?"

"Yes indeed. How about you, Jackie?"

"I've never been happier," she said seriously.

Her husband put an arm around her. "See what the love of a good man can do, Rod?" Jimmy said. "When I found this poor child she was beaten, bedraggled, doing your cooking and afraid to admit her name. Now look at her!—fat and sassy."

"I'm not *that* fat!"

"Pleasingly plump."

Rod glanced up at the cave. "Jackie, remember the night I showed up?"

"I'm not likely to forget."

"And the silly notion I had that this was Africa? Tell me—if you had it to do over, would you rather I had been right?"

"I never thought about it. I knew it was not."

"Yes, but 'if'? You would have been home long ago."

Her hand took her husband's. "I would not have met James."

"Oh, yes, you would. You had already met me. You could not have avoided it—my best friend."

"Possibly. But I would not change it. I have no yearning to go 'home,' Rod. *This* is home."

"Me neither," asserted Jimmy. "You know what? This colony gets a little bigger—and it's getting bigger fast—Goldie and I are going to open a law office. We won't have any competition and can pick our clients. He'll handle the criminal end, I'll specialize in divorce, and we'll collaborate on corporate skulduggery. We'll make *millions*. I'll drive a big limousine drawn by eight

180

spanking buck, smoking a big cigar and sneering at the peasants." He called out, "Right, Goldie?"

"Precisely, colleague. I'm making us a shingle: 'Goldstein & Throxton—Get bailed, not jailed!' "

"Keerect. But make that: 'Throxton & Goldstein.' "

"I'm senior. I've got two more years of law."

"A quibble. Rod, are you going to let this Teller U. character insult an old Patrick Henry man?"

"Probably. Jimmy, I don't see how you are going to work this. I don't think we have a divorce law. Let's ask Caroline."

"A trifle. You perform the marriages, Rod; I'll take care of the divorces."

"Ask Caroline what?" asked Caroline.

"Do we have a divorce law?"

"Huh? We don't even have a getting-married law."

"Unnecessary," explained Goldstein. "Indigenous in the culture. Besides, we ran out of paper."

"Correct, Counselor," agreed Jimmy.

"Why ask?" Caroline demanded. "Nobody is thinking about divorce or I would know before they would."

"We weren't talking about that," Rod explained. "Jackie said that she had no wish to go back to Terra and Jimmy was elaborating. Uselessly, as usual."

Caroline stared. "Why would anybody want to go back?"

"Sure," agreed Jimmy. "This is the place. No income tax. No traffic, no crowds, no commercials, no telephones. Seriously, Rod, every one here was aiming for the Outlands or we wouldn't have been taking a survival test. So what difference does it make? Except that we've got everything sooner." He squeezed his wife's hand. "I was fooling about that big cigar; I'm rich now, boy, rich!"

Agnes and Curt had drawn into the circle, listening. Agnes nodded and said, "For once you aren't joking, Jimmy. The first months we were here I cried myself to sleep every night, wondering if they would ever find us. Now I know they never will—and I don't care! I wouldn't go back if I could; the only thing I miss is lipstick."

Her husband's laugh boomed out. "There you have the truth, Rod. The fleshpots of Egypt . . . put a cosmetics counter across this creek and every woman here will walk on water."

"That's not fair, Curt! Anyhow, you promised to make lipstick."

"Give me time."

Bob Baxter came up and sat down by Rod. "Missed you at the meeting this morning, Rod."

"Tied up. I'll make it next week."

"Good." Bob, being of a sect which did not require ordination, had made himself chaplain as well as medical officer simply by starting to hold meetings. His undogmatic ways were such that Christian, Jew, Monist, or Moslem felt at ease; his meetings were well attended.

"Bob, would *you* go back?"

"Go where, Caroline?"

"Back to Terra."

"Yes."

Jimmy looked horrified. "Boil me for breakfast! *Why?*"

"Oh, I'd want to come back! But I need to graduate from medical school." He smiled shyly. "I may be the best surgeon in the neighborhood, but that isn't saying much."

"Well . . ." admitted Jimmy, "I see your point. But you already suit us. Eh, Jackie?"

"Yes, Jimmy."

"It's my only regret," Bob went on. "I've lost ones I should have saved. But it's a hypothetical question. 'Here we rest.' "

The question spread. Jimmy's attitude was overwhelmingly popular, even though Bob's motives were respected. Rod said goodnight; he heard them still batting it around after he had gone to bed; it caused him to discuss it with himself.

He had decided long ago that they would never be in touch with Earth; he had not thought of it for—how long?—over a year. At first it had been mental hygiene, protection of his morale. Later it was logic: a delay in recall of a week might be a power failure, a few weeks could be a technical difficulty—but months on months was cosmic disaster; each day added a cipher to the infinitesimal probability that they would ever be in touch again.

He was now able to ask himself: was this what he wanted?

Jackie was right; this was home. Then he admitted that he *liked* being big frog in a small puddle, he loved his job. He was not meant to be a scientist, nor a scholar, he had never wanted to be a businessman—but what he was doing suited him . . . and he seemed to do it well enough to get by.

" 'Here we rest!' "

He went to sleep in a warm glow.

Cliff wanted help with the experimental crops. Rod did not take it too seriously; Cliff always wanted something; given his head he would have everybody working dawn to dark on his farm. But it was well to find out what he wanted—Rod did not underrate the importance of domesticating plants; that was basic for all colonies and triply so for them. It was simply that he did not know much about it.

Cliff stuck his head into the mayor's hut. "Ready?"

"Sure." Rod got his spear. It was no longer improvised but bore a point patiently sharpened from steel salvaged from Braun's Thunderbolt. Rod had tried wrought iron but could not get it to hold an edge. "Let's pick up a couple of boys and get a few stobor."

"Okay."

Rod looked around. Jimmy was at his potter's wheel, kicking the treadle and shaping clay with his thumb. "Jim! Quit that and grab your pike. We're going to have some fun."

Throxton wiped at sweat. "You've talked me into it."

They added Kenny and Mick, then Cliff led them upstream. "I want you to look at the animals."

"All right," agreed Rod. "Cliff, I had been meaning to speak to you. If you are going to raise those brutes inside the wall, you'll have to be careful about their droppings. Carol has been muttering."

"Rod, I can't do everything! And you can't put them outside, not if you expect them to live."

"Sure, sure! Well, we'll get you more help, that's the only— Just a second!"

They were about to pass the last hut; Bruce Mc-Gowan was stretched in front of it, apparently asleep.

Rod did not speak at once; he was fighting down rage. He wrestled with himself, aware that the next moment could change his future, damage the entire colony. But his rational self was struggling in a torrent of anger, bitter and self-righteous. He wanted to do away with this parasite, destroy it. He took a deep breath and tried to keep his mouth from trembling.

"Bruce!" he called softly.

McGowan opened his eyes. "Huh?"

"Isn't Art working his plant today?"

"Could be," Bruce admitted.

"Well?"

" 'Well' what? I've had a week and it's not my dish. Get somebody else."

Bruce wore his knife, as did each of them; a colonist was more likely to be caught naked than without his knife. It was the all-purpose tool, for cutting leather, preparing food, eating, whittling, building, basketmaking, and as make-do for a thousand other tools; their wealth came from knives, arrows were now used to hunt —but knives shaped the bows and arrows.

But a knife had not been used by one colonist against another since that disastrous day when Bruce's brother had defied Rod. Over the same issue, Rod recalled; the wheel had turned full circle. But today he would have immediate backing if Bruce reached for his knife.

But he knew that this must not be settled by five against one; he alone must make this dog come to heel, or his days as leader were numbered.

It did not occur to Rod to challenge Bruce to settle it with bare hands. Rod had read many a historical romance in which the hero invited someone to settle it "man to man," in a stylized imitation fighting called "boxing." Rod had enjoyed such stories but did not apply them to himself any more than he considered personally the sword play of *The Three Musketeers;* nevertheless, he knew what "boxing" meant—they folded their hands and struck certain restricted blows with fists. Usually no one was hurt.

The fighting that Rod was trained in was not simply strenuous athletics. It did not matter whether they were armed; if he and Bruce fought bare hands or otherwise,

184

someone would be killed or badly hurt. The *only* dangerous weapon was man himself.

Bruce stared sullenly. "Bruce," Rod said, striving to keep his voice steady, "a long time ago I told you that people worked around here or got out. You and your brother didn't believe me so we had to chuck you out. Then you crawled back with a tale about how Jock had been killed and could you please join up? You were a sorry sight. Remember?"

McGowan scowled. "You promised to be a little angel," Rod went on. "People thought I was foolish—and I was. But I thought you might behave."

Bruce pulled a blade of grass, bit it. "Bub, you remind me of Jock. He was always throwing his weight around, too."

"Bruce, get up and get out of town! I don't care where, but if you are smart, you will shag over and tell Art you've made a mistake—then start pumping that bellows. I'll stop by later. If sweat isn't pouring off you when I arrive . . . then you'll never come back. You'll be banished for life."

McGowan looked uncertain. He glanced past Rod, and Rod wondered what expressions the others wore. But Rod kept his eyes on Bruce. "Get moving. Get to work, or don't come back."

Bruce got a sly look. "You can't order me kicked out. It takes a majority vote."

Jimmy spoke up. "Aw, quit taking his guff, Rod. Kick him out now."

Rod shook his head. "No. Bruce, if that is your answer, I'll call them together and we'll put you in exile before lunch—and I'll bet my best knife that you won't get three votes to let you stay. Want to bet?"

Bruce sat up and looked at the others, sizing his chances. He looked back at Rod. "Runt," he said slowly, "you aren't worth a hoot without stooges . . . or a couple of girls to do your fighting."

Jimmy whispered, "Watch it, Rod!" Rod licked dry lips, knowing that it was too late for reason, too late for talk. He would have to try to take him . . . he was not sure he could.

"I'll fight you," he said hoarsely. "Right now!"

Cliff said urgently, "Don't, Rod. We'll manage him."

185

"No. Come on, McGowan." Rod added one unforgivable word.

McGowan did not move. "Get rid of that joe sticker."

Rod said, "Hold my spear, Cliff."

Cliff snapped, "Now wait! I'm not going to stand by and watch this. He might get lucky and kill you, Rod."

"Get out of the way, Cliff."

"No." Cliff hesitated, then added, "Bruce, throw your knife away. Go ahead—or so help me I'll poke a joesticker in your belly myself. Give me your knife, Rod."

Rod looked at Bruce, then drew Colonel Bowie and handed it to Cliff. Bruce straightened up and flipped his knife at Cliff's feet. Cliff rasped, "I still say not to, Rod. Say the word and we'll take him apart."

"Back off. Give us room."

"Well—no bone breakers. You hear me, Bruce? Make a mistake and you'll never make another."

" 'No bone breakers,' " Rod repeated, and knew dismally that the rule would work against him; Bruce had him on height and reach and weight.

"Okay," McGowan agreed. "Just cat clawing. I am going to show this rube that one McGowan is worth two of him."

Cliff sighed. "Back off, everybody. Okay—get going!"

Crouched, they sashayed around, not touching. Only the preliminaries could use up much time; the textbook used in most high schools and colleges listed twenty-seven ways to destroy or disable a man hand to hand; none of the methods took as long as three seconds once contact was made. They chopped at each other, feinting with their hands, too wary to close.

Rod was confused by the injunction not to let the fight go to conclusion. Bruce grinned at him. "What's the matter? Scared? I've been waiting for this, you loud-mouthed pimple—now you're going to get it!" He rushed him.

Rod gave back, ready to turn Bruce's rush into his undoing. But Bruce did not carry it through; it had been a feint and Rod had reacted too strongly. Bruce laughed. "Scared silly, huh? You had better be."

Rod realized that he *was* scared, more scared than he had ever been. The conviction flooded over him that Bruce intended to kill him . . . the agreement about

186

bonebreakers meant nothing; this ape meant to finish him.

He backed away, more confused than ever . . . knowing that he must forget rules if he was to live through it . . . but knowing, too, that he *had* to abide by the silly restriction even if it meant the end of him. Panic shook him; he wanted to run.

He did not quite do so. From despair itself he got a cold feeling of nothing to lose and decided to finish it. He exposed his groin to a *savate* attack.

He saw Bruce's foot come up in the expected kick; with fierce joy he reached in the proper *shinobi* counter. He showed the merest of hesitation, knowing that a full twist would break Bruce's ankle.

Then he was flying through air; his hands had never touched Bruce. He had time for sick realization that Bruce had seen the gambit, countered with another—when he struck ground and Bruce was on him.

"Can you move your arm, Rod?"

He tried to focus his eyes, and saw Bob Baxter's face floating over him. "I licked him?"

Baxter did not answer. An angry voice answered, "Cripes, no! He almost chewed you to pieces."

Rod stirred and said thickly, "Where is he? I've got to whip him."

Baxter said sharply, "Lie still!" Cliff added, "Don't worry, Rod. We fixed him." Baxter insisted, "Shut up. See if you can move your left arm."

Rod moved the arm, felt pain shoot through it, jerked and felt pain everywhere. "It's not broken," Baxter decided. "Maybe a green-stick break. We'll put it in sling. Can you sit up? I'll help."

"I want to stand." He made it with help, stood swaying. Most of the villagers seemed to be there; they moved jerkily. It made him dizzy and he blinked.

"Take it easy, boy," he heard Jimmy say. "Bruce pretty near ruined you. You were crazy to give him the chance."

"I'm all right," Rod answered and winced. "Where is he?"

"Behind you. Don't worry, we fixed him."

"Yes," agreed Cliff. "We worked him over. Who does

he think he is? Trying to shove the Mayor around!" He spat angrily.

Bruce was face down, features hidden in one arm; he was sobbing. "How bad is he hurt?" Rod asked.

"Him?" Jimmy said scornfully. "He's not hurt. I mean, he hurts all right—but he's not hurt. Carol wouldn't let us."

Caroline squatted beside Bruce, guarding him. She got up. "I should have let 'em," she said angrily. "But I knew you would be mad at me if I did." She put hands on hips. "Roddie Walker, when are you going to get sense enough to yell for me when you're in trouble? These four dopes stood around and let it happen."

"Wait a minute, Carol," Cliff protested. "I tried to stop it. We all tried, but—"

"But I wouldn't listen," Rod interrupted. "Never mind, Carol, I flubbed it."

"If you would listen to me—"

"Never mind!" Rod went to McGowan, prodded him. "Turn over."

Bruce slowly rolled over. Rod wondered if he himself looked as bad. Bruce's body was dirt and blood and bruises; his face looked as if someone had tried to file the features off. "Stand up."

Bruce started to speak, then got painfully to his feet. Rod said, "I tod you to report to Art, Bruce. Get over the wall and get moving."

McGowan looked startled. "Huh?"

"You heard me. I can't waste time playing games. Check in with Art and get to work. Or keep moving and don't come back. Now *move!*"

Bruce stared, then hobbled toward the wall. Rod turned and said, "Get back to work, folks. The fun is over. Cliff, you were going to show me the animals."

"Huh? Look Rod, it'll keep."

"Yes, Rod," Baxter agreed. "I want to put a sling on that arm. Then you should rest."

Rod moved his arm gingerly. "I'll try to get along without it. Come on, Cliff. Just you and me—we'll skip the stobor hunt."

He had trouble concentrating on what Cliff talked about . . . something about gelding a pair of fawns and getting them used to harness. What use was harness

188

when they had no wagons? His head ached, his arm hurt and his brain felt fuzzy. What would Grant have done? He had failed . . . but what should he have said, or not said? Some days it wasn't worth it.

"—so we've got to. You see, Rod?"

"Huh? Sure, Cliff." He made a great effort to recall what Cliff had been saying. "Maybe wooden axles would do. I'll see if Bill thinks he can build a cart."

"But besides a cart, we need—"

Rod stopped him. "Cliff, if you say so, we'll try it. I think I'll take a shower. Uh, we'll look at the field tomorrow."

A shower made him feel better and much cleaner, although the water spilling milk-warm from the flume seemed too hot, then icy cold. He stumbled back to his hut and lay down. When he woke he found Shorty guarding his door to keep him from being disturbed.

It was three days before he felt up to inspecting the farm. Nielsen reported that McGowan was working, although sullenly. Caroline reported that Theo was obeying sanitary regulations and wearing a black eye. Rod was self-conscious about appearing in public, had even considered one restless night the advisability of resigning and letting someone who had not lost face take over the responsibility. But to his surprise his position seemed firmer than ever. A minority from Teller University, which he had thought of wryly as "loyal opposition," now no longer seemed disposed to be critical. Curt Pulvermacher, their unofficial leader, looked Rod up and offered help. "Bruce is a bad apple, Rod. Don't let him get down wind again. Let me know instead."

"Thanks, Curt."

"I mean it. It's hard enough to get anywhere around here if we all pull together. We can't have him riding roughshod over us. But don't stick your chin out. We'll teach him."

Rod slept well that night. Perhaps he had not handled it as Grant would have, but it had worked out. Cowpertown was safe. Oh, there would be more troubles but the colony would sweat through them. Someday there would be a city here and this would be Cowper Square. Upstream would be the Nielsen Steel Works. There might even be a Walker Avenue . . .

He felt up to looking over the farm the next day. He told Cliff so and gathered the same party, Jimmy, Kent, and Mick. Spears in hand they climbed the stile at the wall and descended the ladder on the far side. Cliff gathered up a handful of dirt, tasted it. "The soil is all right. A little acid, maybe. We won't know until we can run soil chemistry tests. But the structure is good. If you tell that dumb Swede that the next thing he has to make is a plough . . ."

"Waxie isn't dumb. Give him time. He'll make you ploughs and tractors, too."

"I'll settle for a hand plough, drawn by a team of buck. Rod, my notion is this. We weed and it's an invitation to the buck to eat the crops. If we built another wall, all around and just as high—"

"A wall! Any idea how many man-hours that would take, Cliff?"

"That's not the point."

Rod looked around the alluvial flat, several times as large as the land enclosed in the city walls. A thorn fence, possibly, but not a wall, not yet . . . Cliff's ambitions were too big. "Look, let's comb the field for stobor, then send the others back. You and I can figure out afterwards what can be done."

"All right. But tell them to watch where they put their big feet."

Rod spread them in skirmish line with himself in the center. "Keep dressed up," he warned, "and don't let any get past you. Remember, every one we kill now means six less on S-Day."

They moved forward. Kenny made a kill, Jimmy immediately made two more. The stobor hardly tried to escape, being in the "dopy joe" phase of their cycle.

Rod paused to spear one and looked up to speak to the man on his right. But there was no one there. "Hold it! Where's Mick?"

"Huh? Why, he was right here a second ago."

Rod looked back. Aside from a shimmer over the hot field, there was nothing where Mick should have been. Something must have sneaked up in the grass, pulled him down— "Watch it, everybody! Something's wrong. Close in . . . and keep your eyes peeled." He turned back, moved diagonally toward where Mick had disappeared.

Suddenly two figures appeared in front of his eyes—Mick and a stranger.

A stranger in coveralls and shoes . . . The man looked around, called over his shoulder, "Okay, Jake! Put her on automatic and clamp it." He glanced toward Rod but did not seem to see him, walked toward him, and disappeared.

With heart pounding Rod began to run. He turned and found himself facing into an open gate . . . and down a long, closed corridor.

The man in the coveralls stepped into the frame. "Everybody back off," he ordered. "We're going to match in with the Gap. There may be local disturbance."

15

In Achilles' Tent

IT HAD BEEN A HALF HOUR SINCE MICK HAD STUMBLED through the gate as it had focused, fallen flat in the low gravity of Luna. Rod was trying to bring order out of confusion, trying to piece together his own wits. Most of the villagers were out on the field, or sitting on top of the wall, watching technicians set up apparatus to turn the locus into a permanent gate, with controls and communications on both sides. Rod tried to tell one that they were exposed, that they should not run around unarmed; without looking up the man had said, "Speak to Mr. Johnson."

He found Mr. Johnson, tried again, was interrupted. "Will you kids *please* let us work? We're glad to see you

—but we've got to get a power fence around this area. No telling what might be in that tall grass."

"Oh," Rod answered. "Look, I'll set guards. We know what to expect. I'm in ch—"

"Beat it, will you? You kids mustn't be impatient."

So Rod went back inside his city, hurt and angry. Several strangers came in, poked around as if they owned the place, spoke to the excited villagers, went out again. One stopped to look at Jimmy's drum, rapped it and laughed. Rod wanted to strangle him.

"Rod?"

"Uh?" He whirled around. "Yes, Margery?"

"Do I cook lunch, or don't I? All my girls have left and Mel says it's silly because we'll all be gone by lunch time—and I don't know *what* to do."

"Huh? Nobody's leaving . . . that I know of."

"Well, maybe not but that's the talk."

He was not given time to consider this as one of the ubiquitous strangers came up and said briskly, "Can you tell me where to find a lad named Roderick Welker?"

"Walker," Rod corrected. "I'm Rod Walker. What do you want?"

"My name is Sansom, Clyde B. Sansom—Administrative Officer in the Emigration Control Service. Now, Welker, I understand you are group leader for these students. You can—"

"I am Mayor of Cowpertown," Rod said stonily. "What do you want?"

"Yes, yes, that's what the youngster called you. 'Mayor.'" Sansom smiled briefly and went on. "Now, Walker, we want to keep things orderly. I know you are anxious to get out of your predicament as quickly as possible—but we must do things systematically. We are going to make it easy—just delousing and physical examination, followed by psychological tests and a relocation interview. Then you will all be free to return to your homes—after signing a waiver-of-liability form, but the legal officer will take care of that. If you will have your little band line up alphabetically—uh, here in this open space, I think, then I will—" He fumbled with his briefcase.

"Who the deuce are you to give orders around here?"

Sansom looked surprised. "Eh? I told you. If you

192

want to be technical, I embody the authority of the Terran Corporation. I put it as a request—but under field conditions I can compel co-operation, you know."

Rod felt himself turn red. "I don't know anything of the sort! You may be a squad of angels back on Terra . . . but you are in Cowpertown."

Mr. Sansom looked interested but not impressed. "And what, may I ask, is Cowpertown?"

"Huh? *This* is Cowpertown, a sovereign nation, with its own constitution, its own laws—and its own territory." Rod took a breath. "If the Terran Corporation wants anything, they can send somebody and arrange it. But don't tell us to line up alphabetically!"

"Atta boy, Roddie!"

Rod said, "Stick around, Carol," then added to Sansom, "Understand me?"

"Do I understand," Sansom said slowly, "that you are suggesting that the Corporation should appoint an *ambassador* to your group?"

"Well . . . that's the general idea."

"Mmmm . . . an interesting theory, Welker."

" 'Walker.' And until you do, you can darn well clear the sightseers out—and get out yourself. We aren't a zoo."

Sansom looked at Rod's ribs, glanced at his dirty, calloused feet and smiled. Rod said, "Show him out, Carol. Put him out, if you have to."

"Yes, *sir!*" She advanced on Sansom, grinning.

"Oh, I'm leaving," Sansom said quickly. "Better a delay than a mistake in protocol. An ingenious theory, young man. Good-by. We shall see each other later. Uh . . . a word of advice? May I?"

"Huh? All right."

"Don't take yourself too seriously. Ready, young lady?"

Rod stayed in his hut. He wanted badly to see what was going on beyond the wall, but he did not want to run into Sansom. So he sat and gnawed his thumb and thought. Apparently some weak sisters were going back —wave a dish of ice cream under their noses and off they would trot, abandoning their land, throwing away all they had built up. Well, *he* wouldn't! This was home, his place, he had earned it; he wasn't going back and maybe wait half a lifetime for a chance to move to some other planet probably not as good.

Let them go! Cowpertown would be better and stronger without them.

Maybe some just wanted to make a visit, show off grandchildren to grandparents, then come back. Probably . . . in which case they had better make sure that Sansom or somebody gave them written clearance to come back. Maybe he ought to warn them.

But *he* didn't have anyone to visit. Except Sis—and Sis might be anywhere—unlikely that she was on Terra.

Bob and Carmen, carrying Hope, came in to say good-by. Rod shook hands solemnly. "You're coming back, Bob, when you get your degree . . . aren't you?"

"Well, we hope so, if possible. If we are permitted to."

"Who's going to stop you? It's your *right*. And when you do, you'll find us here. In the meantime we'll try not to break legs."

Baxter hesitated. "Have you been to the gate lately, Rod?"

"No. Why?"

"Uh, don't plan too far ahead. I believe some have already gone back."

"How many?"

"Quite a number." Bob would not commit himself further. He gave Rod the addresses of his parents and Carmen's, soberly wished him a blessing, and left.

Margery did not come back and the fire pit remained cold. Rod did not care, he was not hungry. Jimmy came in at what should have been shortly after lunch, nodded and sat down. Presently he said, "I've been out at the gate."

"So?"

"Yup. You know, Rod, a lot of people wondered why you weren't there to say good-by."

"They could come *here* to say good-by!"

"Yes, so they could. But the word got around that you didn't approve. Maybe they were embarrassed."

"Me?" Rod laughed without mirth. "I don't care how many city boys run home to mama. It's a free country." He glanced at Jim. "How many are sticking?"

"Uh, I don't know."

"I've been thinking. If the group gets small, we might move back to the cave—just to sleep, I mean. Until we get more colonists."

"Maybe."

"Don't be so glum! Even if it got down to just you and me and Jackie and Carol, we'd be no worse off than we once were. And it would just be temporary. There'd be the baby, of course—I almost forgot to mention my godson."

"There's the baby," Jimmy agreed.

"What are you pulling a long face about? Jim . . . *you're* not thinking of leaving?"

Jimmy stood up. "Jackie said to tell you that we would stick by whatever you thought was best."

Rod thought over what Jimmy had not said. "You mean she wants to go back? Both of you do."

"Now, Rod, we're partners. But I've got the kid to think about. You see that?"

"Yes. I see."

"Well—"

Rod stuck out his hand. "Good luck, Jim. Tell Jackie good-by for me."

"Oh, she's waiting to say good-by herself. With the kid."

"Uh, tell her not to. Somebody once told me that saying good-by was a mistake. Be seeing you."

"Well—so long, Rod. Take care of yourself."

"You, too. If you see Caroline, tell her to come in."

Caroline was slow appearing; he guessed that she had been at the gate. He said bluntly, "How many are left?"

"Not many," she admitted.

"How many?"

"You and me—and a bunch of gawkers."

"Nobody else?"

"I checked them off the list. Roddie, what do we do now?"

"Huh? It doesn't matter. Do *you* want to go back?"

"You're boss, Roddie. You're the Mayor."

"Mayor of what? Carol, do you *want* to go back?"

"Roddie, I never thought about it. I was happy here. But—"

"But what?"

"The town is gone, the kids are gone—and I've got

195

only a year if I'm ever going to be a cadet Amazon."
She blurted out the last, then added, "But I'll stick if
you do."

"No."

"I will so!"

"No. But I want you to do something when you go
back."

"What?"

"Get in touch with my sister Helen. Find out where
she is stationed. Assault Captain Helen Walker—got it?
Tell her I'm okay . . . and tell her I said to help you
get into the Corps."

"Uh . . . Roddie, I don't *want* to go!"

"Beat it. They might relax the gate and leave you
behind."

"You come, too."

"No. I've got things to do. But you hurry. Don't say
good-by. Just go."

"You're mad at me, Roddie?"

"Of course not. But go, *please,* or you'll have me
bawling, too."

She gave a choked cry, grabbed his head and
smacked his cheek, then galloped away, her sturdy legs
pounding. Rod went into his shack and lay face down.
After a while he got up and began to tidy Cowpertown.
It was littered, dirtier than it had been since the morning of Grant's death.

It was late afternoon before anyone else came into
the village. Rod heard and saw them long before they
saw him—two men and a woman. The men were
dressed in city garb; she was wearing shorts, shirt, and
smart sandals. Rod stepped out and said, "What do you
want?" He was carrying his spear.

The woman squealed, then looked and added, "Wonderful!"

One man was carrying a pack and tripod which Rod
recognized as multi-recorder of the all-purpose sight-
smell-sound-touch sort used by news services and expeditions. He said nothing, set his tripod down, plugged
in cables and started fiddling with dials. The other man,
smaller, ginger haired, and with a terrier mustache,

said, "You're Walker? The one the others call 'the Mayor'?"

"Yes."

"Kosmic hasn't been in here?"

"Cosmic what?"

"Kosmic Keynotes, of course. Or anybody? LIFE-TIME-SPACE? Galaxy Features?"

"I don't know what you mean. There hasn't been anybody here since morning."

The stranger twitched his mustache and sighed. "That's all I want to know. Go into your trance, Ellie. Start your box, Mac."

"Wait a minute," Rod demanded. "Who are you and what do you want?"

"Eh? I'm Evans of Empire . . . Empire Enterprises."

"Pulitzer Prize," the other man said and went on working.

"With Mac's help," Evans added quickly. "The lady is Ellie Ellens herself."

Rod looked puzzled. Evans said, "You don't *know?* Son, where have you—never mind. She's the highest paid emotional writer in the system. She'll interpret you so that every woman reader from the *Outlands Overseer* to the *London Times* will cry over you and want to comfort you. She's a *great* artist."

Miss Ellens did not seem to hear the tribute. She wandered around with a blank face, stopping occasionally to look or touch.

She turned and said to Rod, "Is this where you held your primitive dances?"

"What? We held square dances here, once a week."

"'Square dances' . . . Well, we can change that." She went back into her private world.

"The point is, brother," Evans went on, "we don't want just an interview. Plenty of that as they came through. That's how we found out you were here—and dropped everything to see you. I'm not going to dicker; name your own price—but it's got to be exclusive, news, features, commercial rights, everything. Uh . . ." Evans looked around. "Advisory service, too, when the actors arrive."

"Actors?!"

"Of course. If the Control Service had the sense to

sneeze, they would have held you all here until a record was shot. But we can do it better with actors. I want you at my elbow every minute—we'll have somebody play your part. Besides that—"

"Wait a minute!" Rod butted in. "Either I'm crazy or you are. In the first place I don't want your money."

"Huh? You signed with somebody? That guard let another outfit in ahead of us?"

"What guard? I haven't seen anybody."

Evans looked relieved. "We'll work it out. The guard they've got to keep anybody from crossing your wall— I thought he might have both hands out. But don't say you don't need money; that's immoral."

"Well, I don't. We don't use money here."

"Sure, sure . . . but you've got a family, haven't you? Families always need money. Look, let's not fuss. We'll treat you right and you can let it pile up in the bank. I just want you to get signed up."

"I don't see why I should."

"Binder," said Mac.

"Mmm . . . yes, Mac. See here, brother, think it over. Just let us have a binder that you won't sign with anybody else. You can still stick us for anything your conscience will let you. Just a binder, with a thousand plutons on the side."

"I'm not going to sign with anybody else."

"Got that, Mac?"

"Canned."

Evans turned to Rod. "You don't object to answering questions in the meantime, do you? And maybe a few pictures?"

"Uh, I don't care." Rod was finding them puzzling and a little annoying, but they were company and he was bitterly lonely.

"Fine!" Evans drew him out with speed and great skill. Rod found himself telling more than he realized he knew. At one point Evans asked about dangerous animals. "I understand they are pretty rough here. Much trouble?"

"Why, no," Rod answered with sincerity. "We never had real trouble with animals. What trouble we had was with people . . . and not much of that."

"You figure this will be a premium colony?"

"Of course. The others were fools to leave. This place is like Terra, only safer and richer and plenty of land. In a few years—say!"

"Say what?"

"How did it happen that they left us here? We were only supposed to be here ten days."

"Didn't they tell you?"

"Well . . . maybe the others were told. I never heard."

"It was the supernova, of course. Delta, uh—"

"Delta Gamma one thirteen," supplied Mac.

"That's it. Space-time distortion, but I'm no mathematician."

"Fluxion," said Mac.

"Whatever that is. They've been fishing for you ever since. As I understand it, the wave front messed up their figures for this whole region. Incidentally, brother, when you go back—"

"I'm not going back."

"Well, even on a visit. Don't sign a waiver. The Board is trying to call it an 'Act of God' and duck responsibility. So let me put a bug in your ear: don't sign away your rights. A friendly hint, huh?"

"Thanks. I won't—well, thanks anyhow."

"Now how about action pix for the lead stories?"

"Well . . . okay."

"Spear," said Mac.

"Yeah, I believe you had some sort of spear. Mind holding it?"

Rod got it as the great Ellie joined them. "Wonderful!" she breathed. "I can feel it. It shows how thin the line is between man and beast. A hundred cultured boys and girls slipping back to illiteracy, back to the stone age, the veneer sloughing away . . . reverting to savagery. Glorious!"

"Look here!" Rod said angrily. "Cowpertown wasn't that way at all! We had laws, we had a constitution, we kept clean. We—" He stopped; Miss Ellens wasn't listening.

"Savage ceremonies," she said dreamily. "A village witch doctor pitting ignorance and superstition against nature. Primitive fertility rites—" She stopped and said to Mac in a businesslike voice, "We'll shoot the dances three times. Cover 'em a little for 'A' list; cover 'em up a lot for the family list—and peel them down for the 'B' list. Got it?"

"Got it," agreed Mac.

"I'll do three commentaries," she added. "It will be worth the trouble." She reverted to her trance.

"Wait a minute!" Rod protested. "If she means what I think she means, there won't be any pictures, with or without actors."

"Take it easy," Evans advised. "I said you would be technical supervisor, didn't I? Or would you rather we did it without you? Ellie is all right, brother. What you don't know—and *she* does—is that you have to shade the truth to get at the real truth, the underlying truth. You'll see."

"But—"

Mac stepped up to him. "Hold still."

Rod did so, as Mac raised his hand. Rod felt the cool touch of an air brush.

"Hey! What are you doing?"

"Make up." Mac returned to his gear.

"Just a little war paint," Evans explained. "The pic needs color. It will wash off."

Rod opened his mouth and eyes in utter indignation; without knowing it he raised his spear. "Get it, Mac!" Evans ordered.

"Got it," Mac answered calmly.

Rod fought to bring his anger down to where he could talk. "Take that tape out," he said softly. "Throw it on the ground. Then get out."

"Slow down," Evans advised. "You'll like that pic. We'll send you one."

"Take it out. Or I'll bust the box and anybody who gets in my way!" He aimed his spear at the multiple lens.

Mac slipped in front, protected it with his body. Evans called out, "Better look at *this*."

Evans had him covered with a small but businesslike gun. "We go a lot of funny places, brother, but we go prepared. You damage that recorder, or hurt one of us, and you'll be sued from here to breakfast. It's a serious matter to interfere with a news service, brother. The public has rights, you know." He raised his voice. "Ellie! We're leaving."

"Not yet," she answered dreamily. "I must steep myself in—"

"Right now! It's an 'eight-six' with the Reuben Steuben!"

"Okay!" she snapped in her other voice.

Rod let them go. Once they were over the wall he went back to the city hall, sat down, held his knees and shook.

Later he climbed the stile and looked around. A guard was on duty below him; the guard looked up but said nothing. The gate was relaxed to a mere control hole but a loading platform had been set up and a power fence surrounded it and joined the wall. Someone was working at a control board set up on a flatbed truck; Rod decided that they must be getting ready for major immigration. He went back and prepared a solitary meal, the poorest he had eaten in more than a year. Then he went to bed and listened to the jungle "Grand Opera" until he went to sleep.

"Anybody home?"

Rod came awake instantly, realized that it was morning—and that not all nightmares were dreams. "Who's there?"

"Friend of yours." B. P. Matson stuck his head in the door. "Put that whittler away. I'm harmless."

Rod bounced up. "Deacon! I mean 'Doctor.'"

"'Deacon,'" Matson corrected. "I've got a visitor for you." He stepped aside and Rod saw his sister.

Some moments later Matson said mildly, "If you two can unwind and blow your noses, we might get this on a coherent basis."

Rod backed off and looked at his sister. "My, you look *wonderful,* Helen." She was in mufti, dressed in a gay tabard and briefs. "You've lost weight."

"Not much. Better distributed, maybe. You've gained, Rod. My baby brother is a man."

"How did you—" Rod stopped, struck by suspicion. "You didn't come here to talk me into going back? If you did, you can save your breath."

Matson answered hastily. "No, no, no! Farthest

thought from our minds. But we heard about your decision and we wanted to see you—so I did a little politicking and got us a pass." He added, "Nominally I'm a temporary field agent for the service."

"Oh. Well, I'm certainly glad to see you . . . as long as that is understood."

"Sure, sure!" Matson took out a pipe, stoked and fired it. "I admire your choice, Rod. First time I've been on Tangaroa."

"On what?"

"Huh? Oh. Tangaroa. Polynesian goddess, I believe. Did you folks give it another name?"

Rod considered it. "To tell the truth, we never got around to it. It . . . well, it just *was.*"

Matson nodded. "Takes two of anything before you need names. But it's lovely, Rod. I can see you made a lot of progress."

"We would have done all right," Rod said bitterly, "if they hadn't jerked the rug out." He shrugged. "Like to look around?"

"I surely would."

"All right. Come on, Sis. Wait a minute—I haven't had breakfast; how about you?"

"Well, when we left the Gap it was pushing lunch time. I could do with a bite. Helen?"

"Yes, indeed."

Rod scrounged in Margery's supplies. The haunch on which he had supped was not at its best. He passed it to Matson. "Too high?"

Matson sniffed it. "Pretty gamy. I can eat it if you can."

"We should have hunted yesterday, but . . . things happened." He frowned. "Sit tight. I'll get cured meat." He ran up to the cave, found a smoked side and some salted strips. When he got back Matson had a fire going. There was nothing else to serve; no fruit had been gathered the day before. Rod was uneasily aware that their breakfasts must have been very different.

But he got over it in showing off how much they had done—potter's wheel, Sue's loom with a piece half finished, the flume with the village fountain and the showers that ran continuously, iron artifacts that Art and Doug had hammered out. "I'd like to take you up

202

to Art's iron works but there is no telling what we might run into."

"Come now, Rod, I'm not a city boy. Nor is your sister helpless."

Rod shook his head. "I know this country; you don't. I can go up there at a trot. But the only way for you would be a slow sneak, because I can't cover you both."

Matson nodded. "You're right. It seems odd to have one of my students solicitous over my health. But you are right. We don't know this set up."

Rod showed them the stobor traps and described the annual berserk migration. "Stobor pour through those holes and fall in the pits. The other animals swarm past, as solid as city traffic for hours."

"Catastrophic adjustment," Matson remarked.

"Huh? Oh, yes, we figured that out. Cyclic catastrophic balance, just like human beings. If we had facilities, we could ship thousands of carcasses back to Earth every dry season." He considered it. "Maybe we will, now."

"Probably."

"But up to now it has been just a troublesome nuisance. These stobor especially—I'll show you one out in the field when—say!" Rod looked thoughtful. "These *are* stobor, aren't they? Little carnivores heavy in front, about the size of a tom cat and eight times as nasty?"

"Why ask me?"

"Well, you warned us against stobor. All the classes were warned."

"I suppose these must be stobor," Matson admitted, "but I did not know what they looked like."

"Huh?"

"Rod, every planet has its 'stobor' . . . all different. Sometimes more than one sort." He stopped to tap his pipe. "You remember me telling the class that every planet has unique dangers, different from every other planet in the Galaxy?"

"Yes . . ."

"Sure, and it meant nothing, a mere intellectual concept. But you have to be afraid of the thing behind the concept, if you are to stay alive. So we personify it . . . but we don't tell you what it is. We do it differently each year. It is to warn you that the unknown and deadly can lurk anywhere . . . and to plant it deep in your guts instead of in your head."

"Well, I'll be a— Then there *weren't* any stobor! There never were!"

"Sure there were. You built these traps for them, didn't you?"

When they returned, Matson sat on the ground and said, "We can't stay long, you know."

"I realize that. Wait a moment." Rod went into his hut, dug out Lady Macbeth, rejoined them. "Here's your knife, Sis. It saved my skin more than once. Thanks."

She took the knife and caressed it, then cradled it and looked past Rod's head. It flashed by him, went tuck-*spong!* in a corner post. She recovered it, came back and handed it to Rod. "Keep it, dear, wear it always in safety and health."

"Gee, Sis, I shouldn't. I've had it too long now."

"Please. I'd like to know that Lady Macbeth is watching over you wherever you are. And I don't need a knife much now."

"Huh? Why not?"

"Because I married her," Matson answered.

Rod was caught speechless. His sister looked at him and said, "What's the matter, Buddy? Don't you approve?"

"Huh? Oh, sure! It's . . ." He dug into his memory, fell back on quoted ritual: " 'May the Principle make you one. May your union be fruitful.' "

"Then come here and kiss me."

Rod did so, remembered to shake hands with the Deacon. It was all right, he guessed, but—well, how old were they? Sis must be thirtyish and the Deacon . . . why the Deacon was *old*—probably past forty.

It did not seem quite decent.

But he did his best to make them feel that he approved. After he thought it over he decided that if two people, with their lives behind them, wanted company in their old age, why, it was probably a good thing.

"So you see," Matson went on, "I had a double reason to look you up. In the first place, though I am no longer teaching, it is vexing to mislay an entire class. In the second place, when one of them is your brother-in-law it is downright embarrassing."

"You've quit teaching?"

"Yes. The Board and I don't see eye to eye on policy. Secondly, I'm leading a party out . . . and this time your sister and I are going to settle down and prove a farm." Matson looked at him. "Wouldn't be interested, would you? I need a salted lieutenant."

"Huh? Thanks, but as I told you, this is my place. Uh, where are you going?"

"Territa, out toward the Hyades. Nice place—they are charging a stiff premium."

Rod shrugged. "Then I couldn't afford it."

"As my lieutenant, you'd be exempt. But I wasn't twisting your arm; I just thought you ought to have a chance to turn it down. I have to get along with your sister, you know."

Rod glanced at Helen. "Sorry, Sis."

"It's all right, Buddy. We're not trying to live your life."

"Mmm . . . no." Matson puffed hard, then went on. "However, as your putative brother and former teacher I feel obligated to mention a couple of things. I'm not trying to sell you anything, but I'll appreciate it if you'll listen. Okay?"

"Well . . . go ahead."

"This is a good spot. But you might go back to school, you know. Acquire recognized professional status. If you refuse recall, here you stay . . . forever. You won't see the rest of the Outlands. They won't give you free passage back later. But a professional gets around, he sees the world. Your sister and I have been on some fifty planets. School does not look attractive now—you're a man and it will be hard to wear boy's shoes. But—" Matson swept an arm, encompassed all of Cowpertown, "—this counts. You can skip courses, get field credit. I have some drag with the Chancellor of Central Tech. Hmmm?"

Rod sat with stony face, then shook his head. "Okay," said Matson briskly. "No harm done."

"Wait. Let me tell you." Rod tried to think how to explain how he felt . . . "Nothing, I guess," he said gruffly.

Matson smoked in silence. "You were leader here," he said at last.

"Mayor," Rod corrected. "Mayor of Cowpertown. I *was* the Mayor, I mean."

"You *are* the Mayor. Population one, but you are still boss. And even those bureaucrats in the control service wouldn't dispute that you've proved the land. Technically you are an autonomous colony—I hear you told Sansom that." Matson grinned. "You're alone, however. You can't live alone, Rod . . . not and stay human."

"Well, yes—but aren't they going to settle this planet?"

"Sure. Probably fifty thousand this year, four times that many in two years. But, Rod, you would be part of the mob. They'll bring their own leaders."

"*I* don't have to be boss! I just—well, I don't want to give up Cowpertown."

"Rod, Cowpertown is safe in history, along with Plymouth Rock, Botany Bay, and Dakin's Colony. The citizens of Tangaroa will undoubtedly preserve it as a historical shrine. Whether you stay is another matter. Nor am I trying to persuade you. I was simply pointing out alternatives." He stood up. "About time we started, Helen."

"Yes, dear." She accepted his hand and stood up.

"Wait a minute!" insisted Rod. "Deacon . . . Sis! I know I sound like a fool. I know this is gone . . . the town, and the kids, and everything. But I *can't* go back." He added, "It's not that I don't want to."

Matson nodded. "I understand you."

"I don't see how. *I* don't."

"Maybe I've been there. Rod, everyone of us is beset by two things: a need to go home, and the impossibility of doing it. You are at the age when these hurt worst. You've been thrown into a situation that makes the crisis doubly acute. You—don't interrupt me—you've been a man here, the old man of the tribe, the bull of the herd. That is why the others could go back but you can't. Wait, please! I suggested that you might find it well to go back and be an adolescent for a while . . . and it seems unbearable. I'm not surprised. It would be easier to be a small child. Children are another race and adults deal with them as such. But adolescents are neither adult nor child. They have the impossible, unsolvable, tragic problems of all fringe cultures. They don't belong, they are second-class citizens, economically and socially insecure. It is a difficult period and I don't blame you for not wanting to return to it. I simply think it might pay. But you have been king of a whole world; I imagine that term papers and being told to wipe your feet and such are out of the question. So good luck. Coming, dear?"

"Deacon," his wife said, "Aren't you going to *tell* him?"

"It has no bearing. It would be an unfair way to influence his judgment."

"You *men!* I'm glad I'm not male!"

"So am I," Matson agreed pleasantly.

"I didn't mean that. Men behave as if logic were stepping on a crack in a sidewalk. I'm going to tell him."

"On your head be it."

"Tell me *what?*" demanded Rod.

"She means," said Matson, "that your parents are back."

"*What?*"

"Yes, Buddy. They left stasis a week ago and Daddy came out of the hospital today. He's well. But we haven't told him all about you—we haven't known *what* to say."

The facts were simple, although Rod found them hard to soak up. Medical techniques had developed in two years, not a pessimistic twenty; it had been possible to relax the stasis, operate, and restore Mr. Walker to the world. Helen had known for months that such outcome was likely but their father's physician had not approved until he was sure. It had been mere coincidence that Tangaroa had been located at almost the same time. To Rod one event was as startling as the other; his parents had been dead to him for a long time.

"My dear," Matson said sternly, "now that you have thrown him into a whingding, shall we go?"

"Yes. But I had to tell him." Helen kissed Rod quickly, turned to her husband. They started to walk away.

Rod watched them, his face contorted in an agony of indecision.

Suddenly he called out, "Wait! I'm coming with you."

"All right," Matson answered. He turned his good eye toward his wife and drooped the lid in a look of satisfaction that was not quite a wink. "If you are sure that is what you want to do, I'll help you get your gear together."

"Oh, I haven't any baggage. Let's go."

Rod stopped only long enough to free the penned animals.

16

The Endless Road

MATSON CHAPERONED HIM THROUGH EMIGRANTS' GAP, saved from possible injury a functionary who wanted to give Rod psychological tests, and saw to it that he signed no waivers. He had him bathed, shaved, and barbered, then fetched him clothes, before he let him be exposed to the Terran world. Matson accompanied them only to Kaibab Gate. "I'm supposed to have a lodge dinner, or something, so that you four can be alone as a family. About nine, dear. See you, Rod." He kissed his wife and left.

"Sis? Dad doesn't know I'm coming?"

Helen hesitated. "He knows. I screened him while Deacon was primping you." She added, "Remember, Rod, Dad has been ill . . . and the time has been only a couple of weeks to him."

"Oh, that's so, isn't it?" Used all his life to Ramsbotham anomalies, Rod nevertheless found those concerned with time confusing—planet-hopping via the gates did not seem odd. Besides, he was extremely edgy without knowing why, the truth being that he was having an attack of fear of crowds. The Matsons had anticipated it but had not warned him lest they make him worse.

The walk through tall trees just before reaching home calmed him. The necessity for checking all cover for dangerous animals and keeping a tree near him always in mind gave his subconscious something familiar to chew on. He arrived home almost cheerful without being aware either that he had been frightened by crowds or soothed by non-existent dangers of an urban forest.

His father looked browned and healthy—but shorter and smaller. He embraced his son and his mother kissed him and wept. "It's good to have you home, son. I understand you had quite a trip."

"It's good to be home, Dad."

"I think these tests are much too strenuous, I really do."

Rod started to explain that it really had not been a test, that it had not been strenuous, and that Cowpertown—Tangaroa, rather—had been a soft touch. But he got mixed up and was disturbed by the presence of "Aunt" Nora Peascoat—no relation but a childhood friend of his mother. Besides, his father was not listening.

But Mrs. Peascoat was listening, and looking—peering with little eyes through folds of flesh. "Why, Roderick Walter, I *knew* that couldn't have been a picture of you."

"Eh?" asked his father. "What picture?"

"Why, that wild-man picture that had Roddie's name on it. You must have seen it; it was on facsimile and Empire Hour both. I knew it wasn't him. I said to Joseph, 'Joseph,' I said, 'that's not a picture of Rod Walker—it's a fake.'"

"I must have missed it. As you know, I—"

"I'll send it to you; I clipped it. I knew it was a fake. It's a horrible thing, a great naked savage with pointed teeth and a fiendish grin and a long spear and war paint all over its ugly face. I said to Joseph—"

"As you know, I returned from hospital just this morning, Nora. Rod, there was no picture of you on the news services, surely?"

"Uh, yes and no. Maybe."

"I don't follow you. Why should there be a picture of you?"

"There wasn't any reason. This bloke just took it."

"Then there *was* a picture?"

"Yes." Rod saw that "Aunt" Nora was eyeing him avidly. "But it was a fake—sort of."

"I still don't follow you."

"Please, Pater," Helen intervened. "Rod had a tiring trip. This can wait."

"Oh, surely. I don't see how a picture can be 'a sort of a fake.' "

"Well, Dad, this man painted my face when I wasn't looking. I—" Rod stopped, realizing that it sounded ridiculous.

"Then it *was* your picture?" "Aunt" Nora insisted.

"I'm not going to say any more."

Mr. Walker blinked. "Perhaps that is best."

"Aunt" Nora looked ruffled. "Well, I suppose *anything* can happen 'way off in those odd places. From the teaser on Empire Hour I understand some *very* strange things did happen . . . not all of them *nice.*"

She looked as if daring Rod to deny it. Rod said nothing. She went on, "I don't know what you were thinking of, letting a boy do such things. My father always said that if the Almighty had intended us to use those gate things instead of rocket ships He would have provided His own holes in the sky."

Helen said sharply, "Mrs. Peascoat, in what way is a rocket ship more natural than a gate?"

"Why, Helen Walker! I've been 'Aunt Nora' all your life. 'Mrs. Peascoat' indeed!"

Helen shrugged. "And *my* name is Matson, not Walker—as you know."

Mrs. Walker, distressed and quite innocent, broke in to ask Mrs. Peascoat to stay for dinner. Mr. Walker added, "Yes, Nora, join us Under the Lamp."

Rod counted to ten. But Mrs. Peascoat said she was *sure* they wanted to be *alone,* they had so *much* to talk about . . . and his father did not insist.

Rod quieted during ritual, although he stumbled in responses and once left an awkward silence. Dinner was wonderfully good, but he was astonished by the small

210

portions; Terra must be under severe rationing. But everyone seemed happy and so he was.

"I'm sorry about this mix-up," his father told him. "I suppose it means that you will have to repeat a semester at Patrick Henry."

"On the contrary, Pater," Helen answered, "Deacon is sure that Rod can enter Central Tech with advanced standing."

"Really? They were more strict in my day."

"All of that group will get special credit. What they learned cannot be learned in classrooms."

Seeing that his father was inclined to argue Rod changed the subject. "Sis, that reminds me. I gave one of the girls your name, thinking you were still in the Corps—she wants to be appointed cadet, you see. You can still help her, can't you?"

"I can advise her and perhaps coach her for the exams. Is this important to you, Buddy?"

"Well, yes. And she is number-one officer material. She's a big girl, even bigger than you are—and she looks a bit like you. She is smart like you, too, around genius, and always good-natured and willing—but strong and fast and incredibly violent when you need it . . . sudden death in all directions."

"Roderick." His father glanced at the lamp.

"Uh, sorry, Dad. I was just describing her."

"Very well. Son . . . when did you start picking up your meat with your fingers?"

Rod dropped the tidbit and blushed. "Excuse me. We didn't have forks."

Helen chuckled. "Never mind, Rod. Pater, it's perfectly natural. Whenever we paid off any of our girls we always put them through reorientation to prepare them for the perils of civil life. And fingers were made before forks."

"Mmm . . no doubt. Speaking of reorientation there is something we must do, daughter, before this family will be organized again."

"So?"

"Yes. I mean the transfer of guardianship. Now that I am well, by a miracle, I must reassume my responsibilities."

Rod's mind slipped several cogs before it penetrated

211

that Dad was talking about *him*. Guardian? Oh . . . Sis was his guardian, wasn't she? But it didn't mean anything.

Helen hesitated. "I suppose so, Pater," she said, her eyes on Rod, "if Buddy wants to."

"Eh? That is not a factor, daughter. Your husband won't want the responsibility of supervising a young boy—and it is my obligation . . . and privilege."

Helen looked annoyed. Rod said, "I can't see that it matters, Dad. I'll be away at college—and after all I am nearly old enough to vote."

His mother looked startled. "Why, Roddie dear!"

"Yes," agreed his father. "I'm afraid I can't regard a gap of three years as negligible."

"What do you mean, Dad? I'll be of age in January."

Mrs. Walker clasped a hand to her mouth. "Jerome . . . we've forgotten the time lag again. Oh, my baby boy!"

Mr. Walker looked astonished, muttered something about "—very difficult" and gave attention to his plate. Presently he looked up. "You'll pardon me, Rod. Nevertheless, until you are of age I must do what I can; I hardly think I want you to live away from home while at college."

"Sir? Why not?"

"Well—I feel that we have drifted apart, and not all for the best. Take this girl you spoke of in such surprising terms. Am I correct in implying that she was, eh . . . a close chum?"

Rod felt himself getting warm. "She was my city manager," he said flatly.

"Your *what?*"

"My executive officer. She was captain of the guard, chief of police, anything you want to call her. She did everything. She hunted, too, but that was just because she liked to. Carol is, uh—well, Carol is *swell*."

"Roderick, are you *involved* with this girl?"

"Me? Gosh, no! She was more like a big sister. Oh, Carol was sweet on half a dozen fellows, one time or another, but it never lasted."

"I am very glad to hear that you are not seriously interested in her. She does not sound like desirable companionship for a young boy."

212

"Dad—you don't know what you are saying!"

"Perhaps. I intend to find out. But what is this other matter? 'City Manager!' What were *you?*"

"I," Rod said proudly, "was Mayor of Cowpertown."

His father looked at him, then shook his head. "We'll speak of this later. Possibly you need, eh—medical help." He looked at Helen. "We'll attend to the change in guardianship tomorrow. I can see that there is much I must take care of."

Helen met his eyes. "Not unless Buddy consents."

"Daughter!"

"The transfer was irrevocable. He will have to agree —or I won't do it!"

Mr. Walker looked shocked, Mrs. Walker looked stricken. Rod got up and left the room . . . the first time anyone had ever done so while the Lamp of Peace was burning. He heard his father call after him but he did not turn back.

He found Matson in his room, smoking and reading. "I grabbed a bite and let myself in quietly," Matson explained. He inspected Rod's face. "I told you," he said slowly, "that it would be rough. Well, sweat it out, son, sweat it out."

"I can't *stand* it!"

"Yes, you can."

In Emigrants' Gap the sturdy cross-country wagons were drawn up in echelon, as they had been so often before and would be so many times again. The gate was not ready; drivers gathered at the booth under Liberty's skirts, drinking coffee and joking through the nervous wait. Their professional captain was with them, a lean, homely young man with deep lines in his face, from sun and laughing and perhaps some from worry. But he did not seem to be worrying now; he was grinning and drinking coffee and sharing a doughnut with a boy child. He was dressed in fringed buckskin, in imitation of a very old style; he wore a Bill Cody beard and rather long hair. His mount was a little pinto, standing patiently by with reins hanging. There was a boot scabbard holding a hunting rifle on the nigh side of the saddle, but the captain carried no guns on his person; instead he wore two knives, one on each side.

A siren sounded and a speaker above the Salvation Army booth uttered: "Captain Walker, ready with gate four."

Rod waved at the control booth and shouted, "Call off!" then turned back to Jim and Jacqueline. "Tell Carol I'm sorry she couldn't get leave. I'll be seeing you."

"Might be sooner than you think," asserted Jim. "My firm is going to bid this contract."

"Your firm? Where do you get that noise? Have they made him a partner, Jackie?"

"No," she answered serenely, "but I'm sure they will as soon as he is admitted to the Outlands bar. Kiss Uncle Rod good-by, Grant."

"No," the youngster answered firmly.

"Just like his father," Jimmy said proudly. "Kisses women only."

The count was running back down; Rod heard it and swung into saddle. "Take it easy, kids." The count passed him, finished with a shouted, *"ONE!"*

"Reins up! Reeeiins *UP!*" He waited with arm raised and glanced through the fully-dilated gate past rolling prairie at snow-touched peaks beyond. His nostrils widened.

The control light turned green. He brought his arm down hard and shouted, "Roll 'em! *Ho!*" as he squeezed and released the little horse with his knees. The pinto sprang forward, cut in front of the lead wagon, and Captain Walker headed out on his long road.

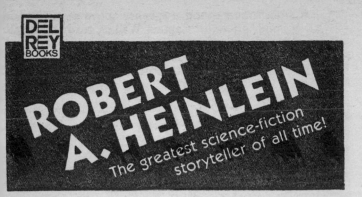